JAMEELA GREEN RUINS EVERYTHING

BOOKS BY ZARQA NAWAZ

Laughing All the Way to the Mosque

Jameela Green Ruins Everything

ZARQA NAWAZ

JAMEELA GREEN RUINS EVERYTHING

HARPER

An Imprint of HarperCollinsPublishers

JAMEELA GREEN RUINS EVERYTHING. Copyright © 2022 by Zarqa Nawaz. All rights reserved. Printed in the United States of America. No part of this book may be used or reproduced in any manner whatsoever without written permission except in the case of brief quotations embodied in critical articles and reviews. For information, address HarperCollins Publishers, 195 Broadway, New York, NY 10007.

HarperCollins books may be purchased for educational, business, or sales promotional use. For information, please email the Special Markets Department at SPsales@harpercollins.com.

FIRST EDITION

Designed by Emily Snyder

Library of Congress Cataloging-in-Publication Data has been applied for.

ISBN 978-0-358-62123-2

22 23 24 25 26 LSC 10 9 8 7 6 5 4 3 2 1

To my children, Maysa, Inaya, Rashad, and Zayn,
who needed proof that I wasn't online shopping for eight years.

OK, maybe I was, but I still finished the book.

Lee Lee, Fajr Prayer, 6:07 a.m., Oct. 6

Dear Allah,

Mom's disappeared. The CIA says she's killed people. And that she's a terrorist. She is. But the kind who will fight you at a Kate Spade flash sale. Religion's never been her thing.

I know she's been acting weird lately, but people don't get radicalized and run off to the Middle East to fight in a holy war that quickly. Unless terrorists sit around watching comedy specials on Netflix while online shopping, their lifestyle wouldn't appeal to her.

I'm really scared. She could be a better person and mom, but I love her. Dad says her life has been complicated. And the complications have caught up to her.

I'm doing what the imam at the mosque, Brother Ibrahim, taught me: be patient and ask You for help. So please help.

But Brother Ibrahim is missing, too. Something is very, very wrong.

NINE DAYS EARLIER

1

MAYBE THE PRAYERS HAD FINALLY WORKED. JAMEELA
scanned the growing crowd in the New York Public Library's sixth floor.
She was impressed. Her publicist, Arlene Baker, waved. She had on her
uniform: a powder blue pantsuit last seen on Hillary Clinton or Chairman Mao. Jameela waved back.

"Great crowd," gushed Arlene as she tottered up to Jameela in matching heels, windmilling her arms to maintain her balance. She air-kissed
Jameela with her perfect raspberry pout. Jameela wondered how her lipstick never came off. Maybe it was tattooed on.

"I haven't seen a book launch this big in a while," Arlene said. "And I've
been to two others already this week."

"I know why they're here," said Jameela. "I've been trying something
new."

"What?"

"Praying."

Jameela hadn't prayed since Jamal. But now there was something she
needed badly. After decades of work, Jameela had finished her memoir.
She looked up, trying to find God in the tin-stamped ceiling.

Remember what we talked about, she thought. *You will make my book
go right to the top of the* New York Times *bestseller list like You do for all
the white people You love so much: J. K. Rowling, George R. R. Martin, or
even better, Margaret Atwood. That woman doesn't need any more number one books. And she has enough hair on her head to stuff a whole pillow.*

Do any of those people even believe in You? Probably not. In the Qur'an, Prophet Solomon asked for a kingdom greater than anyone's before or after, plus to talk to animals, and You gave it to him. So now it's my turn. I want a literary career greater than anyone else's. I don't want to talk to ants or anything. Unless they know how to order a book from Amazon. So that's it. IMMORTAL LITERARY SUCCESS. If You need to send me a sign, use a grilled cheese sandwich. That's what You do for Christians, right?

Arlene touched Jameela's arm and brought her back to earth. "That's so funny, sweetie, I thought you said 'praying.' So much press here. So fantastic. And your mom and her friends came, too. How sweet."

Jameela turned to see her mother, Nusrat, arriving with five of her Pakistani friends, all wearing bright, jewel-toned shalwar chemises. She acknowledged them with a curt nod, her right hand in her jacket pocket, rubbing the blue marble prayer beads her brother, Jamal, had given her as a child. People streamed in by the dozens. She should have tried praying long ago. Who knew God could be so responsive?

But then Courtney Leland entered. Jameela froze. The familiar chill of dread ran up her spine, even after all these years. Why was that woman here?

Oh no. Suddenly it made sense why people were rushing to get front row seats. Jameela clutched her prayer beads so tightly her fingers hurt. Fear and anxiety sparked through her body. She was instantly transported back to high school, a time when she and her mother had constantly fought over her clothing choices. She was forced to wear pants under her dresses, and any hairstyle besides pigtails was deemed too alluring. If Anne of Green Gables had been brown, with a unibrow and a mustache, Jameela would have been her doppelgänger.

During that tumultuous period, her brother had convinced her to join the yearbook staff to gain experience as a writer and develop confidence. By her senior year, she had become editor of the school yearbook and eked out a niche for herself—until Courtney joined the team and, like a black hole, absorbed all whose eyes gazed upon her. In that year's yearbook, their group photograph featured a smiling Courtney standing in the front of everyone, hands on hips, partly blocking Jameela's face. The caption *editor* was typed under her photo.

She looked exactly the same now as she had back then, maybe a bit thinner and blonder. Her clothing choices perhaps had become more cutting edge. She wore knee-high black suede boots with stiletto heels over black leggings, a miniskirt, and an orange jacket with metal zippers everywhere. It looked like she'd just thrown the outfit together, but Jameela could tell that it was all high-end designer. *I am not in high school anymore. I am an accomplished woman. Please, everyone look at me,* she thought. The cameras swung toward Courtney. Arlene came and sat beside a devastated Jameela.

"How did she know about this event?" Jameela whispered through clenched teeth. Reporters mobbed Courtney, who was turning her head at an angle perfected by a thousand Instagram photos. Her lips were parted just so, and her eyes looked off into an unknown distance. She even took out a pair of tortoiseshell glasses and posed with one of the ends lightly touching her lip. *Was that even sanitary?* Courtney put them on while tossing her hair, which also seemed to know exactly where to land. She screamed "sexy librarian," while Jameela suddenly felt matronly in her sensible brown walking shoes.

Arlene picked a piece of fluff off her lapel.

The truth finally hit Jameela. "You didn't!"

"Jameela, listen to me. You're a first-time author of a good book, yes, but you don't have name recognition yet. We have a hard time getting people to Margaret Atwood anymore. It was the only way."

"What do you mean, 'the only way'? It's my book launch! Why does she get top billing?"

"I may have suggested to her that it was going to be an interview-style launch with —"

"Courtney's going to interview me?"

"You were best friends in high school, so it makes perfect sense."

"We were not best —"

Arlene stepped on Jameela's toe as Courtney approached the women, a cloud of perfume following her like low-lying cumulus clouds.

"Arlene, thanks for asking me to be part of your event. It was so kind of you."

"Thanks for fitting us in," replied Arlene.

Jameela could sense Arlene was trying hard not to gush. If they hadn't been surrounded by people, Jameela would have throttled Arlene for picking the one person on earth who had betrayed her during her most vulnerable time. She had to appear gracious, or people would suspect the truth: she was jealous of Courtney's career success.

"Yeah, thanks," she added.

"Oh, you're so welcome," said Courtney, turning her attention to Jameela. "We were besties in high school," she told Arlene. "Jameela let me take over the yearbook so I could use it on my résumé. And it worked! I became the editor in chief of *Dazzle*. Launched my literary career. Under my leadership, we now have more subscribers than *Cosmo*."

"That's so kind of Jameela," exclaimed Arlene. "Always thinking of others before herself."

"Yes, so how could I keep away when I heard about Jameela's book? I wanted to be part of the excitement."

Jameela's fingers dug deeply into Arlene's arm.

"Ouch!" she yelped, pulling her arm away.

Thank God guns aren't allowed in public libraries. "You shouldn't have. Really, you must be so busy with your own book promotion." Jameela tried to slow down her breathing.

"Think nothing of it. My own parties are getting exhausting. But enough about me. Nothing like the first book. Almost like having a baby, isn't it? Except that it doesn't ruin your body. Oh, but you look great, considering. Did you only have one?" Courtney looked critically at Jameela's stomach.

"Thanks," said Jameela, pulling her cardigan protectively around her. "Is that gray hair?"

Arlene yanked Jameela toward her and whispered fiercely, "Behave. She brings more publicity to your event. Look, she's already onstage. Follow her." Arlene went up to the mic and took some papers out of her powder blue purse. Jameela wondered if she'd had each piece of her outfit dyed together in the same vat.

"I'd like to welcome everyone to the official launch of Jameela Green's *Mainly Muslim*, a tour de force memoir about a woman born in suburbia to conservative Pakistani parents. To help us celebrate, we have a special guest, Courtney Leland, the author of *Will Anyone Save Me?*— a book about her harrowing year in captivity in Iraq before her dramatic rescue by Navy SEALs. It's been on the *New York Times* bestseller list for more than thirty weeks with no sign of slowing down."

Courtney sat in a plush burgundy velvet chair opposite Jameela, who saw her short skirt get shorter. She reeked of sophistication and glamour, while Jameela felt like a frumpy, middled-aged mother. After the applause died down, Courtney took off her orange jacket to reveal a transparent black blouse with a racy red bra underneath. Every eye turned to her. Even Jameela had a hard time looking away. Courtney took the mic, which was sitting on a small table between them.

"So, Jameela, I've read your book. It was very funny."

"Thank you. I thought I could read from the first chapter?"

Courtney looked like she'd just realized the event was about Jameela and not her.

"Is it a short chapter?"

Jameela ignored her and opened her book to the section she'd marked, and began reading.

I picked up a bottle of soda from the grocery shelf, but my mother snatched it and eyed the label suspiciously. "It says root beer." She put it back.

"But, Ummi, it's not real alcohol, it's just a name, and it tastes good," I whined.

My mother stared at me. "Where did you drink it?"

It was a rare fatal error.

"My friend Emily shared her can with me at school."

My mother was furious. "What kind of principal runs your high school? They ban peanuts but allow pretend alcohol? No wonder this society is so dangerous, full of alcoholics and drug users. I'll be speaking to him about indoctrination on Monday."

I silently returned the root beer to the soft drink —

"Was your mother always so strict?" interrupted Courtney.

Not always, thought Jameela. She remembered trips to the West Coast when she and Jamal were young. Those were the days when her mother didn't care about the scantily clad men and women lying on the beach or what anyone was drinking. She was another person. Jameela had been fourteen and had just started high school where Jamal was a senior. He died a week before his graduation. "She became strict when I started high school."

"Speaking of high school, didn't your mother have an issue with the shorts that were mandatory in gym class? You rebelled by wearing them at school behind her back, even though you didn't know how to shave your legs. You describe yourself as looking like a hairy tarantula in boxers, but I thought you looked adorable."

Jameela bristled at Courtney for trivializing her personal stories of assimilation. "My mother wasn't exposed to hair removal. Boys and girls both wore cotton shalwar chemises at school. That's a long shirt with baggy trousers, so their legs were always covered and not judged the way they are here."

Jamal had been the one to tell her to be patient with their parents. Shorts and gym class were foreign to her mother, who had grown up in Pakistan and needed time to adjust. He came up with the idea of Jameela wearing track pants, and even went to talk to the principal about changing the dress code, which allowed Jameela to participate in sports at her mother's comfort level. But after Jamal died, there was no one to mediate, and a wall went up between Jameela and her parents. They wanted her to become a doctor, but she wanted to study creative writing and become a writer. She might as well have told them she wanted to become a ferret. If Jamal had lived, she would have had an ally. But after he died, she had no one until she met Murray in college, where Jameela secretly took writing classes and started chronicling her experiences growing up in an eccentric American-Muslim-Pakistani household. It had taken her a decade and half to finish her memoir and find a publisher, but here she was.

Courtney turned to Jameela. "But the cultural differences are deeper than clothes. Some Muslims don't date in high school. Why is that?"

Jameela was glad that brown skin could hide the color rushing to her face. She knew what Courtney was trying to get out of her. She hadn't written about Jamal.

"Some Muslims, like some Christians, believe dating or 'getting to know' someone is a means to an end, specifically marriage. And if they're not ready for marriage, they don't date."

"Oh, please. What's wrong with just dating for fun and sex? This isn't the eighteenth century," Courtney snorted, while looking at the audience for support. Some people tittered uncomfortably.

"Some Muslims want to have sex after marriage. It's a religious thing."

Jamal had been handsome and popular in school, and girls prayed he'd notice them, not realizing that if they'd prayed, literally, he probably would have. Jamal started congregational Juma prayers every Friday for the Muslim students, but sometimes non-Muslim students came to listen to his sermons because they offered solace, especially during exams. Jamal lived for soothing souls. He always talked about becoming a social worker.

Jameela gave Arlene a look. But it was too late.

"There were some cute guys in high school who were missing out," said Courtney, twisting a strand of her hair. "I remember one guy in particular who didn't seem interested in women at all unless they were Mother Teresa."

Jameela's hand was too damp to rub the prayer beads in her pocket.

"When we were in high school together, your brother was killed. Why isn't he in the book?"

A train whistle blared in Jameela's head, which started to throb. She had deliberately chosen to omit that part of her life from the memoir. Her editor realized she wasn't ready to write about Jamal yet. Arlene, despite her faults, could read the panic in Jameela's face and leapt up.

Before the audience could even register Courtney's question, Arlene was at the mic. "There are so few memoirs of women of color. White women get a chance to tell our stories in print all the time. And quite frankly get more of the shelf space than we deserve. It's time to rectify that. Jameela, what inspired you to write your book?"

Jameela knew she needed to derail Courtney with her answer so she'd abandon her line of questioning. There was only one way forward. "I thought a funny book about the life of an ordinary Muslim woman would help the world see us as regular people, just people who may have stricter parents. If female Muslims exist in literature, it's usually as a victim of Muslim men, who are portrayed as being brutal and violent."

She felt a pang of guilt, but it was too late. There had been rumbling in the literary community that Courtney had purposefully set out to be kidnapped in Iraq. She was supposed to be meeting with her Middle East counterpart for *Dazzle* when she decided to head out for a "tour" of the war-ravaged country against the advice of locals. She immediately got kidnapped by insurgents, who thought she was a spy. It caused an international outcry and an equally spectacular rescue. The book and subsequent movie deal meant Courtney could quit her job at *Dazzle* and ride the speaking circuit for the rest of her life.

Courtney's smile wavered. The camera swerved back to her as she shrugged a blond lock over her shoulder. "Did I mention that I've just sold my book rights to Warner Studios?"

"Who'll play you?" yelled a woman in the front row.

"I'm hoping for Jennifer Lawrence. We have the same eyes. And she's just as slender as I am. Well, maybe not quite, but it's important for people to see women with different body types."

There was a moment of silence, and then a woman wearing a turtleneck under a floral muumuu put up her hand. "Jameela's trying to break down stereotypes by writing about ordinary Muslim women, and your film is going to portray Muslim men as evil, oppressive monsters. Aren't the two of you on opposite sides of the fence?"

The room fell silent. Jameela could sense Courtney fidgeting. She put her orange jacket back on and hugged herself. "I was kept captive in a tiny room with no window for over three hundred and seventy days. I thought I'd never see my mother again. She'd just been diagnosed with breast cancer when I was captured —" Her voice cracked, and she started to cry. There was a sudden commotion as audience members got up and tried to comfort her. One woman offered her a tissue, which Courtney accepted and used to delicately dab her eyes. Jameela noted that she was careful not to smudge her eyeliner.

Arlene gripped the microphone. "Okay, everyone, I think that's enough of the interview portion of tonight's event. Jameela and Courtney will be in the atrium to sign books."

Jameela moved toward Arlene, but there were so many people swarming around Courtney that it took a few minutes to reach her. "No more questions for me? I thought this was my book launch."

"We'd never recover after that performance," said Arlene. "We should just salvage what we can from the day."

"Courtney is selling her books here?" Indignation filled Jameela. It had been decades since high school, and Courtney still managed to upstage her. She had more money and fame than Jameela, so why keep haunting her?

"It was the only way we could get her to come." Arlene swallowed, noticing Jameela's growing anger. "She charges fifty thousand dollars per appearance. We were lucky we could get her for free. Now, match my breathing. It'll help you deal with your rage and jealousy issues." Arlene held Jameela's shoulders and stared at her until their breathing was in sync.

Jameela's heart rate came down, and she looked at the long lineup at the book table. Arlene had a point. Books about Muslim women leading boring lives in the suburbs didn't exactly burn up the bestseller lists — even if they were funny. "Women's Vic Lit" was a genre unto itself, and if you happened to be a victim of Muslims, even better. How could she compete with that?

Jameela took out her favorite purple gel pen and moved to the table where a pile of her books sat untouched. With a cover illustration of a tree with bright yellow and orange leaves, it could have been a book about nursery rhymes. Courtney's had a photo of her with perfect winged eyeliner in a formfitting fuchsia dress. She was peering out from behind a chain-link fence. Like a snake self-correcting, the long line of people shifted so it was in front of Courtney. The only people left standing in front of Jameela's table were her mother and her friends. Nusrat picked up one of her books. "I've just started a book club."

"Since when do you read anything other than the Qur'an?" asked Jameela.

"Since I discovered J. K. Rowling. Have you heard of her?"

"*Harry Potter*?"

"Yes, there are seven books in the series. You should read them."

"Isn't that a sin, with all the wizards and magic?"

"It's just make-believe, Jameela. Don't be such a fundamentalist. I love that white woman. Now, *she* can write."

It drove Jameela nuts when her mother flip-flopped on issues that used to be sacrosanct. After Jamal's death, her mother cracked down on anything that seemed too Western. Jameela wasn't allowed to trick-or-treat because Halloween was a giant pagan candy fest celebrating the devil himself. It didn't help that little children in red devil costumes, complete with pitchforks, rang their doorbell. It was a miracle that Satan himself didn't emerge from the bowels of Hell, possess people and make them murder their neighbors, or have sex with them, the latter being worse. Nusrat forced the family to sit in the basement while the doorbell rang all evening, until Jameela heard eggs break against the windows. And now, after ruining her childhood, Nusrat had turned the rules around when it suited her. The only good thing that had come out of Jameela's wretched memories was this memoir.

Nusrat flicked through the copy she was holding. "If you cut us a deal, maybe we'll read your book next month."

Jameela took in the scene. God was clearly screwing with her. She needed professional help. There was only one place to go.

2

MOSQUES ARE LIKE BAD BOYFRIENDS. JAMEELA PARKED in front of the squat, sandy-colored building. *You always feel judged.* She looked up in the sky, where surely God was looking down at her disapprovingly.

"I hate this place," said Jameela, getting out of the car. "And You of all ... You should know why." Yesterday's disastrous book launch had forced her hand. God was out to get her, and Jameela needed to do damage control before something worse happened, like she got transformed into an ant that only Malcolm Gladwell could hear.

When Jamal was alive, going to their mosque back home in Brooklyn had been an adventure. The mosque was always fuller on the Fridays when he gave the sermon. He talked about avoiding the forbidden, or haram, like alcohol and drugs, but also about taqwa, the feeling of God flowing through your heart, and always ended his sermon with his favorite verse in the Qur'an: "And your Lord says, Call upon Me and I will respond to you."

But Jameela had stopped talking to God long ago. What was the point? Faith, fun, and frivolity had extinguished when Jamal suddenly died. That had been twenty-five years ago. Now thirty-nine, Jameela had hoped over a decade of marriage and motherhood would have eased her pain. But instead, she found herself drifting further and further away from the people she loved.

The stucco walls of the mosque had cracks near the door and windows. The grass near the entrance hadn't been mowed, and weeds were threatening the small flower garden. It was fall in Liverspot, North Dakota, and red and yellow leaves clogged the rain gutters.

"You should really take out the halfwits who run this place. Aren't burning hailstones Your weapon of choice?"

Jameela sighed. She was pretty sure that asking God to murder idiots was haram. Why was she always such a bitch? Her daughter, Lee Lee, would tell her life itself seemed to make her angry. "And whose fault is that?" she mouthed while staring at the sky, leery about attracting the hailstones. Atheists had it easy. God wasn't ruining their lives. Then she remembered the last words Jamal had spoken to her.

Don't whine, wine is haram.

She took a breath. This was harder than she originally thought. Jameela hadn't entered a mosque since Jamal's funeral. But Lee Lee raved about the imam here; he was the only one who had given her solace when their cat, Billie, died of cancer. Somehow Jameela's motherly exhortations of "life is cruel" hadn't helped. She wiped away a tear, felt for Jamal's prayer beads in her jacket pocket, gave them a quick rub, and reached for the scarf in her purse.

Ibrahim vacuumed the stairs after prayers were over and the mosque was almost empty. The board of the mosque believed it was unseemly for the imam to perform this lowly task, especially since they had hired someone else to do it. But Ibrahim felt that a weekly cleaning wasn't enough. He had visited the local church across the street. The wood was polished and buffed to such a high shine that it looked like glass. He had been putting off having the minister visit the mosque until he felt the mosque was just as pristine. It was a matter of pride for him. Remembering the hadith of the prophet doing his own household chores, washing and mending his own garments, he wanted to be the imam of the most spotless mosque anyone had ever seen. And to be perfectly honest, the cleaning helped soothe his nerves in this new land.

As he finished the stairs and started toward the front lobby, he saw a black Honda CRV parked in front of the doors. A woman with black shoulder-length hair emerged from the car and stood staring at the mosque with what appeared to be great interest. He wondered if it was her first time.

The woman put on a turquoise scarf dotted with an orange paisley pattern and entered the building. She stared at the shoe rack for a few seconds. He decided to break her reverie.

"There is much room for your shoes here," he said gently, knowing his Arabic-inflected voice would identify him as a newcomer to this country. The woman jumped slightly.

"Thank you," she said, as she bent down to put her shoes in one of the slots.

He noticed a string of blue marble prayer beads on the floor and put them in his pocket. "You've just missed Zuhr prayer," he said. "But you're welcome to stay and wait for Asr."

"I'm sorry for interrupting your vacuuming. I'm looking for the imam. Do you know where he is?"

"I am the imam." Ibrahim could see the look of disbelief on her face. She had mistaken him for the janitor even though he wore his imam garb, which was composed of a long white robe and a black skullcap. Maybe he should consider a name tag, as one board member had suggested.

"You're a little too young to be the imam," she said, scrutinizing him. "Usually the imam is older and . . . angrier."

Ibrahim felt defensive. "I am twenty-five, but I finished my training in Al-Azhar. It is one of the most respected Islamic institutions in the world."

"Yeah, I don't care if you were trained at the Vatican, as long as you're the real deal."

Ibrahim unplugged the vacuum and wound up the long yellow electrical cord. There was a knot. The woman took it from him and started to undo it.

"Where did you grow up?" asked Jameela.

Ibrahim stepped back, unhappy with the question. It always made him feel inadequate.

"In a small village in Egypt. I am new to the West. But I feel I have already learned much from this community. And I can offer —"

She put out her hand to stop him. "You had me at 'small village.' That's good, you haven't been corrupted yet."

"Corrupted by what?"

"Life. God likes people like you. All innocent and idealistic. People who still think life is about hope and meaning."

Her words sounded like a compliment, but Ibrahim knew they were not.

She stared at the knot of the cord as if she could undo it with her eyes alone. "God is messing with me. I did nothing to God. Well, maybe I stopped believing in Her . . . Him. Does that offend you?"

"Not believing in God?" he asked. He wanted to say, *Yes, very much.*

"Thinking that God might be a woman and then not believing in Her."

He took a moment. This was the first time he'd had to think about such a thing, and he hoped his eyes would not betray him.

"In Islam, God does not belong to any gender. It is a limitation of the English language to insist on a gendered pronoun, but in Arabic, the word *God,* or *Allah,* is genderless, so you can refer to God as a woman if you prefer. There is no insult since there is nothing insulting about women." Had this concept ever occurred to his instructors at Al-Azhar? Probably not.

"As for not believing in God, this worries me. But you are here in a mosque, so that is a good sign."

"Oh, I've decided to believe in God, but I'm having some issues. Man, this place is a dump."

Ibrahim could not argue with her there. In Egypt, a mosque was made of stone and marble, and was the pride of the community. But here, it resembled a dusty pawnshop. He chastised himself for thinking this way. He realized that his mind had drifted for a few seconds, and now they were both standing awkwardly in the lobby.

"My name is Jameela, by the way," she said, sticking out her hand.

Ibrahim stared at the hand as if it were a creature from outer space. He knew shaking hands with the opposite sex was a custom here, but it seemed too forward to him. He needed more time to get used to it.

Jameela pulled her hand back.

An ant crawled onto Ibrahim's arm, and he took out his pocket handkerchief, gently brushed the ant onto it, closed the fabric around it like a protective parachute, and opened the door and flung the creature outside. Jameela watched his actions closely.

"My daughter does the same thing. She said you inspired her with the story of Prophet Sulayman and the ants."

Ibrahim didn't know what shocked him more, that God may be a woman, or a teenager being inspired by him. He thought for a moment. Definitely the teenager.

"Let us continue our discussion in here," he said, as he took off a chain from around his neck with several keys on a ring. He unlocked a door beside the shoe filing cabinet and led her into the mosque library.

The woman sat down on a dilapidated brown leather sofa that gave off a tired hiss. The imam sat opposite her on a ratty green and yellow plaid sofa.

"My brother encouraged . . . had encouraged me to be a writer. He died, but I kept writing, and my memoir finally got published. And I prayed for my book launch to go well, and God screwed me over."

The woman was tired and needed someone to talk to. She had circles under her eyes and seemed sad.

"That does not sound like God," he said.

"Yeah, well, clearly God doesn't have a problem with you. You probably believed in Her your whole life, so you get a free pass. Me, however, She's sticking it to." She looked into his eyes imploringly.

He picked up two books from the table. When he put them back in their designated spots on the second shelf, as if by magic, a single Arabic word embossed in gold stretched across the spines of the set, like a glittering dragon. "So, you want me to help you —"

"Get God to give me the thing I want. And deserve. Especially after taking away my brother. That's the only way I'll stop believing God is a monster."

Ibrahim felt nausea rise to his throat. He poured himself water from the dispenser in the room, but it didn't help. Thank God his lunch had digested by now so that he didn't 'toss his cookies,' a saying in the West that had never made sense to him, given the variety of things one could expel during times of spiritual crisis. He took out a pocket handkerchief and wiped the perspiration off his brow and upper lip. God wasn't a vengeful creator. After all, every chapter of the Qur'an started with a reminder of His . . . Her mercy and while it was true that sometimes God's tests were difficult, Ibrahim believed in God's promise that after every hardship was ease. But he had never encountered someone so bitter before. Go back to basics. Ibrahim moved to the next shelf and straightened those books as well. "You must be patient."

"I'm done being patient. My brother died over twenty years ago, so I've done my time. Now I have a major ask." Jameela jumped up and snatched a paper cup from the pile beside the water dispenser. Ibrahim assumed she was about to fill it; instead, she crushed it in her hand and threw it in the garbage can. "I want my book to become number one on the *New York Times* bestseller list. Tell me how to get what I want from God." She sat back down and dug her finger into the cracked leather of the sofa and made a hole. "You have a degree from Al-Azhar, for God's sake. What's your name, anyway?"

Ibrahim plucked the cup from the garbage can and placed it in the blue recycling bin. His nausea seemed to abate. "Ibrahim."

"Like the prophet?"

"Yes, my mother, as people here would say, was a fan." He smiled at the memory of his mother. "She died last year. It was pancreatic cancer, which I did not know could spread so rapidly. But, by the grace of God, there was not too much pain." Her only wish for him was to be an imam, and he had succeeded. Ibrahim opened the dark mahogany cabinet and rooted around until he found a bottle of Windex and a box of rags. Joy unfurled in his chest. He made a silent prayer of thanks to God. This was what heaven must feel like.

"How do I make God answer my prayers?" said Jameela. She crossed her arms, reminding Ibrahim of one of his five-year-old students.

"It is a question many have asked before you," said Ibrahim, trying to sound profound. Despite this woman's unorthodox language and approach, she was asking the same question all people who struggle with faith ask. And it was his duty to help her. If he couldn't save her soul, then what use was he as an imam? "Why is this prayer so important to you?"

"Because being number one in the *New York Times* means you have made it as a writer. I'm pushing forty. If I don't succeed at writing, I'll be stuck selling crop insurance to farmers in Liverspot, North Dakota, for the rest of my life. And my brother would be . . ."

She stopped talking and seemed to lose herself in thought. Ibrahim brought her a paper cup that she gratefully crushed. As Ibrahim ran the rag over the window, he pondered her question again. At least with marriage problems or drug excess, one could recommend counselors. But God coercion was different.

"Make God listen!"

Another man in a shalwar chemise approached. He must have come early for Asr prayer and had overheard Jameela's raised voice from the lobby. "Do you need help, brother?" he asked.

"Yes, could you clean the outside of this window? There is dirt on the other side." Ibrahim handed him a fresh rag and spray bottle.

"Actually, I meant, can I help you with . . . other matters," said the unhappy man, taking the tools and nodding toward Jameela.

"Sister Jameela is in need of my advice. But the window outside has not been cleaned in years," said Ibrahim, and shut the door. His pride was pricked at the suggestion that he might need assistance. The man appeared outside and stared dejectedly at the two of them through the window while he sprayed. Ibrahim found his disconsolate face distracting, so he shut the drapes.

Ibrahim had taken a course in counseling before he took this job. His advisors had recommended it, and now he was grateful. This woman was clearly on the edge, and it was his moral duty to help her. He straightened the pamphlets on the wall unit. The cleaning had reinvigorated him.

"You have to prove to God that you are sincere. You cannot expect something for nothing."

"But I've started praying."

"No, you have to show more . . . how do you say, concrete effort."

"Like what? Volunteering at a soup kitchen, giving money to charity, that sort of thing?"

Ibrahim thought for a second. Those were good things, but she would do them as robotic acts and be unsatisfied. He needed something that would alter her mental state. He saw a pamphlet entitled *Be a Good Muslim Neighbor,* with an illustration of a woman giving a coin to a person sitting cross-legged in a street.

"You have to find a homeless person and help solve their problems."

Jameela's eyes widened. "What? No. You can't help the homeless. They want to live on the streets. I'm pretty sure there are studies that prove it."

Ibrahim's nausea returned. He made a mental note to stock Imodium in the library for the future spiritual guidance sessions with this woman. "No, that is what you must do. Otherwise, God won't answer your prayers."

"How do you know that? God's not speaking to you, is She? Is there a grilled cheese sandwich with words on it?"

"I only eat falafels," he said, wondering how a grilled cheese sandwich was connected to the divine. He would google that later. He was nervous about having presumed God's will. He needed to pray for absolution, but if he went into the prayer hall now, this obsessed woman would follow him. *Please God, just don't let me ruin her life and mine along with it.* He'd never thought being an imam could be this dangerous. His father had always told him to go into plumbing.

"Just do as I say, and then come back," he said. Usually, he'd recommend extra prayers or charitable donations; this was the first time he'd recommended someone actually leave their home and change someone else's life. He hoped his advice would humble her to tune in to the needs of those around her.

Jameela looked at him, but her thoughts were clearly elsewhere. He cleared his throat, and she came out of her dreamlike state. "I'll do it on one condition," said Jameela. "You come with me."

Jameela, Zuhr Prayer, 1:30 p.m., Sept. 30

You are God, and You can do anything. You can make my book a best-seller without me having to save a homeless person. Jamal was killed by a hitchhiker who was also homeless. Someone he was trying to help. So why should I help them?

And does that imam even know what he's doing? It's like he's an es-capee from Magical Maids. But those tend to be the type of people You like. The ones who are all humble and good and pray all day. Just like Ja-mal.

Ibrahim, Zuhr Prayer, 1:30 p.m., Sept. 30

My Lord, I hope to be guided by You, but I am afraid. I have never met a homeless person in the West. In Egypt, as You know, there are many beggars in the street, but we are a poor country. I do not know why there are homeless people in the West when even the animals have houses. Here, people put little bags on their hands and actually pick up the excrement of dogs and put it in their pocket until they can find an appropriate receptacle. It is truly a remarkable country. I will go with the strange woman and assume this is Your will. Please protect me and help me help her.

Oh, and can I get married? It is difficult to find a wife here in the West. My mother was right about not allowing a computer in our home growing up — I have accidentally come across unclothed people engaged in what I have to assume is a form of procreation. I feel marriage would protect me from thinking about this act in a way that will become all-consuming.

3

"DO WE HAVE ANY JUICE BOXES?" ASKED JAMEELA AS she threw a loaf of bread and some apples into a knapsack. Lee Lee was measuring cut-up cauliflower. It had been two days since the book launch, and Jameela felt Ibrahim had the power to put a curse on her if she didn't feed the homeless.

"I threw them out last year when Dad got diagnosed with diabetes," Lee Lee said. "Plus, the straws are bad for the environment. Why?"

"I thought they'd be convenient for the homeless to drink from. But we wouldn't want to trigger Armageddon too early. I'll just take some leftover coffee." Jameela poured the last dregs from the coffee maker into her thermos. "They can drink it straight out of the bottle, like booze."

"You're taking stale coffee and giving it to the homeless?" asked Lee Lee slowly. "Since when did you start caring for people?"

Jameela pretended she didn't hear. "Maybe I can offer some leftover steak from last night's dinner, too," said Jameela, as she reached into the fridge. The garage door rumbled, and Murray emerged with a pickleball racket over his shoulder. Jameela greeted him at the front door with a piece of steak on a fork.

"You weren't planning on eating this, were you?" she asked.

"I love you, too," replied Murray, setting down the racket and kissing her on the lips. "You can have it."

Jameela headed back to the kitchen and started to slice it up. "It's not moldy, so it should be fine."

"How was your game?" asked Lee Lee as she sauteed some mushrooms and cauliflower.

"Pulled a muscle while yanking a bicuspid. I'll try again next week. What's happening?" Murray asked Lee Lee, while throwing a glance at Jameela.

"You're making up lame excuses not to exercise, I'm making you a stir-fry with the recommended amount of vegetables, according to the USDA Food Guidelines," she said. "And Mom is attempting to feed the homeless by giving them questionable meat in a baggie."

Murray turned just in time to see Jameela put the pieces of meat into a Ziploc bag.

"That's great," said Murray. "Especially after you said you'd never help a homeless person since —"

Jameela disappeared into the hallway closet, where she found an old overcoat Murray never wore anymore. In the pocket was an unfinished scarf and knitting needles stuck in a ball of wool that she removed, stuffing the jacket into her backpack. Hiding from Murray when he was just trying to be supportive was unkind, but she didn't want to explore her "feelings" right now.

Jameela had met Murray in college, and he was the only one she felt safe talking about her past with. She'd introduced Islam to him as the religion that had brought her nothing but pain, and still, he'd decided to convert. That decision almost broke them up. But Murray felt that Jameela's issues with her parents had more to do with culture than faith. Wanting her to marry someone from the same ethnic tribe in Pakistan, forbidding her from playing street hockey with boys from the neighborhood, their kooky ideas about Halloween — these were the concerns of parents trying to find their way in the West, not religious zealots.

After they finished their undergraduate degrees, Murray was accepted into dentistry school, but Jameela's dismal marks kept her out of medical school. Instead, she got a job at an insurance company and the two kept seeing each other. He proposed in his last year of school and wanted Jameela to introduce him to her parents. Their unhappiness at the engagement gave Jameela some satisfaction, but Murray insisted they postpone the wedding until her parents came around.

They waited over a year until Nusrat started to worry about the depreciation of Jameela's ovaries, so for the sake of fleeting fertility, her parents reluctantly agreed to the marriage. Jameela overheard her mother tell some scandalized guests that Murray came from the northern regions of Pakistan, hence the white skin.

"Where are you going to find them, honey?" Murray's voice pulled her back to the present.

"They're homeless; it's not like they have addresses," Jameela said.

"Remember they're people, Mom," said Lee Lee.

Jameela ignored her. "The imam is coming with me."

"Brother Ibrahim from the mosque?" asked Lee Lee, dropping the spatula.

Jameela found herself resenting Lee Lee for being so shocked. But it wasn't her fault. Jameela always spoke about the mosque as if it were hosting a reunion of the Third Reich. "The one and only," said Jameela. "It was his brilliant idea. Something about God answering my prayers if I changed the life of a homeless person."

"I love his Qur'an study classes, but the other kids think he's a little weird."

"Those kids know when to call it."

The doorbell rang. Jameela was stuffing some socks into the knapsack, so Lee Lee went to answer it and came back with Ibrahim, who was holding a large bag. Lee Lee was chattering away.

"And I read the verses you assigned last week. The story about Adam being sent to Earth. What I don't understand is that even the angels didn't think creating humans was a good idea. They told God that we were going to mess things up on Earth, so we really weren't worth it. And all God said was, 'I know what you don't know.' What did God know about us, Brother Ibrahim?"

Lee Lee's eyes shone with delight as she talked to him. They never shone that way when she talked to Jameela.

"This is the question humans have been trying to answer since we were created," Ibrahim said. "But I feel the answer may be that there are people like you, Maleeha, who are trying to make the Earth a better place by caring so much about it."

"Call me Lee Lee, everyone else does."

Ibrahim turned to Jameela. "Your daughter is the best student in my class. And so . . . different from you."

"She takes after her father and uncle," said Jameela. She was proud of Lee Lee. *The one thing I did right.*

Suddenly, Ibrahim saw Murray and looked guilty. He introduced himself and shook Murray's hand.

"I've enjoyed listening to your Friday sermons," said Murray. "More informative and livelier than the last guy."

"You also attend the mosque?" asked Ibrahim.

"Since I converted, and I bring Lee Lee to your classes every week. And since you came, I've never seen her so enthusiastic about going to the mosque."

No one mentioned that Jameela was the holdout in the family.

"I hope you do not mind that I'm traveling alone with your wife. We will be in public at all times."

"Oh, it's totally fine," said Murray, keeping a straight face.

"I will make sure my hands are on the driver's wheel, so no one will get the wrong impression."

"Relax, Ibrahim," said Jameela. "People aren't going to think we're having an affair."

Ibrahim winced. He pulled a scarf and mitts out of his bag. "I was given many of these by people when I came to Liverspot, so I feel that I can pass them on." He pulled out a plastic container with a sandwich in it. "I learned how to make a grilled cheese sandwich, too, which I understand from your wife is a powerful symbol in Western culture."

"Yeah, it's pretty powerful, all right," said Murray.

"I am not sure how Westerners came to believe that God speaks to them through a sandwich, but we must not disrespect their customs," said Ibrahim.

"White people do a lot of weird things," Jameela said. "Like getting themselves kidnapped on purpose to sell a book."

Murray and Lee Lee looked at each other, and then at Jameela, who continued to pack things.

"Don't give me the side eye like I'm crazy. You two weren't in New York to see Courtney Leland sabotage my book launch."

"Mom, you think everyone's evil and out to get you."

"That's because they are. Has anyone seen Jamal's prayer beads?" asked Jameela, patting her coat pocket. "I lost them yesterday."

Ibrahim pulled out a string of marble beads from inside his jacket.

"I'm sorry, I didn't realize they belonged to you. They were on the floor of the mosque." He handed them back to her.

Jameela gazed at them for a moment. "They were his favorite. He never left the house without them." She tucked them away in her knapsack.

"Where are the two of you going, exactly?" asked Murray.

"My friend Anwar told me that many homeless people congregate at the park downtown near the shopping mall. It would be a good place to start," said Ibrahim.

"Well, no time like the present," said Jameela, as she filled another thermos with coffee.

When she was done, Murray kissed Jameela on the lips and held her hands. "I'm really proud of you, honey. You've been trying new things lately, and that's good. But remember to look after yourself, too. If you get overwhelmed, just come home, and we'll talk."

"Why would I get overwhelmed?" Jameela pulled her hands away. She didn't like it when Murray worried about her like this. It made her feel like a child. "I'm over his death, Murray. I'm not doing this for some airy-fairy recovery process. I'm on a mission. Feed the homeless. Make God happy. Get onto the bestseller list. A simple quid pro quo arrangement."

Murray saw Ibrahim squirm.

"I feel that we're missing an important part of the equation," said Ibrahim. "We do it to please God."

Jameela tightened the lid on the thermos, and then turned it upside down to make sure it didn't leak. "No, we do it so God gives us what we want and stops screwing us over with privileged white women."

4

JAMEELA GOT OUT OF THE CAR, AND THE REALITY OF what they were doing hit her. Large Dutch elms flanked the perimeter of the park, making it difficult to see the walking paths inside. Streetlamps illuminated small patches of dead grass, but for the most part it was dark, except when someone lit a cigarette. The outdoors made Jameela feel a little melancholy about her days at Muslim summer camp. The Muslims there were relaxed and made religion fun. Jamal volunteered as a counselor, but after he died, she stopped going.

Ibrahim and Jameela got out of the car, and she had started toward the park when she noticed that Ibrahim was frozen to the ground. She went back for him, and he grabbed her arm. "I am so sorry for touching you in this manner," he said. He looked pale and frightened as he let go. She looked up and could make out three men huddling for warmth. Two of them were sharing a bottle of beer.

"Is that alcohol?" asked Ibrahim. Jameela could tell this was the first time he'd seen anyone drink.

"It's no big deal," she said. "They're not drunk, and they won't hurt you." Her heart sped up. She was not going to have a panic attack and give Murray the satisfaction of being right. As they stood immobile, staring at the men, getting colder by the minute, Jameela forced herself to walk toward them. After Jamal's death, she'd seen knives hiding in the pockets of people passing in the street. Her parents had forced her to see a therapist, who taught her techniques to stop projecting her fear onto strangers. These men were just ordinary people doing ordinary things, like smoking and drinking. It helped that Ibrahim was more frightened than she was. He'd risk getting hypothermia before talking to a man who smelled like beer. If anything happened to him, Lee Lee would never forgive her. Their relationship was already strained from Jameela's bitter view of life. She took Ibrahim's arm and marched him to where the men were standing and offered up a shaky thermos. "Would you guys like some coffee?"

Two men walked away, but the third man turned around. He was easily over six and half feet tall, and had matted sandy-colored hair, combat boots caked in mud, and biceps that bulged under his green army camouflage coat, giving him the appearance of a military-issue Jolly Green Giant. His height and size were so overwhelming, Jameela wondered if both she and Ibrahim could fit into his arms and be crushed to death. She felt relieved that he was not drinking and wondered how someone so menacing but clean-cut had wound up here. The man seemed equally curious and looked at Jameela, and then at Ibrahim, who was wearing a robe and skullcap.

"Is it organic? And do you have any milk or raw sugar?" he asked in a friendly voice. His smile reached his eyes.

Jameela hadn't even considered adding milk and sugar. She'd thought a homeless person would be thrilled with just getting coffee.

"I don't drink black coffee," he said. "It stains my teeth."

Good Lord, thought Jameela. Of course, they'd find the one homeless guy who thought they were running a pop-up Starbucks.

"Would you like a pair of mittens?" asked Ibrahim.

The man looked at the gray woolen mitts that Ibrahim held out. "Wow, they're from the Gap," he said, and put them on. "I like these, thanks. What else you got?"

Ibrahim took the hat and a scarf out of his bag.

The man put them on immediately. "Ah, that's more like it. I didn't think it would be so cold this evening. You forget that fall nights get nippy 'round these parts."

"You can keep them," said Ibrahim, elated at his success.

"Would you like some meat?" asked Jameela taking out a bag with a squished, brown lump stuck to the side. She put it back. "Or an apple?"

The man ignored her, addressing Ibrahim instead. "You look like a decent guy."

Ibrahim looked joyful. "I'm trying to do God's work," he said. "He . . . or She as people in the West like to think of God . . . wants us to look after the poor and less fortunate."

"Well, I'm poor. And God wants us to drink decent coffee. My favorite place is just down here. Come with me." The two of them trooped behind as if pulled by a tractor beam.

Inside the coffee shop, the man ordered three lattes, one for each of them. The order came to sixteen dollars and forty cents. Jameela looked at Ibrahim, who looked just as imploringly at her.

"They do not pay me very much at the mosque," he said, "so, as you say in this country, I am broke."

The horror struck Jameela: neither had brought any money — she had left her wallet at home to avoid being robbed by a homeless person. This was humiliating.

Their companion dug into his pockets. He pulled out a five and a ten dollar bill, and some nickels and dimes. Shamed, the two of them sat down in a plastic booth waiting for their benefactor to return with their drinks.

"Thank you so much," said Ibrahim, accepting his latte. "Can we ask you your name?"

"Barkley," he said, as he took a small brown paper package and slowly poured the large golden crystals into his latte. "I love this place. I read an article in the *New York Times* that artificial sweeteners can cause glucose levels to spike, so I switched."

"In my country, we love real sugar in our coffees, too," said Ibrahim. He emptied five white packages into his drink. Jameela was more of a tea drinker, so she had nothing to contribute to the conversation.

"I also love merino wool," said Barkley, as he fingered the gloves. "Did you know those goats are the most winter hardy?"

"I did not know that. You are knowledgeable about so many areas of life, Barkley," said an impressed Ibrahim.

"Thanks, Ibrahim. You're a pretty worldly guy yourself."

Jameela envied Ibrahim's ability to put people at ease and engage them quickly. She couldn't connect with people after Jamal's death. Murray had been the first person she trusted. Friends were a foreign concept.

"You seem like an educated and cultured man," said Ibrahim. "May I ask how you became homeless and made friends with others who are similarly affected?"

Jameela choked. "Ibrahim," she whispered. "You can't ask that."

"Ah, no worries," Barkley said. "In a nutshell, I'm mentally ill. I went off my meds, pissed off my family, my employer, and all my friends, and lost everything. Now I'm homeless."

"Why didn't you take your medication?"

"'Cause I hate the way the pills make me feel. Sluggish and dead inside."

"But your life is such a tragedy," said Ibrahim.

Jameela couldn't clear her throat hard enough. Ibrahim got her a cup of water.

"It's not so bad. I make a decent living. But the winter gets to me. It's hard to find places to keep warm."

"Where do you sleep?"

"Sometimes on heating grates, or inside doorways, but usually someone throws me out."

"That sounds very painful."

"I wear extra padding around my ribs, so I don't feel the kicks."

A look of horror swept over Ibrahim's face. "Would you like to live in our mosque?" he asked.

Jameela spat out her latte. She looked at him. "Can I talk to you?"

"You are talking to me," said Ibrahim.

"In private," she hissed.

The two moved to the next booth.

"You can't just do that; you don't know who he is. He could kill you while you sleep." A part of Jameela couldn't believe she'd just said that, but she was afraid for Ibrahim.

"We only die when God decrees," said Ibrahim.

"Okay, fine, but God also said in the Qur'an, 'Don't do stupid things.'"

Jameela knew she was on shaky ground and wished she had more of a grasp of Islam for moments like this.

"I do not believe such a verse exists, and I do know the book very well."

Jameela racked her brain for every lesson that she had ignored thirty years ago in her Islamic Sunday school classes. "But there's another source of knowledge that's ... got something to say about things like this ..."

"You mean hadith, where the sayings, actions, and approvals of the Prophet Muhammad, may God's peace and blessings be upon him, were recorded?"

Ibrahim sounded like a talking version of Wikipedia. "Yes, and there's one about a camel," said Jameela, whose head hurt from trying to remember the saying.

"Tie your camel before you leave it," said Ibrahim.

"Exactly. You just invited a camel who is off his meds into your mosque."

"Okay, I understand what you are saying. We do not know enough about this man to let him live in the mosque."

Jameela breathed deeply and took a sip from her latte, which was, as Barkley promised, very good. "Yes, that's exactly what I'm saying," she said.

They returned to their booth.

"I go to the library where there's free Wi-Fi, and I've made some Muslim friends online," said Barkley. "They taught me verses of the Qur'an."

"Really?" asked Ibrahim, getting excited. "What did you think?"

"I loved that allegory about the light in the oil lamp."

"Oh, Surah twenty-four, verse thirty-five. That is my favorite, too," said Ibrahim. "Many Muslims, Sufis and mystics, have spent their entire lives trying to decipher the meaning of that verse."

Barkley swallowed a sip of his latte. "But to me, it's so obvious. God is the light that illuminates everything."

"Yes, I agree, the meaning is so beautiful."

"Allah is the Light of the heavens and the earth," said Barkley and Ibrahim together.

They quoted the verse by heart to each other. Jameela couldn't believe it: first, they were bonding over sugar crystals, and now they were reciting Qur'anic verses. She felt like a third wheel on their date.

"I want to become a Muslim," said Barkley suddenly, his eyes full of light.

Ibrahim took a deep breath and closed his eyes. "You can live with me."

Jameela, Isha Prayer, 10:37 p.m., Sept. 30

The imam said, "Feed a homeless person, and God will answer your prayers." Simple proposition, and I expected a quick turnaround for results.

Barkley may have had to buy his own coffee, but let's not quibble. I put an apple in his pocket. But instead of my prayers being answered, Barkley is now moving in with the imam, a man who clearly should never go into contract negotiation. So I have a new problem — this crazy, not-so-homeless guy may kill the imam, just like the hitchhiker killed my brother.

You have taken me down this road before. I can't go through this again. I'll save Ibrahim from Barkley, but I would appreciate some reciprocation regarding the bestseller list.

I'll get Ibrahim's address from Lee Lee. She mentioned that he's always trying to have the youth over to his apartment to study the Qur'an, but no one ever wants to go. Poor guy. He's ripe for the picking.

Ibrahim, Isha Prayer, 11:08 p.m., Sept. 30th

A friend! By Your grace and Your mercy, You have provided me with companionship! True, he is not a wife, but to have someone in the apartment is still the most incredible gift a man could ask for. And he wants to convert to Islam! A miracle. I cannot thank You enough. Now I can tell Abdul Jaleel, my supervisor at Al-Azhar, that I have a convert. He will be so proud of me. I had a suspicion that they felt I was too stiff for this job, but now I have proven them wrong. Or You have.

I apologize for being so arrogant; it is a terrible defect that I am working on.

5

IBRAHIM CRACKED AN EGG INTO THE FRYING PAN. HE'D never made breakfast for anyone else before. A sense of contentment and joy overcame him.

Barkley snored on Ibrahim's futon in the living room. The board members had found him an apartment close to the mosque and had canvassed the local community for donations to make it cozier. As a result, the apartment had an eclectic arrangement of furnishings. The dining room had a round oak table with the word *Mudhamud* carved into it by a child who had tried to spell the prophet's name and failed.

A burgundy wall hanging with gold sequins sewn in an elaborate Indian pattern hung on a metal rod above the teal suede sofa, which had seen better, nonstained days. Plastic vases of artificial flowers were strewn about the place, interspersed with a few small turquoise hand-painted Turkish ceramic bowls. Ibrahim used some of them to store his miswaks, and pens. One of his elderly non-Muslim neighbors told him his apartment looked as if it had been decorated by an eccentric Martha Stewart unleashed on a Middle Eastern thrift shop: Islamic shabby chic, she called it. He did not know who Martha Stewart was, but he was grateful that the community had tried so hard to make him feel at home.

Ibrahim's favorite piece of art in his home was a velvet panel with ninety-nine squares, each embroidered with a different name of God in gold thread. The tapestry was encased in a dented gold frame and hung in the kitchen. Ibrahim loved looking at a different name each day. To-day, he looked at al-Wali, which meant "protecting friend."

It was a relief to have company after months of loneliness in Liverspot. The city was small, only twelve thousand people. The gentle undulations of the landscape reminded him of the sand dunes of his home in Egypt. But, unlike in Egypt, it was difficult to connect with people here. Until now. Barkley had taught him how to make microwave popcorn, which they ate while watching *Jurassic Park*. Dinosaurs were his favorite extinct beings. To think that Allah had allowed such fierce and majestic creatures to roam the earth. Ibrahim wished he had lived in simpler times like that.

He didn't have any friends at the mosque. People felt awkward around him, and he was caught between generations. Growing up in Egypt, it was unthinkable to even talk to a girl; the other day, he confiscated a boy's iPhone and saw photos of the boy's seminude fellow classmate. He returned the iPhone at the end of class and said nothing. To get his students to trust him, he would have to be lenient, or they would turn away from Islam entirely. Their parents, on the other hand, thought he shouldn't let the girls and boys sit in the same room in case they developed feelings for one another. Ibrahim had observed "hookup" culture in his classroom, and he knew the parents had no idea what was going on. He wanted the teenagers to talk to him about their lives, but everyone thought him too odd. Whenever he used slang to fit in, such as "cowabunga" or "get jiggy with it," the kids would laugh, google the words, and tell him those expressions went out several decades ago. *How to become groovy in the West?* With Barkley, he felt normal. Barkley didn't think he was strange at all.

"Smells good, Ibby," said Barkley, sauntering over to the frying pan. "Can I call you that?"

"You may call me Ibby, if it satisfies you," said Ibrahim. He would have to tell his friends at Al-Azhar that he now had a nickname. "I have made you eggs with buttered toast."

"Ahh, that's so sweet," said Barkley. "Do you have any grape jelly?"

As Ibrahim handed him the jar, the doorbell rang, and he headed to the entrance and saw Jameela's angry face through the peephole.

"You're alive," she spat at him as he opened the door. "I thought I was gonna find your dead body in a pool of blood."

"But why would I be in such a terrible state?" asked Ibrahim, taking Jameela's jacket and hanging it on an old wooden coat hanger. Jameela walked in and looked at the spartan quarters. Ibrahim was secretly proud of his apartment. It was a mansion compared to his tiny room in Egypt.

"Because a certain someone had killed you," said Jameela, who suddenly saw Barkley eating his breakfast in the tiny kitchenette.

"Who?" asked Ibrahim, confused. "I keep my door locked at all times." He feared he had missed something, which happened to him quite often here.

"Great eggs, Ibby," Barkley called from the kitchenette. "You're a natural-born cook. Is that cumin I taste?"

"Yes! And Sister Jameela has come for a visit."

"Why is he still here?" whispered Jameela, as she pulled Ibrahim into the tiny living room.

"Why shouldn't he be?"

"Okay, I know you're new to this culture, but we don't just let homeless live with us. It's not normal."

"What do you normally do?"

"We give them a quarter and walk away."

"That doesn't sound very useful. It's difficult to buy a meal with so little money."

"No, lots of people give them quarters, and then they buy themselves food."

"But where do they live?"

"I don't know, the streets. No one uses them at night, so taxpayers are getting their money's worth."

"That sounds like it would not be very comfortable, or safe. It is okay for Barkley to live with me," said Ibrahim. "I have an extra room, and I enjoy his company. I will start his Arabic lessons right away so he can start praying." Sister Jameela's words were starting to make him feel uneasy. Even his mother said he was too trusting, but being kind and merciful were the attributes of God Herself, so how could it be wrong?

"He's using you," whispered Jameela. "He's pretending to be Muslim so you'll feel sorry for him, and it's working. You're giving him a free place to live and making him breakfast."

"Why does this bother you so much?" said Ibrahim. "He is living with me, so you have no worries." Even if Sister Jameela was correct and Barkley wasn't sincere in his friendship, there wasn't anything wrong with sharing food and space with a needy person. In time, their friendship could become deeper and more meaningful. This was such a rare opportunity to have someone in his life, he wasn't going to be dissuaded.

Jameela took a deep breath. "My brother was killed by a hitchhiker when I was fourteen. He was transient and lived in people's homes, like Barkley. That's why this entire situation is freaking me out."

Ibrahim had heard the Western word *epiphany*. He suddenly understood its meaning.

"I am saddened to hear about your brother. From your face, I know he meant much to you. Sometimes God takes someone away to teach us about life."

"My life was ruined after he died. That's what it taught me!" Jameela quickly wiped away tears, hoping Ibrahim hadn't noticed.

"You must be patient. It takes time to understand God's plan for us."

"That plan will be me organizing your funeral. Jameela jammed her hands into her jacket pockets.

She was inconsolable.

"Have you ever spoken to anyone else about your brother's death?"

She shook her head. "The therapist my parents forced me to see. And then Murray. Lee Lee knows I had a brother, but I've never talked to her about what happened."

Ibrahim's heart swelled. He was among the first people she'd opened up to. *Please, God, help me with the next step. I am not sure how to proceed.*

"I want to talk to you about your brother." Ibrahim passed Jameela a Kleenex. "I feel there is much unresolved grief that is affecting many parts of your life."

"Ibby!" yelled Barkley from the kitchen. "Can I check my email on your computer?"

Jameela wiped away her tears, and they both walked to the kitchenette.

"I don't have Wi-Fi," said Ibrahim.

"What? That's cray-cray," said Barkley.

"The board of the mosque said that I would have to pay for Wi-Fi out of my wages, but after food and rent, and money I send home to relatives in need, there is not enough left over to afford it."

"Dude, Wi-Fi is a basic human right."

"I have shelter, food, heat, and electricity, so I feel that my basic human rights are being met."

"You've come from a Third World country, so I can see how that makes sense. But being able to check your email is a big deal here," said Jameela.

"I do check it. The mosque has Wi-Fi, and I spend most of my day there."

"Ibby, I need to know how my homies are doing. Email is the only way I can keep tabs on my friends. Some of us are always on the move."

That did make sense, thought Ibrahim. And then he had another epiphany! The mosque computer was in the library. All the children's Islamic educational books were there as well. He could kill two birds with one stone. He shuddered. That Western saying was too violent. It reminded him of the biblical ordinance of stoning adulterers to death, which some Muslims had tried to emulate. He had feelings about the misappropriation of Christian biblical ordinances but felt that it was a subject that would not go over well during Christian-Muslim dialogue day at the church.

"We will go to the mosque. There are books on beginner Arabic in the library. I can sign them out and start your Arabic lessons right away."

"Giddyup," said Barkley.

6

JAMEELA OPENED THE HEAVY GLASS DOORS TO THE mosque to let Ibrahim and Barkley in. Barkley watched Ibrahim take off his shoes and did the same. She had just knelt to take off her shoes when she heard a familiar voice.

"Mom?"

Jameela spun around and saw Lee Lee coming out of a classroom. She was wearing a pale pink scarf with blue butterflies. She was trailed by several five-year-olds.

"What are you doing here?" asked Jameela.

"I just finished teaching Arabic to the kindergarten class."

Jameela had forgotten that Lee Lee taught in the mosque on weekends. As far as mother-daughter relationships went, Jameela wasn't winning prizes for communication. Her own mother's parenting style had been more akin to Chairman Mao barking out orders.

I'm so proud of you, Jameela wanted to say. But when Lee Lee asked her what she was doing in the mosque, she found herself saying, "Why shouldn't I be here?"

"I've never seen you at the mosque. Like, ever. You said hell would have to freeze over. And with climate change, you were worried that was a possibility, so then you said —"

"Yes, I know what I said," snapped Jameela, immediately regretting her tone. "I'm here with Brother Ibrahim and Barkley."

Barkley stepped forward and stuck out his hand to a surprised Lee Lee. She shook it.

"Hey, little lady, it's so cool that you're teaching the little ones."

"Thanks, I want to go into education one day."

I didn't know that, thought Jameela.

"Sister Lee Lee, I have a new roommate, and he wants to become Muslim," gushed Ibrahim. "Would you like to help me teach him Arabic?"

Jameela was growing fond of Ibrahim, but his naivete continued to alarm her.

"We found Barkley in the park, and he's living with the imam now," said Jameela.

Lee Lee regarded Barkley and Ibrahim with a concerned look. "That's so great. But do you guys think that maybe things are moving a little too quickly? Becoming Muslim is a big decision."

Jameela felt relief. She may have been a crap mother, but her daughter still had more common sense than these two birdbrains.

"Well, little lady," Barkley said. "I do have some Muslim friends I've made online. They've taught me a lot of stuff already, speaking of which, there's Wi-Fi here, right?"

"Let me show you the library," said Ibrahim, taking his key out.

When Ibrahim got the door open, Barkley ran toward the communal computer as if it were a long-lost friend.

Lee Lee looked at Brother Ibrahim with worry.

"Brother Ibrahim, many marginalized people convert to Islam because they're looking for a sense of community and belonging."

"And I am providing those things to him."

"True, and that's a good thing, but if you guys found Barkley in the park, there may be things he needs that you can't give him," said Lee Lee.

Jameela felt a sense of pride. Lee Lee reminded her of Jamal.

"What things do you speak of, Sister Maleeha, I mean, Lee Lee?" asked Ibrahim.

"His medical history, for sure. A doctor's visit would be good to make sure he's okay."

"He doesn't like doctors, Sister Lee Lee. He already told us he decided to get off his medicine for his mind because of the way it made him feel."

"That's a huge issue, Brother Ibrahim. Mental health is a really big deal," said Lee Lee. "Even when people don't want help."

Ibrahim looked thoughtful as he took in Lee Lee's advice.

"You are correct, Sister Lee Lee. I have put my feelings before Brother Barkley's mental welfare. Thank you for seeing through my selfishness."

"Guys, I need to get back home, pronto," said Barkley, catching everyone off guard as he walked out of the library and started to put his shoes on.

"Perhaps we should make an appointment at the nearby walk-in clinic first," said Ibrahim. "A doctor there helped me get rid of a painful rash I acquired while teaching the kindergarten class. I believe it was called 'Hand, foot, and mouth disease.'"

"No time, Ibby. I got things to do right this minute," said Barkley as he tied his shoes.

"But you are homeless, and have few friends and likely no future. What could possibly be so pressing?" said Ibrahim, watching in anguish.

Jameela winced.

"No time to explain," yelled Barkley, as he bolted out of the mosque.

7

IBRAHIM AND JAMEELA ENTERED THE APARTMENT TO find Barkley packing up his belongings.

"Brother Barkley, where are you going? You have just arrived." Ibrahim was frightened. Something had clearly gone wrong in the mosque. Was it the Wi-Fi password he had chosen? IslamIsTheOneTrueFaith123 seemed innocuous enough. Perhaps it came across as too arrogant. He would think of a more neutral message.

"One of my Muslim friends online told me to get out of the mosque as fast as possible. That people will try and influence me."

"I promise to change the password," said a mollified Ibrahim. "How about IslamIsAGoodReligion?"

"He said you would try and talk me out of my Islamic duty."

Ibrahim felt a wave of relief. "To pray five times a day. It is onerous at first, but we can take it very slowly. As Sister Lee Lee said, there are other more important issues, like your mental health."

"That's what my friend told me you'd say. You'd try and take me to a doctor, so I gotta vamoose."

"I am not familiar with this Western term," said Ibrahim, who felt he would never get a grip on the English language. The word had an ominous ring to it.

"It means 'leave in a hurry,'" said Jameela.

Ibrahim felt his world lose color.

"But where will you vamoose to?"

"Syria."

Ibrahim and Jameela stopped breathing at the same time and stared at Barkley as if he had just grown horns. This wouldn't be solved by a new Wi-Fi password.

"My friend made all the travel arrangements," Barkley said.

"I thought you were just checking your emails at the mosque," Ibrahim said.

"I was, and one of my friends sent me a cool website," continued Barkley.

"Show me," said Jameela, passing her cell phone to Barkley. He typed into it and passed it back.

Jameela and Ibrahim watched a sleek YouTube video that featured several men dressed like ninjas with rifles, running in slow motion. Suddenly a young man with a blond beard, wearing a white turban and robe started speaking.

"Do you feel helpless to change the world when there is so much suffering?" He was standing in what looked like a bombed-out building. "Join the Dominion of the Islamic Caliphate and Kingdom today, and we'll give you the tools you need to help feed orphans, take care of the homeless, support widowed women, and bring peace and justice to the world." The video then showed men dressed in camouflage passing cartons of food from a truck to a group of veiled women and giving a crutch to a man sitting on the ground. One of them ruffled a child's hair.

Jameela was mesmerized. It looked like a recruitment video for the American Armed Forces. Music swelled as a shepherd walked with his flock toward the sunset. She thought Jesus was about to make an appearance, but the video ended with the words *A World at Peace . . . Finally.*

The two of them stood there in silence for a minute, absorbing what they'd just seen. Ibrahim was familiar with the video, having seen the Arabic version. His instructors at Al-Azhar made them watch it and then discussed its contents, since the DICK was becoming successful in recruiting young, idealistic men and women. But Ibrahim was also aware of how difficult it was to dissuade someone who'd been infected with their message. The Al-Azhar institute tried inoculating their students early by teaching them critical thinking skills. But without that intervention, it was virtually impossible to change someone's mind.

"Come with me," said Barkley. "Life here is too hard. We'll have a whole posse to hang with, and we can be tent buddies."

"No, this is not a good group," said Ibrahim. "They say they are good, but they do very bad things to innocent people." Ever since the DICK emerged, they had devastated the Muslim world with their cruelty and resurrection of ancient practices such as slavery.

"But did you see that video?" said Barkley. "They take care of babies."

"This is all an illusion," said Ibrahim. "I come from that part of the world. If it were true, what they are claiming, I would be the first to sign up, but they are lying to you."

As he spoke, Ibrahim could see the romantic dream of the desert in Barkley's eyes.

"My friend sent me that video, Ibby. He's there, and says it's exactly like the video."

Ibrahim's heart sank. His roommate's cousin had joined this group, and no one had been able to dissuade him, not even his own mother, who cried for days after he left.

"It is like that in the beginning, but as time passes, your friend will realize that things are not what they seem."

"Are you saying my friend is a liar?"

"I am saying that your friend is being manipulated. He may not even be writing those emails. This group has people who specialize in recruiting Westerners. Someone else may have written that email with your friend's name."

"No way, man. My intel is legit. I got three friends on that side of the world who are telling me it's the real deal. One of them even sent me pictures of himself in his last email. He looked so happy with his new life."

Ibrahim could tell he was losing.

"Plus, they said the longer I stayed with you, the more you'd try and convince me this group was bad. And they were right."

"But we had decided that you would live with me," said Ibrahim. It was like watching someone deliberately set themselves on fire and refuse help. He knew that Barkley wouldn't last long in Syria. They'd see his size and immediately send him out on dangerous combat missions.

Jameela looked pensive. "Yeah, maybe you should stay here for a while and learn Arabic. Trust me, it's not that easy."

"That video said there were Islamic classes for people. They provide everything: education, food, shelter. It's the complete deal, man."

"This group, they are a ... How do you say it in English?" Ibrahim pondered, searching for the word.

"Cult!" yelled Jameela. "They're a cult! Like the Moonies or David Koresh or those guys who drank the Kool-Aid. It's the same philosophy: build a utopian society where nothing bad ever happens. They brainwash people into joining, and then you can't leave."

Barkley started collecting his things. "Thanks for the food and clean clothes. I really appreciate it."

Ibrahim stood in his way. "You cannot join this group."

Barkley had a foot on Ibrahim and outweighed him by a hundred pounds. He picked Ibrahim up and tossed him on the sofa as if he were a rag doll.

"If you try to stop me again, I'm gonna make sure you can't get off that couch. Sorry, man."

And then he was gone.

Jameela went to the couch and helped Ibrahim sit back up. They sat in silence for a few moments. Ibrahim wondered if the last hour had even happened, it seemed so unreal.

"I don't understand," said Jameela. "He was fine just a few hours ago."

Ibrahim moved to fill a banged-up kettle from the sink. As the familiar click of gas started, he put it on the blue flames, and then dampened a cloth and wiped down the oak table. His friends in Egypt had told him stories of relatives and neighbors he knew who had joined the DICK, but until today he had never met someone who had been radicalized.

"He must have been in contact with them for some time," said Ibrahim. "They send money to recruits to help build trust. Remember how he paid for our lattes?" He moved from the table to the cupboards and started polishing them.

Jameela had found that odd, but she had been overcome by embarrassment and hadn't questioned it.

"I've met men who come to the mosque who are like Barkley. They've found out about Islam from this group, the Dominion of the Islamic Caliphate and Kingdom, on the computer. I speak to them about Islam, and gradually they understand they have been manipulated." *If only I'd had more time with him,* thought Ibrahim.

"Do you really think he can make it all the way to Syria?" asked Jameela.

"Yes. But he will still need money for airfare. This is how the DICK tests people. After building trust, they ask the person to fund their own way to Syria. Barkley doesn't have that money, so there is hope."

"You don't keep cash in your apartment, do you?"

"I just keep the donation box from the Juma prayers. Why?"

"Where's the box?" asked Jameela.

"Barkley would never take money from me," said Ibrahim. He reached up to the top of the refrigerator and took down a metal box. It was marked *Donations* in black marker. The padlock had been pried open. Ibrahim opened the box. It was empty, except for a few coins. He felt angry now. It was one thing to be seduced by a cult, but to steal from a fellow human being? It made him hate Barkley. *Don't do that,* Ibrahim reprimanded himself. It was what the DICK wanted, to pit Muslims against Muslims.

"How much was in there?" asked Jameela.

"Almost two thousand dollars. I gave a particularly inspiring khutba about taking care of the poor, so people were more generous."

"That's probably just enough to fly to Turkey and then get transported to Syria. I wonder if he was already a convert and looking for a way to get the money when we stumbled on him. We were an easy target."

"He did know much about the Qur'an," agreed Ibrahim. "When he declared he wanted to become Muslim, he knew I would take him in. I was played."

Jameela smiled at his use of a Western colloquialism, but then quickly got to business. "We have to go to the police."

8

JAMEELA AND IBRAHIM WALKED UP THE GRAY CON-
crete steps of what resembled a sleek industrial warehouse but was actually the Liverspot Police Station. Beyond a set of dark glass doors, they
found a policeman behind a bulletproof barrier. He asked them their
business and then pressed a button allowing a second set of dark glass
doors to open. Jameela took a number from a metal box and sat with
Ibrahim in the waiting area. It could have been a doctor's office, except
it was so cavernous. They could hear a man arguing with the police officer behind a Plexiglas barricade.

"Sorry, sir, we can't arrest your neighbor for putting up Christmas
lights."

"But it's only October!"

The police officer dismissed him and called out the next number.

Jameela and Ibrahim walked up to the barricade and sat down in the
chairs in front of it. They could read the red-haired officer's name tag:
INSPECTOR MATHESON.

"How can I help you?" the inspector asked.

"We're worried that someone we know has joined DICK," said Jameela, leaning forward to talk through the hole in the barricade, and realizing too late that the two of them should have worked on their story.
Not that there was a story.

Inspector Matheson sat up straight. Clearly, a full day of complaints about cats, dogs, and Christmas lights could not compete with international terrorism.

"Come with me," said Inspector Matheson, directing them into another room at the back of the office. He instructed them to sit on black metal chairs.

"Are you scared?" Jameela whispered to Ibrahim out of the corner of her mouth.

"I trust my Lord," said Ibrahim. "She will protect us."

"I knew you were going to say that," said Jameela. "But bad things happen to people who believe."

"They happen so God may test us and make us stronger in our spiritual resilience."

Jameela wished this were true. But she felt that tragedy had just made her angrier and more bitter.

"But what if we get overcome by the test?"

"Just pray and have patience, and all will be resolved."

"That's a lot of —"

Before she could answer, two male officers with dirty-blond crew cuts entered the room. They introduced themselves as Officers MacMillan and Morris. Jameela wondered if having a last name starting with *M* was a requirement for entering the police force in Liverspot.

Jameela and Ibrahim told them the whole story.

"You said his name was Barkley," said MacMillan. "Did he have a last name?"

"We never asked," said Jameela, feeling stupid. She remembered wanting to leave the park as soon as possible. If she had shown an iota of interest in his life, things might have ended differently.

"I felt it would be rude to be so personal," said Ibrahim.

"And yet you let him sleep in your home," said Morris.

"He seemed very trustworthy," said Ibrahim. "I realize now it was a foolish thing to have done, but we were just trying to do some good."

"And how was he communicating with DICK while in your home?"

"We took him to the mosque," said Jameela. "He wanted to communicate with his friends, and Ibrahim doesn't have Wi-Fi in his apartment." Jameela hoped that would make Ibrahim look more innocent. *He is innocent,* she reminded herself. Being here, being interrogated like this, was making her feel guilty for something she didn't do. *I should have been the one to protect Ibrahim, and I failed him,* was all she could think.

"While using the mosque computer, Barkley's friend forwarded him the recruitment site for the DICK. You have to answer some questions before they let you access it," said Ibrahim.

"How did he learn those answers?" asked Officer MacMillan.

"He may have learned them from other Muslims he's met. They are not difficult questions."

"You seem to know about their recruitment tactics," said Officer Morris unkindly. He put down his pen and notepad and stared at Ibrahim.

"I have had some friends who joined them," said Ibrahim. "They were also tricked into believing that the DICK was doing good in the world."

Officers MacMillan and Morris gave each other the side eye.

"So, you know current DICK operatives?"

Before Jameela could stop him, Ibrahim answered. "If my friends are still alive, then yes."

Dread enveloped Jameela's heart and squeezed it. Tight.

The officers left the room without saying a word.

"Do you think they will be able to find Barkley and bring him back?" asked Ibrahim.

"You should stop talking about your association with DICK," said Jameela, her palms clammy.

"I do not have an association with them," said Ibrahim. "I have some friends who disappeared after joining them."

"I know, but in this country, when you say you have friends who belong to a crazy, homicidal cult group, it makes it sound like you have a connection."

"But I tried to stop them. I have not done anything wrong. And this is a good country. The police will understand."

"That's debatable. You're a citizen, right?"

"I am not yet a citizen of this country," said Ibrahim, slowly.

Jameela didn't want to make Ibrahim any more frightened than he already looked. She took a sip of water to hide her face.

An hour later, both officers came back.

"We'd like to keep you here for some more questioning," said Officer Morris to Ibrahim. "Ms. Green, you are free to leave."

"Why am I leaving, if he has to stay?" asked Jameela.

"Our background on you came out clean. You work for Act of God Insurance. Your manager confirmed your job history."

"You were checking my background when we came to you for help?" This was not a good time to be brown and suspected of terrorism.

"Your friend's background is more problematic."

"He just came from Egypt to work as an imam. And those idiots at the mosque would have checked his background, too. Ask them!" It occurred to her now that she should have brought one of the mosque board members with her. They would have vouched for Ibrahim's character.

"We will," said the officer, opening the door. "It's time for you to leave."

She could see Ibrahim starting to polish the table with his sleeve. He needed something to distract him. Jameela could see dust bunnies in the corners of the room but doubted they would agree to let Ibrahim mop the floor to calm his nerves. "Wait," said Jameela, as she lunged toward Ibrahim. "Take my brother's prayer beads. I always believed that they brought luck —"

"There's no such thing as luck, only what God —"

"Okay, that's enough talk," said Officer Morris.

"Do not worry about me," said Ibrahim. "This is a good country, and nothing bad will happen."

Jameela could see him advance each bead through his fingers while he said "Subhanallah" under his breath. *Glory be to God.* He was praying, which would soothe him, the way it used to soothe Jamal. "Going to the park was about helping me become a better person. I put him in this position. You should be detaining me."

The police officer had his hand on her arm and steered her toward the door.

"What about a lawyer? Surely he gets a lawyer?"

"This may be a serious international terrorism case, ma'am. We are beyond lawyers at this point."

Jameela was pretty sure that wasn't a thing, but when it came to arresting Muslims, anything was possible these days.

"Can I ask a favor, Sister Jameela?" asked Ibrahim as the officer put handcuffs on him. "Tell Lee Lee the assignment for next Sunday's class is about Surah Maryum, the verses where Maryum wishes she wasn't born just before she gave birth to Prophet Isa. It's a lesson that it's okay to be afraid, even if you believe in God. Can you tell her?"

Jameela could not believe that Ibrahim was worried about Lee Lee's lessons. No wonder Lee Lee loved him. He cared more about other people than himself, just like Jamal.

"You can tell Lee Lee yourself, "Jameela said, but it was too late. Officer Morris had moved her outside.

"I don't understand what's happening," she said.

"It's not for you to worry about, ma'am. We'll handle it from here."

Jameela knew what that meant. There were numerous stories of Muslims being deported to countries the US used to outsource torture. This entire situation was her fault. How on earth would she explain this to Lee Lee? If Ibrahim never came back, Lee Lee would be as devastated as Jameela had been when Jamal died. And Lee Lee would never forgive her.

9

LEE LEE, DRESSED IN AN ORANGE FLEECE ONESIE, WAS chopping spinach and ginger in the kitchen. Jameela entered, slumped into the chair, and put her head down on the table. If yesterday had been frustrating and scary, today was the reckoning. She felt too exhausted to even talk.

"Are you okay, Mom?"

Jameela didn't respond. Murray whistled as he strode down the stairs. He winced at the sight of the spinach.

"Oh no, Lee Lee, not the power shake," he said, reaching for the coffeepot.

"Dad, I think there's something wrong with Mom. She's acting weird . . . weirder than normal."

Murray looked at Jameela. "Babe, are you okay?" Jameela lifted her head up. "Your eyes are so bloodshot."

"I think the world is a horrible place, and nothing good will ever happen," she croaked.

Murray put down the coffeepot he'd picked up. "What's wrong, darling? Arlene left a message. You have an NPR interview this afternoon. That's terrific. Your book is starting to get some traction. Things are looking up."

She couldn't do the interview. And that was the problem. She had no idea what to do, she felt paralyzed. "I'd be better off dead."

"I know Jeff Dermont isn't the greatest interviewer, but isn't that a bit extreme?"

"Whatever I touch turns to ashes. I should never have been born." Jameela dragged her hands down her face.

Lee Lee concentrated harder on the task at hand. She put the spinach and ginger into the blender, and the mixture turned a bright bottle green. She threw in some chopped-up carrots and apple. The machine struggled with the harder vegetables and made a whining noise.

Murray signaled for her to stop. He made Jameela stand up and looked at her drawn face.

"Babe, you don't look so good." He wrapped his arms around her. "Maybe it's time for us to play pickleball together. You could use some exercise."

"*You* could use some exercise," chastised Lee Lee as she brought over a tall glass of green liquid with small pieces of carrots bobbing about and joined her parents at the kitchen table. "You always say you're gonna start but never do."

Murray ignored both the glass and Lee Lee. "I know the book launch didn't go the way you hoped, but it's going to be okay. Things will turn around. Remember when your parents said we couldn't get married? And look at us now!" He tried twirling Jameela around, but she stopped him and held tightly on to him as they swayed in unison.

"Why do you look so sad, Mom?" asked Lee Lee. She rubbed her mother's back.

Jameela felt her small, warm hand.

"Let's go sit on the couch," said Murray as he led Jameela to the dark blue leather sectional in their open-concept family room. Lee Lee followed, flicked away one of her dad's origami birds, and sat on an ottoman across from her parents. She put the power shake on a side table beside her father.

"That homeless guy, Barkley, that Ibrahim brought to the mosque yesterday?"

"I remember, he seemed sweet," said Lee Lee.

"Ibrahim let him move in. And then Barkley stole the mosque's money to join DICK."

"The Middle Eastern terrorist group?" asked Murray.

"Yeah, so in the afternoon, we went to the police to report the theft and his disappearance, but instead they were suspicious of Ibrahim and kept him for extra questioning. When I called his apartment a few hours later, his answering machine said his mother was sick and he had to rush back to Egypt. I called the mosque board, and they said Ibrahim told them the same thing."

"That's it? That's what's gotten you this upset? But that sounds like a normal thing the imam would do," said Lee Lee. "Rush to visit his sick mother, especially after he's been in North Dakota for six months."

Jameela knew it would be difficult to explain his disappearance. They hadn't seen the looks of steely determination on the officers' faces. She could practically smell their glee.

"I was with him the last two days," replied Jameela. "He told me his mother died of pancreatic cancer last year. I know he's been taken."

"Taken by whom?" asked Murray.

"Taken by the same people who take people—Homeland Security, FBI, CIA, the Iraqi security forces. They're probably all in cahoots with each other."

"Cahoots?" said Murray.

Jameela could tell she was losing him and Lee Lee.

"Yes! To torture him for information about DICK!"

"That sounds ... a little crazy, Mom," said Lee Lee. "It makes more sense that Brother Ibrahim rushed back home to be with his sick mom than him getting secretly deported for torture. That only happens in the movies."

"Lee Lee, you have to believe me. You care about Ibrahim the most," said Jameela as she reached out to touch her daughter.

Lee Lee recoiled. "And you don't care about him at all. He got roped into your help-the-homeless-get-what-I-want-from-God crap, and now you're freaked out because he had to look after his mother instead of you."

"Lee Lee!" Murray shouted. "Don't talk to your mother like that. Apologize right now."

Lee Lee stood up and strode back toward the kitchen. "Sorry," she mumbled.

Jameela dug her fingers into Murray's shoulders. "I called the police again a few minutes ago. They have no record of him coming in," she implored, in a last-ditch attempt to get them to believe her.

Murray pried her fingers from his arms. "Probably the police lost his file. They're not the most organized outfit. I mean, this is Liverspot."

"No, they're hiding something. The security camera will prove we were there!"

"Even if you find the footage, it doesn't matter, Mom. Brother Ibrahim wouldn't lie on his answering machine. He's too honest," called Lee Lee from the kitchen.

"But that's it, someone forced him to say those things, and he's speaking in code. Plus the police are denying ever seeing him. It's a conspiracy. Don't you see it?"

Jameela's head hurt.

"Babe, you just got back from your book launch in New York, which ended badly. You should rest. I'm a little worried about you."

Murray tried tucking a blanket around her, but she tossed it to the other side of the couch. "I got the imam deported because I wanted a bestseller. He's probably being tortured somewhere, and it's all my fault." Where did they torture people? Probably in some grimy cell, which, for Ibrahim, would be torture enough.

"Sweetheart, would you like to see someone, a counselor maybe? The stress of seeing a homeless person has probably been more than you can handle."

"Why would seeing a homeless person trigger Mom?" asked Lee Lee as she put a slice of cheese between two pieces of bread and buttered the outside pieces. She plunked the whole thing in the frying pan, where the bread sizzled and the cheese started oozing out the sides.

"That's a conversation for another time," said Murray, giving Lee Lee not-now eyes.

"I'll tell you if you listen to me," tried Jameela.

"No," said Murray. "You're too stressed out."

"Mom, we want to believe you, but Dad's right," said Lee Lee. "At school, we learned about the importance of taking care of your mental health." She compressed the bread with the spatula to make it fry faster.

"Wow," said Jameela, "you guys would commit me before looking into any of this?"

"No one's saying anything about committing anyone," said Murray. "Talking about past trauma can be therapeutic. I'll take some time off work."

"Stop looking at me like that!" said Jameela.

"Dad is just worried about you," Lee Lee said. "You've been acting weird lately."

"Name one thing that's been different about me."

"Well, for starters, the praying," said Murray.

"You've been wanting me to become more spiritual, and when I finally pray, you think I'm insane?"

Lee Lee put the oily sandwich on a white plate and walked to her mother.

"And looking after poor people. It's not really you, Mom," said Lee Lee, handing Jameela the grilled cheese. "Eat it. It'll make you feel better. You always make it for me when I'm feeling sad." She hovered over her mother like a protective orangutan.

Jameela looked at the sandwich, golden and crispy, just the way she liked it. She knew it was an apology.

Murray ran his fingers through Jameela's hair. "You've been working on that book since college. It's an incredible achievement. But take things slowly. You don't need to change who you are."

Jameela ignored them. "Guys, look at this! Do you see?"

Murray and Lee Lee looked at the sandwich.

"What?" asked Murray. "Is the sandwich talking? Because if it is, I'm calling a doctor right now."

Jameela knew they weren't taking her seriously. She took a bite of the sandwich and tried not to stare at the rest of it too closely. Murray and Lee Lee watched her with worry. Lee Lee absentmindedly handed her father the forgotten glass of liquefied spinach. He drank it in three gulps.

Jameela reluctantly took a few more bites of the sandwich and then washed it down with a glass of water.

"No, no," she said. "You guys are right. The stress of the book launch really got to me. I just need to relax. I haven't been sleeping or eating properly for days. This sandwich was all I needed, really."

"I'll stay home from work today," said Murray. "I'll get Steve to cover for me."

"No, I'm going to do my NPR interview, and then I'll book a flight to Brooklyn to visit my parents. There are some bookstores in New York and New Jersey that want me to do signings for them. And some retail therapy in a big city is better than actual therapy."

Murray kissed Jameela on the head.

"Buy whatever you want, darling. It's going to be okay."

Murray, Zuhr Prayer, 12:57 p.m., Oct. 2

It's been a while since we've had a heart-to-heart. When you have an easy life, you get kind of complacent, and I've been coasting lately. I tried origami and knitting, but I'm a sad sack when it comes to new things. Lee Lee doesn't believe watching Netflix counts as a hobby. It's Jameela. Ever since Jamal died, she's had trouble bonding with people. When she made friends with the imam, I thought it was great. She never makes friends and has always resisted coming out to my dentist functions. Getting her book published was supposed to make things better, get her out of the funk she's been in for years, but instead she's starting to imagine things. I don't know if she's hallucinating or just stressed out. Before all this, being a good husband was letting her vent and being patient while making sure Lee Lee didn't notice what was happening, but things are unraveling fast.

Please help me understand what's going on with my wife. While I wait for an answer, I'll start knitting again. Lee Lee was right, it reduces stress. I'll make a scarf to prove I can follow through on something.

Jameela, Zuhr Prayer, 1:35 p.m., Oct. 2

I got Your message on the grilled cheese sandwich. Nobody could see it except for me. You said "GO" very clearly in black, charred lettering, so I'm going to trust You. But go where? That message was a little vague. Moses got clearer instructions with the Ten Commandments. I guess beggars can't be divine-communication choosers. I'll go visit my parents, for starters. There may be people in a bigger city who can help me find Ibrahim. Liverspot is a dead end. But I want brownie points for doing that. If we're gonna talk about looking after your mental health, I shouldn't be anywhere near them. They suck the sanity right out of you. But I'll go. In the meantime, please don't let anything happen to Ibrahim. I'm risking the health of my brain cells to find information to bring him back. Quid pro quo?

Ibrahim, Asr Prayer, 4:57 p.m., Oct. 2

My Lord, I think I am in trouble. I have not sinned, but in this country, if you are a Muslim, you do not have to sin to be in trouble. I know we are to be tested in this world to find out how strong our faith is, but please, no torture, especially the kind where they use electric cables on your sensitive areas. I am not married, but that kind of torture would interfere with my duties as a husband, if You understand my meaning. I am sorry I had to bring that subject up. I could handle waterboarding, though. My brothers would do that to me at home when they wanted to play Cops and Americans. I've learned how to concentrate underwater as a result.

10

NUSRAT BUTT, A ROTUND PAKISTANI WOMAN DRESSED in a striped green and orange shalwar chemise, watched with a satisfied look as cumin and cubed onions sizzled in a hot frying pan. A pleasing aroma filled her small but well-kept kitchen in Brooklyn.

Jameela sat in a kitchen chair and watched her mother. Nusrat had bought all the food she loved growing up. As Jameela ate her curry chicken with whole wheat roti, she was reminded of her childhood — the good parts, anyway. Her parents had lived in this brownstone since she and Jamal were in elementary school. After his death, they had thought about moving, but this was the house where Jamal grew up. Keeping it meant keeping his memory alive. Jameela rarely visited her parents these days, but whenever she did, she would go into Jamal's room and sleep in his bed. The smell of his musk incense still permeated his things.

Jameela was dying to tell someone else about Ibrahim, and her mother loved conspiracy theories; her racism, sexism, and general irrationality always played a part in how she thought. After 9/11, she had said confidently, "It couldn't have been Muslims, we're not that organized. It had to be the Jews." She felt that God might have let the whites colonize her people, but She made sure they got wrinkles faster as payback. Jameela couldn't risk telling her mother, because if Nusrat didn't believe her, she'd call Murray and he'd be here in a heartbeat and she'd probably be put in a straitjacket, medicated, and placed in the nearest psychiatric hospital. Then again, her mother hated Murray and everything about him. And, as if on cue . . .

"I don't know why you took your husband's last name," she said to Jameela, as she added a teaspoon each of paprika and turmeric to the pan. The color of the onions changed to a bright orange hue, and she placed a piece of fish on top. "You always said you were a feminist, and feminists don't change their last names. So, what did you do when you finally married? Change it." She waved a black spatula in the air like an oily sword.

Jameela sighed. "Ma, our last name is Butt. I couldn't do it anymore."

"Butt is a good name, a solid Pakistani name. Are you ashamed of your own name?"

"Yes." Was staying with her mother worth it? No, it wasn't. It was killing her. After Jamal's death, they fought all the time.

"What's so special about Green? It's the color of mold, overboiled eggs, and dead white people." Nusrat flipped a piece of fish and examined the black crust with satisfaction. She sprinkled it with sea salt.

Jameela ate diced mangos out of a bowl. At least she wouldn't die of starvation here. The last time she'd stayed with her parents, she'd gained four pounds. An endless supply of nuts, cut-up fruit, and sweet tea just materialized. "The Qur'an mentions the color green in the descriptions of heaven," said Jameela. "Plus, it's my husband's last name."

"Your white husband," said Nusrat.

"Ma, you love Murray." She was regretting her trip more and more.

"Yes, we love Murray, but we would love him even more if he was Pakistani and could speak Urdu." Nusrat took her spatula and slid the piece of fish onto a plate covered in a paper towel. The oil turned the paper towel translucent. "We could have taken trips to Karachi with his parents."

"You could still take trips with Len and Trish," said Jameela. "They'd love to go to Karachi. It would be exotic for them."

"No, Len and Trish just want to go to the cottage." Nusrat pronounced their names as if it pained her. "Once they invited your father and me to their place in Muskogee. A building without electricity or running water. You had to go to an outhouse to relieve yourself. We didn't come to the US so we could live like we were back in your father's village in Pakistan. It's unbelievable what white people find fascinating. They should go to Rawalpindi and cook hot dogs over the burning dung pits; it would be the perfect vacation for them."

Jameela felt the familiar instinct to flee but willed herself to remain calm. *Remember, you're here to save Ibrahim. There's a clue somewhere in this house. Be patient and find it,* she thought. At least they were talking. Whenever she came to her parents' house, they bickered about everything as a substitute for talking about Jamal. Anytime she probed about his death, they would refuse to discuss it further. *He's gone, and nothing good will come from constantly digging at his grave,* her mother would say.

As if on cue, her mother changed the subject again as she chopped up tomatoes. "So, you are selling your book at McNally Jackson tomorrow afternoon."

"Yeah, it's a way of pushing book sales," said Jameela. "Kind of like being a vacuum salesperson." Jameela hated the idea of being gawked at by white people. It was like being in a zoo but harder. At least the animals could walk away and eat their bowl of insects. She had to fraternize with the insects.

"Can your father and I come?" asked Nusrat.

"No."

"Why not?"

"Because you'll embarrass me."

"Nonsense," her mother said. She reached for her long chemise and used it to mop her forehead, exposing her round, bulbous, dappled belly, which Jameela always associated with motherhood and oppression.

Jameela's father, Faisal, walked into the kitchen wearing a white cotton muscle shirt with a giant Pakistani flag on the front. He kissed Jameela on the forehead. He believed women were superior to men and the best thing for them was to earn six-figure salaries and never marry. Murray had encouraged her to pursue her dream of writing, so Faisal tolerated him. He believed writing was a noble, if tragically underpaid, profession. He tried to spear a piece of fish from the serving platter.

"Stop that," said Nusrat, slapping his hand. "You're not an animal. Wait until I put it on the table."

"Look what I found in the halal meat store. Isn't it beautiful?" Faisal lovingly rubbed the Pakistani flag. "I can't wait to wear this outside. The armholes will allow my pits to breathe."

"You can't wear that outside, Faisal."

"Why not?"

"It's called a wife-beater. It's inappropriate."

"But I don't beat you. And you can just as easily call it a sleeveless T-shirt."

"Or call it tacky," said Jameela, turning to her mother. "And you wonder why I'm going alone."

Nusrat plated a piece of fish and placed it in front of her husband along with a tomato and radish salad. "I'll just go with you, and your father can invite his friends here and talk about his new look."

"Your next book should be about American foreign policy and how much damage it's caused to the Muslim world," said Faisal, as he poked a piece of tomato with his fork.

Jameela kept her mouth shut. Her father was a retired professor of political science. He worshipped Mahmood Mamdani, professor of government and anthropology at Columbia University, who had written the book *Good Muslim, Bad Muslim*. In it, Mamdani argued that Muslims hadn't engaged in armed jihad for centuries until the Russians invaded Afghanistan in 1979, and the Americans, fearing that the scourge of Communism was spreading, wanted a proxy army to fight the incursion and what better way than to encourage Muslims to jihad. Jameela's mother, although a trained Montessori teacher, could also just as easily have taught a university course on American foreign policy, so dinner conversation often circled around the idea that violent jihad was an American invention, and Jameela didn't have the patience or time to go down this road again.

"How is your book club?" Jameela asked her mother, trying to steer the conversation to neutral territory. "What are they up to?"

"There's been a lot of drama around Aunty Parveen," said Nusrat.

"I don't know any Aunty Parveen," said Jameela.

"She used to be your Uncle Raheel, but we don't use that name anymore. It's called a dead name. She's transitioned."

Well, this was definitely new. Uncle Raheel was married to Aunty Alia and they were the most romantic couple she had ever met. And her mother knew what deadnaming was.

"People are trying to convince Aunty Alia to divorce Aunty Parveen, but she's having none of it. She's going to support the gender-affirming surgery and continue as if nothing happened. The two of them are happier than they've ever been. Our book club is about to have its first lesbian couple."

It was odd for Jameela to hear her mother talking about transgender issues as if she were discussing whether store-bought masala could compete with homemade.

"And you're okay with all this?"

"This is what happens when the End of Days is close. But not everyone is as open-minded as me. Aunty Parveen's brother Aziz is visiting from Pakistan. Her family has organized an intervention, at our book club, of all places."

Jameela felt solidarity for Aunty Parveen. "Who is this uncle?"

"Aziz? He's the head of ISI back home, so her family thinks he'll be able to talk sense into her."

"What's ISI?" asked Jameela.

"Inter-Services Intelligence. It's the equivalent of Homeland Security, but for Pakistan. They hunt terrorists," said Faisal. "But that General Aziz is insufferable. He believes he's the most connected man in the world of intelligence."

Jameela dropped her fork.

Jameela, Maghrib Prayer, 7:09 p.m., Oct. 3

I feel a plan coming together. You want me to meet with General What's His Name and figure out where Ibrahim and Barkley went. I can do that. I'm assuming You've got my back. And my front. And my intestines. Please don't let them fall out.

Also, I liked my mother more when she was a card-carrying member of the Taliban. Now she's gotten all progressive and woke, I don't approve. Why wasn't she more open-minded twenty years ago? Your timing is awful. With her, I mean. But keep the timing good with me. Do not send me to Guantanamo. I can't do burlap head sacks. I don't have the chin for it.

11

JAMEELA SAT WITH THE SAME GROUP OF PAKISTANI women who had come to her book launch. Aunty Alia and Aunty Parveen's house was humble but beautifully decorated, with Indian knickknacks on the bookshelves. A small brass candlestick stood on the mantelpiece; beside it, a miniature model of a Pakistani double-decker bus encrusted with beads and small diamond-shaped mirrors. A velvet sofa and love seat with windmills in the fabric pattern were pushed up against the forest green walls. Despite the cacophony of design and color, there was a sense of peace in the home. The coffee table was from Pakistan. Her parents had an identical one, with the legs fashioned after those of a lion. Large platters of samosas and pakoras with various chutneys in small containers sat on its glass surface, which obscured the pattern of dark vines and flowers carved into the wood.

Aunty Parveen was in the kitchen wearing a black velvet shalwar chemise, which had small sparkly balls decorating the hemline. A man with a thin mustache and heavily gelled, center-parted hair was talking to her. He looked like a swarthy villain from a 1930s movie. *It must be Uncle Aziz,* thought Jameela. She stood up and moved closer to the kitchen to hear their conversation.

"We can find you help. There are many fine Pakistani psychiatrists who specialize in this sort of thing."

"I don't need help from your psychiatry friends. I know who I am, and I won't be bullied by you."

"You have a sickness that can be cured."

"Oh, really? Then why does Iran have a progressive attitude toward sex reassignment surgeries? They don't treat it like a sickness."

"The Shia are always a little off when it comes to religion," said Aziz. "They even allow tattoos."

"So, if one Muslim sect disagrees with the all-powerful Sunnis, they must be wrong?"

"That's enough talk for today. I'll be back tomorrow."

"Have a good trip back to Pakistan," snapped Aunty Parveen before rejoining her friends.

She seemed more assertive than before. Nusrat had told Jameela that Aunty Parveen was watching a lot of *Orange Is the New Black* and that Laverne Cox was her new hero.

Jameela walked into the kitchen and popped a piece of bright orange poppadom into her mouth. Its spongy texture stuck on her tongue. As Aziz passed by, Jameela stepped in his path and he bumped into her.

"Excuse me, young lady," he said, as he brushed some crumbs off his jacket and tried to walk around her. The poppadom dissolved on Jameela's tongue just in time.

"I heard you're part of the ISI in Pakistan," she said, taking a white ceramic dish from a stack and spooning out a gulab jaman from a large crystal bowl. She quickly offered him the treat. He thanked her and, after his first bite, observed her closely.

"Who told you that?" he asked, standing straighter. "I'm a respected Pakistani businessman who makes his money selling hand-knotted wool carpets from Waziristan to fine establishments everywhere."

"My mother told me," said Jameela, as she took another spoonful of the silver-frosted gulab jaman. She should have eaten before she came. The whiff of cardamom-infused syrup was intoxicating. This seemed less like a book club and more like a food orgy of all her childhood favorites. "And those women know everything."

"What do you want?" sniffed Aziz. His dessert was clearly taking the edge off.

Jameela told herself to remember this technique as an interrogation tactic. Food before facts. "I have information about DICK."

Aziz smirked. "What could you possibly know about the DICK?" he asked. "Everyone thinks they have some secret knowledge."

"The imam of my mosque was taken away by the police for questioning."

"American law enforcement questions everyone. If you order too much fertilizer for your roses, they think you're a terrorist."

He was arrogant. Her father had been right to describe him as insufferable. But she needed him to save Ibrahim, so she willed herself to remain calm and persuasive. "We went to the authorities to tell them about a homeless man who joined DICK. When they found out Ibrahim had friends who were part of DICK, they kept him for more questioning. I never saw him again."

"Perhaps your friend decided to get a better-paying job in retail. Being an imam in the West is a pauper's errand."

Jameela played her trump card. "A few hours later, I called his number and heard this."

She put her iPhone on speaker, and a clearly shaken Ibrahim spoke: "I am sorry for the inconvenience of leaving my job so suddenly, but my mother is ill in Egypt, and I must go and visit her. I will not be home for a while. Could someone water my plants?"

"So, he's a good son. That doesn't make him a criminal or interesting."

"His mother died a year ago. And he has no plants. It was a signal. He was never planning a trip to the Middle East. The police are covering up his disappearance. And I don't know why."

The third gulab jaman that was headed to Aziz's mouth stopped and came back down. "I hate Americans. Those bastards screwed us over with the bin Laden capture."

"The Navy SEALs? What did you want them to do?"

"They knew where bin Laden was, and instead of sharing their information, they kept it hidden." Aziz thrust the gulab jaman into his mouth and chewed furiously.

"Probably because they thought you would tip off bin Laden," she said. "He'd been living safely in Pakistan for years."

Aziz looked at her with distaste. Oh no, thought Jameela. Why did she always have to be so combative? She needed him as an ally. Placation was necessary.

"You know nothing of Pakistan or its politics," said Aziz, as a fourth gulab jaman finally made it to his mouth.

Jameela had not grown up in a conspiracy-based household for nothing. Her father's obsession was Afghanistan. "I know a little bit. Did you know the Americans had books published in Virginia to promote jihad? They distributed them in elementary schools in Afghanistan, so children would grow up thinking that violence and fighting were the fundamentals of their faith."

She could tell Aziz was impressed. "I actually have some of those books in my office in Pakistan. Few people know about how much material was created."

"In a way, one could say that modern jihad was an American invention."

Aziz snorted. "The Americans will never accept their responsibility in inciting that rage."

Jameela couldn't believe it. She had him. After all those years she had been forced to listen to her father's bellyaching about the Americans, it had finally paid off.

After a decade of arming Afghan mujahideen — Muslim freedom fighters, as they were called then — recruiting Muslims from around the world, including Osama bin Laden, to fight alongside the mujahideen, and turning local schools into institutions that fermented the indoctrination of violence, the Soviets withdrew, but the consequences were devastating. In that time period, bin Laden formed al-Qaeda, and its networks spread globally.

"The Americans created the conditions for men to become radicalized and cause chaos in the Middle East," said Jameela. "They bear responsibility for the creation of DICK."

"Those idiots never learn," said Aziz, plucking a piece of fuzz from his shirt.

"Ibrahim has no involvement with DICK. Why would the CIA take him?" she asked.

"If he knows people who have joined, the CIA can get names from him of current operatives. The DICK keeps their agents secret, so any knowledge is useful. What's his name again?"

"Ibrahim Sultan."

Aziz took out his phone and tapped at it for ten minutes. Jameela couldn't take the tension anymore. "What did you find out?"

"Your friend's name is on the Americans' watch list."

She was right. The message in the sandwich had led her here, to con-firmation. It was a bizarre way for God to guide her, but then, God chose a burning bush to reach Moses. At least She was subtler with her.

"How's that possible? He's not a terrorist. He doesn't even kill ants. He scoops them up with a tissue and flings them outside."

"The usual story," said Aziz. "Someone got captured somewhere, was tortured for names, and blurted out your friend's name in a moment of desperation."

"So the police ran his name, and he came up?"

"Of course. Your police friends think they've captured a real terrorist, and now they're going to outsource his torture to gather more informa-tion."

"Outsource it to whom?" asked Jameela.

"Syria, most likely. They'll jail him, torture him until he gives them enough information, and then he'll have an unfortunate accident."

Jameela was horrified. The gulab jaman turned in her stomach. She reached for a large teapot encased in a quilted red, green, and gold tea cozy. It looked like it was wearing a Christmas snowsuit. She poured some chai.

"Tea?" she asked, passing Aziz the cup. He took it and sipped. She poured herself some too. As the hot sweet liquid flavored with cinna-mon, fennel, and cloves warmed her, she pushed herself to continue. "Can you help me get Ibrahim back?"

"Depends."

"On what?"

"On how far you're willing to go."

GO — that fateful word again. It must be a sign. What else could it be? "What do you mean?"

Aziz watched her conspiratorially. Jameela wondered if he might even twirl his mustache. "To free your imam, you'll have to go to Paki-stan. You cannot tell anyone where you're going, or else the DICK will find out and kill you, and then there will be no hope for Ibrahim."

Jameela jerked as if she had just been shocked with an electric prod. She sat down on a sticky vinyl chair. Riotous sounds came from the liv-ing room as the women discussed *Fifty Shades of Grey,* but the atmo-sphere in the kitchen was menacing. Her hope had been that Aziz would bring Ibrahim home, and she would be off the hook. The word *GO* wasn't supposed to take her out of North America. There was no way she was going. Even to save Ibrahim.

"I can't go to Pakistan," she whispered. "How would that help get Ibrahim back?"

Aziz looked physically pained as he got up and brought back a pomegranate, two clean bowls, two spoons, and a small paring knife. "According to our intelligence, the DICK has been looking for a Western-born Muslim woman for one of their most dangerous operations. It will be the next 9/11."

"Why Western-born?" asked Jameela, trying to hide her terror. "Don't they have enough women in their own ranks?"

Aziz started carving the outside of the shell and then gently separating the fruit without staining his hands. It was impressive. "It's symbolic, because it proves that Western Muslims are unhappy with decades of US imperial interference with their countries and want revenge." He gave Jameela a spoon and divided the pomegranate seeds into the two bowls. "If the West treated the Muslim world fairly, Western Muslims would never join the DICK."

The tart, sweet pomegranate juice exploded in her mouth, leaving the hard seeds, which she ground with her teeth. She swallowed. "So, it's a PR move."

"Of course. Up until now, their recruits have been mostly disaffected Muslim men, silly teenage girls, and overzealous white converts. They don't appeal to the vast majority of well-educated and stable Muslims living in Canada and the US, countries that have historically integrated Muslims well into their societies."

"You want me to be that Western-born woman?" She couldn't believe those words came out of her mouth.

"You fit the profile perfectly."

"Why not just get one of your spies to infiltrate?"

"We've tried. But the DICK always asks the spies an arcane question about Western culture. We have taught them about all the intricacies of the American constitution, for example, but the questions are so obscure that we don't even understand what is being asked."

"Like what?"

"What is the best product in the Fenty Beauty line?"

"The Trophy Wife highlighter. Everyone knows that."

"My God. You are the perfect recruit."

Jameela stifled the feeling of rising pride. "You want me to pretend I've been radicalized and join DICK?"

"Only if you have the courage."

It was a trick. Seduction by pomegranate. "It's not a matter of courage. I'm the reason he's in trouble. But there must be another way to save him."

"'You break it, you fix it,' as Westerners like to say," said Aziz. "Or as Muslims like to say about Westerners, 'They break it, and we have to live with the mess for generations.'"

Jameela couldn't argue with that sentiment, but she needed Aziz to take her seriously so she could figure out a saner plan to rescue Ibrahim.

"Please tell me there's a plan B that doesn't involve me leaving."

"Plan B is that your friend dies. Assuming he's not dead already."

She knew Aziz was right. The American authorities weren't going to listen to her. They had already covered their tracks. And who knew what would happen to her if she went to the media with her story. On a scale of one to Edward Snowden, she needed her foot out the door already. "Let's say I'm willing to go. What's next?"

Aziz took a deep breath, as if this was the moment he had been waiting for. "We'd arrange for you to get to Pakistan and join the DICK. You'd learn about their plans for bombing a Western target. You'd relay that information to us."

"And then?"

"In return, we find your imam and send him home."

"That's suicide, and I'm not doing it," said Jameela.

Aziz tapped his phone for a few minutes and then thrust it toward her. On the screen was a photo of Ibrahim tied up with a piece of fabric covering his mouth. There was a bruise above his left eye and a cut on his forehead.

"Is that your imam?"

"Where did you get that?" said Jameela, gripping the phone. Panic surged through her.

"He's already on his way to be tortured in Syria. But it's not too late to have him rescued. We have operatives there who could intercept and bring him back home."

"So just do it!" Jameela whispered savagely. "Why would you let an innocent man get hurt?"

"This is a war, my dear, and each of us has to play our part. Your part was written when you made friends with this man. And if you cooperate, you could save thousands of lives."

This wasn't a joke. Thousands of innocent people would die in a horrific terrorist attack if she didn't stop it, not to mention Ibrahim was going to be tortured and killed in a Syrian prison. "And if I don't cooperate?"

"I can arrange for his fingernails to be sent to you for sentimental purposes."

He was a monster, but a monster who could save Ibrahim.

"But how would I even find out about this mission? It's not like I can just join DICK and say, 'Hey, guys, what's up?' I'd have to penetrate their ranks at the highest level, and that could take months."

"The operation is imminent, and I'm in a position to recommend you for it. You just have to relay the details to us. After we confirm your information, we will bring back your imam."

"You're in a position to recommend someone for the mission?" Jameela's disdain for Pakistan and her parents' blind loyalty to it had a lot to do with the way their country played two faces when it came to combating terror. They had likely hidden bin Laden, and they wouldn't hesitate to nurture the Taliban and al-Qaeda if they needed those militant groups to suppress nationalist sentiments in their tribal areas. She would argue with her parents that the Pakistani government needed these groups to exist in order to get generous military aid from the US. But they had finally overplayed their hand. The Americans had cut them off.

"If we get details about the next the DICK operation," said Aziz, "the Americans may restore military aid."

Jameela looked at him from the corner of her eye. "You can't extract information from DICK this time, can you? In fact, you can't do this without me."

Aziz sniffed and put his bowl down. "The DICK knows about our . . . relationship with the US, so they are less forthcoming."

"Really? DICK is worried you might double-cross them. And the Americans are tired of being double-crossed."

Aziz concentrated on the bright yellow ladoos sitting beside the shiny orange jalebis as if trying to decide which one to pick. Jameela voted for the jalebi, and as if he could read her mind, Aziz picked up the spiral-shaped confection, broke it into two, and gave one half to Jameela, who immediately took a bite of the sweet, hard outer shell, which released the saffron-drenched juices into her mouth.

"The DICK insist that they want an American Muslim woman to carry out the attack. A woman who is born and raised in America, with a stable job and family, would get far more social media attention than anyone else. The DICK is all about symbolism, and they feel that would send a message to the Western world that they can't trust their Muslim citizens. 9/11 was carried out by Saudi nationals, but the next attack will be from someone homegrown. It will also serve to further sever ties between American Muslims and their non-Muslim counterparts. They are seeking to end that relationship of trust and community."

A religious war. Jameela felt a chill race down her spine. The warm tea wasn't working anymore. The US was probably one of the few non-Muslim countries in the world where Muslims were free to practice their faith and contribute to society. But any attack from a Muslim-American citizen would inspire violent retaliations.

Aziz apparently noticed her unease and put down his teacup. "It's just a matter of time before they find someone who will carry out the mission. And then thousands will die. My hope is to find the right person first, place her with the right people, and get the information to stop it. Do you want to be that person?"

Jameela wondered how this conversation had gone so sideways. She'd come to her mother's book club to manipulate this man into saving Ibrahim. She'd been outmanipulated by him, and now she was being asked to do the unthinkable. She was a wife and mother. Espionage was not in her skill set, unless tracking down obscure vintage items of clothing on eBay counted. Not to mention she could get seriously injured or killed. She should get out while she still could.

Mind you, she thought, pouring herself more tea, *Islamophobia is at an all-time high.* Lee Lee's future and the future of Muslims living in North America were starting to become imperiled as the bonds of trust started to fray. This had been DICK's plan from the beginning. White supremacists were using the same tactics here at home: vandalizing mosques and killing Muslims to start a race war. Even the Liverspot

Mosque had been spray-painted with graffiti — *Muslims Go Home!* — in angry red, puffy letters. She had to make a decision.

"And I'm the closest you've come to finding someone desperate enough to listen to you," said Jameela, with some bitterness.

"You're quick. Spy craft suits you."

Jameela ignored the backhanded compliment. She thought about all the people who would be killed if a bomb went off in a crowded place like an airport or a mall. What if she had been in a position to prevent 9/11? How different would the world be today? But leaving without telling Murray or Lee Lee was unthinkable, and if she told them, they would commit her for sure.

"How do I know the US won't indict and convict me for terrorist activities?"

"The same way I know that I won't suddenly choke on this pomegranate seed. Faith."

Jameela's mind flashed back to the previous week when she had met Ibrahim in the mosque. He was vacuuming the stairs and had no idea that her presence in his life was about to destroy him.

"If I find out about the bomb plot, you'll get Ibrahim back."

"Yes. But you must leave tonight, or it will be too late to save him."

"What? My husband thinks I'm in New York visiting my parents and signing books in McNally Jackson."

"Make sure he keeps thinking that. You have a cell phone. They work from anywhere."

12

AS JAMEELA ENTERED THE BUSY AIRPORT LOUNGE, THE humidity hit her like a wall. The last time she'd been in Karachi, she was five and on a family vacation. She'd forgotten about the heat. People dressed in cotton shalwar chemises and Western-style clothing bustled around her.

A silent, dark-skinned man with a pockmarked face held up a cardboard sign with her name on it.

"My name is Yusuf," he said without emotion. "I'll be taking you to Aziz." He took her bag. Aziz had traveled separately on a private military plane. He said his movements were always tracked by the Americans, and it would be suspicious if they were seen together.

Yusuf was silent for the entire hourlong journey through the winding traffic. The roads were stuffed with cars, buses, minibuses, and motorbikes. Jameela had never seen such traffic congestion in her life. No one stayed in their lanes, vehicles shot into spaces that became available without signaling, and the horns never stopped beeping. The smell of diesel fuel permeated the air. Worried about getting overwhelmed by the stimulation, she shut her eyes.

The hardest thing about the trip was not being able to tell Murray and Lee Lee where she was going. She'd told them she would be staying in New York for an extended period of time doing book signings across the city, and that she'd text and email them often. She left a note for her mother saying she was staying with an old friend. Hopefully this whole adventure could be wrapped up in a few days. Since this lunatic journey started as an act of faith, she might as well continue, and pray that everything would work out.

They drove up to a house behind black iron gates. Two men in military fatigues with automatic rifles stood at attention. They exchanged words with Yusuf and then opened the gates. The house was finished in pink and white stucco and wouldn't have looked out of place in a Florida retirement community.

Once inside, she was led to a small room with dust-coated furniture made of dark wood. She felt like she had been transported back in time. There was a record player on a table with a stack of old, frayed cardboard-sleeved albums. The bookshelf had the usual books on the Qur'an and Islam, but then Jameela stopped. There they were. The anti-Soviet textbooks. She pulled out a yellowed alphabet primer and flipped through the letters in Pashto — *J is for jihad,* with the accompanying sentences *"Jihad is mandatory"* and *"I, too, will go to jihad." T is for topak, or gun. How do you use the word? "My uncle has a gun. He does jihad with a gun." Our religion is Islam. All the Russians and the Infidels are our religion's enemies.* It was the alphabet of jihad. Every word had a picture of a bullet or a sword or some item associated with fighting and killing.

Finally, Aziz came into the room. His thin mustache was artfully sculpted. She wondered how much time he spent maintaining it.

"Mrs. Jameela, I hope your flight was satisfactory," he said in that strained voice that indicated he could not have cared less if she had been trussed up and stored with the luggage.

"It was kind of you to fly me first class," said Jameela.

"Please never talk of it again. I needed you to be able to sleep so you could begin preparations right away."

Yusuf came in with a tray and offered some tea in china cups with the same floral pattern that decorated Aunty Parveen's set. Pakistan's colonial history seemed to continue through Royal Doulton. He put a tin box of chocolate-covered cookies on the table. Each biscuit had the image of a man playing polo pressed into its chocolate topping. Even the cookies were colonized. Her phone pinged. It was a text message from Murray.

Where r u?

"Who is that?" asked Aziz.

"My husband," said Jameela, her heart suddenly thudding. The reality of what she'd done was starting to seep in. They were probably having breakfast together. Murray attempting another new project, the way he had with origami or knitting, to keep his mind "sharp," only to abandon it a week later, inviting the wrath of Lee Lee, which would spur Murray to ask her why she wasn't having fun with friends like a regular teenager. Grief had transformed all their roles, and Jameela suddenly missed the tug-of-war of their mornings. She wanted to go home.

Aziz read her mind. "Do not panic. Just text him something as if you were back in the US."

Jameela remembered that they were twelve hours ahead. It was eight a.m. in Liverspot. She texted him back.

Getting ready for the signing at The Owl Bookstore. Love you.

Moments later, Murray texted back.

Have fun. Call me when you're free.

"I really do have a signing," said Jameela. "I don't suppose we could figure out DICK's plan and get both Ibrahim and myself back to the US before people realize I'm gone and my writing career evaporates? By the way, have you figured out where he is?"

"As I said before, he's on a flight to Syria," said Aziz. "The Americans are trying to extract information about the people who recruited your homeless friend."

"Ibrahim doesn't know anything," Jameela repeated. "He was just trying to help Barkley out, because he's a good Muslim. What's Barkley's deal, anyway?"

"Your homeless friend Barkley was being groomed to be part of the DICK for some time now."

"You're telling me we accidentally bumped into a jihadist wannabe in the park?"

"Did Mr. Barkley seem unusually interested in Islam?"

"Well, yeah, and also in good-quality lattes. Although he also had enough money to pay for them."

"Yes, the DICK befriends people on Facebook, and then sends recruits small amounts of money as gifts to buy their loyalty," said Aziz, looking disgusted as he sipped his tea.

"I don't get it," said Jameela. "DICK recruits homeless guys to do what, exactly?"

"To fight in their war."

"But why?"

"Because Muslims from Muslim homes ask critical questions."

"Like what?"

"Like, 'Why are you killing so many people, mostly Muslims, for no reason?'"

"White people don't ask these questions?"

"Muslims born into the faith have a more nuanced understanding of Islam than converts. Converts are easier to recruit, because they don't have a strong religious knowledge base and, more importantly, are looking to belong to a group that has an identity. But young, disaffected teenage Muslims fall into this category because they are naïve and see the world in black and white."

"What will happen to Barkley?"

"He'll become, as you people say, 'cannon fodder.'"

Jameela's phone pinged again. It was another text from Murray.

Just got a call from your mother. She said you're not staying with your friend and I called the bookstore and they said you canceled. She's worried. So am I. What's going on?

"Uh-oh," said Jameela. "My husband just found out that I'm not selling books like I said I was."

"Careless planning," said Aziz. "You should never lie. I will fix it."

Jameela handed him her phone. Aziz read the text and looked at her coldly.

"Yes, this was to be expected. We must tell him the truth."

"That I came to Pakistan to rescue Ibrahim?"

"No, a different truth. You became radicalized and left to join the DICK. The DICK will be monitoring your phone messages, and so will the American authorities."

"What? No! Why would the Americans be monitoring my phone?"

"Because Yusuf created false Facebook messages between yourself and undercover recruiters for the DICK while you were on the plane to convince them you believe in their cause. You are now a terrorist. Congratulations."

"He did what? I never gave you permission to do that."

"You were encouraging me to go fast so you could sign your books at the bird bookshop."

Jameela watched in horror as Aziz started typing on her phone.

"I want my phone back!" Jameela lunged for it, but Aziz gave it to Yusuf, who left the room. "You lied to me. You made me believe this whole crazy adventure was going to be quick and easy, and now you're creating a new identity for me and lying to my husband. You betrayed me!" Her face felt red and hot.

"I did not betray you. Stop acting like you're in an episode of *Star Wars*. I may not have shared all the details with you, true, but if I did, you may not have agreed so easily."

"I wouldn't have agreed at all!" screamed Jameela, desperately looking around the room for some sort of projectile to implant in Aziz's head. Yusuf had wisely cleared away the china in the meantime and came back quickly for the cookie tin. He must have sensed her rage.

"Stop having a temper tantrum. You are not five years old. The phone must stay with us. We must plant more information on it, so the American authorities continue to believe that you've joined the DICK. And the DICK must believe that you have been radicalized and are not a spy, otherwise they will kill you, and then I must start all over again."

"Well, I wouldn't want to inconvenience you," spat Jameela.

"Thank you for understanding," he said. "We will send messages to the authorities and the press from time to time. And then we must destroy your phone, because after this day, no one must be able to track it using its GPS signal, or they could kill you right away."

"You've told my government that I'm undercover, right? They might kill me otherwise."

Aziz looked at her. "No, everyone must believe you are a real terrorist, or this plan will not work."

Jameela realized that she should have asked these critical questions much earlier. Too late now. "Now everyone will want to kill me."

"I need you to stop talking. We must concentrate on the plan, because, as you mentioned, much can go wrong."

"What did you say to my husband?"

"I stated that you have finally seen your faith in a new light and must pursue different goals. He will understand."

13

MURRAY PUT HIS KNITTING NEEDLES, WHICH WERE AT-
tached to a growing lavender scarf, on his lap and reached for his phone
to read an incoming text.

"What's wrong, Dad?" asked Lee Lee eating breakfast while simultaneously watching her favorite YouTuber, Mr. Aardvark, on her iPhone.

"It's your mom. She just sent me the oddest text."

"Well, she has been a little off lately," said Lee Lee, unperturbed, taking another mouthful of her cereal. "Is she planning on sewing parkas
for polar bears?"

"No, it says —" Murray couldn't believe the words.

Lee Lee looked up and saw his face. She reached over and grabbed
the phone from his hand.

"Lee Lee, don't read it." But it was too late.

Lee Lee dropped her spoon. It clattered to the kitchen floor.

"What's going on, Dad?" she asked, her voice high.

Murray hugged her as she started sobbing. It took Murray all the
courage he could muster not to do the same. It wouldn't help if the two
of them bawled in unison. He needed to pull it together. His mind went
back to when he'd met Jameela twenty years earlier during a physics
class in college. She'd dropped her giant backpack full of textbooks on
the floor beside him and landed in her seat with a loud, exaggerated
sigh. She'd had eyes the size of saucers, dark skin, and long black hair.

The air of desperation emanating from her had triggered a yearning to save her from pain he couldn't yet understand.

As their relationship developed, Jameela had confided in him. How the death of her brother changed everything about her life. How her parents blamed themselves and became hypervigilant about faith to give themselves a sense of security. And how she had given up on that faith.

"Publishing this book has taken a huge toll on your mom," he said to Lee Lee. "Stirring up memories of her lost brother . . ."

He bitterly regretted not staying home from the dental clinic yesterday. Clearly, Jameela had been planning something and thought she couldn't trust him. She'd always been a little high-strung. But this time was different. *Would she really have abandoned him?* He read the text again while carefully holding the phone away from his daughter. Lee Lee was crying on his shoulder, and a pool of snot was collecting there.

I have decided never again to return to the United States. Please accept my decision, your wife, Jameela.

His heart leapt. He hadn't read it carefully before. That wasn't Jameela's voice. It was someone pretending to be her. Jameela was in trouble.

"Lee Lee, I think someone's got your mom's phone and wants us to think she's been radicalized."

Lee Lee stopped crying and pulled away from him. "Really? She didn't decide to leave us? How do you know?"

"Because your mother doesn't end her texts with 'your wife, Jameela,'" he said, giving Lee Lee the phone. Lee Lee stared at the strange combination of words and grew calmer. Lee Lee had inherited the savior complex from her father. It manifested in her obsessive need to fill him with fiber and vitamins to stave off early death by high fructose corn syrup and trans fat.

The phone vibrated in her hand, and she passed it to her father.

It was Nusrat.

"Ummi, how are you?" asked Murray.

"Terrible," snapped Nusrat. "Jameela's been brainwashed, You Idiot, and it's all your fault. Jameela was at my book club talking to Aziz —"

"Who is Aziz?"

"I was just about to tell you that, You Idiot. Let me finish. Aziz is Parveen's psychotic brother who belongs to Pakistan's secret intelligence branch. They talked for an hour, and then she went back to my house and wrote a note that she was visiting Chloe, a friend from high school. When I called Chloe, she didn't know what I was talking about. Jameela must have packed and left for Pakistan right after."

"What did Aziz say to her?" asked Murray.

"I wasn't in the kitchen with the two of them, You Idiot. But whatever he said convinced her to leave the country. The CIA came to my house this morning to tell me there was a woman who matched Jameela's description taking a direct flight from the JFK airport to Karachi."

Murray scrambled through the kitchen desk filing cabinet. Jameela's passport was still there.

"How did she manage to fly without her passport?"

"She sent messages on her Facebook to the DICK telling them she wanted to join," replied Nusrat. "Someone from the DICK arranged for her flight to Pakistan where she would meet her contact and then fly to Syria. The CIA were alerted immediately, and they decided to let her travel in order to track her movements. But her phone was destroyed after she got to Karachi. The CIA believe Jameela has joined the DICK. Did something happen before she left? Did you have a fight with her? What did you do to make her run away? Think, You Idiot, think!"

Oh please, a silly domestic fight wouldn't have caused Jameela to suddenly run out on him and become a terrorist. If that were the case, DICK would be full of disgruntled women.

"She believed that the CIA kidnapped the imam of our local mosque," said Murray, "and sent him abroad to be tortured for information about DICK ... We didn't believe her. She wanted to save him. This doesn't make any sense."

"Of course it doesn't. I knew nothing good would come from marrying you, and now look, she's got herself embroiled in an international terrorist plot." Nusrat started crying.

Murray couldn't be annoyed with her. She was scared, and so was he. Nothing was adding up. The message he had received was cryptic and clearly from someone else.

"Going to Pakistan isn't the same as being a terrorist, Ummi. Why does the CIA think she's joined DICK?"

"Because, You Idiot, the CIA intercepted communications between her and the DICK. She's been recruited to carry out a suicide operation on a Western target."

Murray's head suddenly felt leaden. Sometimes he dismissed Jameela's histrionics, but how could he have missed something this big? Surely, he would have noticed his wife becoming radicalized and joining a homicidal death cult. He thought back to her newfound desire to pray, which was odd, but she didn't spout anti-Western sentiments or talk about the need to avenge Muslim deaths. If anyone should be suspects, it should be Jameela's anti-Western parents. But they mostly terrorized him. This whole crazy thing started after Jameela went to feed the homeless with Ibrahim. He should have realized that coming into contact with Barkley would make her emotionally vulnerable. Jameela's mental state had clearly unraveled right in front of him, and he had done nothing. He needed to sit down.

"Are you okay, Dad?" asked Lee Lee. He noticed she was shaking. He had almost forgotten she was there. He told Nusrat he'd call her back later.

"Everything's fine." He held Lee Lee tight once again.

"No, it's not, Dad," said Lee Lee, dribbling tears that were merging into the puddle of snot on the back of Murray's shirt. "Mom's gone missing, and now Nani's saying she's a terrorist."

That pretty much summed up the last half hour. Their whole lives had just shattered.

"You have to go to school," said Murray, trying to buy time so he could pull himself together.

"It's only seven-thirty," said Lee Lee looking tiny in a Dalmatian-spotted onesie.

Murray thought he was going to have a nervous breakdown. Then his cell phone buzzed again.

"This is Special Agent Carmichael, with the CIA. We'd like to have a word with you, Mr. Green."

Strangely, these words came as a balm. This hallucinatory world had become real. He needed help to understand what was happening with his wife.

"Sure, where can we meet?"

"We're standing outside your door."

14

JAMEELA SAT IN THE DUSTY LIVING ROOM OF AZIZ'S SE-
cret bungalow in Karachi. She'd had time to wash up and change into
a cotton shalwar chemise that had the same red, black, and turquoise
floral design as the carpet in the foyer. But she wasn't complaining; the
outfit was breathable in the poorly air-conditioned room. The humidity was starting to make her normally wavy hair look like a halo of black
netting. She rummaged in her handbag for a brush. Just then, the door
opened and Aziz entered with a man who looked like an Arab Dwayne
Johnson. He wore sandy-colored pants and a T-shirt, which bulged with
what she thought must be chemically enhanced muscles.

"I trust you've had a chance to rest," said Aziz.

"I'm great. The bathrooms are a bit different here, but other than
that, everything's fine. I was hoping we could talk about letting my
family know I'm okay. My husband and daughter are going to be really
freaked —"

"They are the least of my concerns," interrupted Aziz. "This is Abdullah. He is the DICK's number two." Abdullah was gazing at her like a sali-
vating lion stares at a gazelle.

"Nice to meet you, Abdullah," said Jameela, in what seemed an inappropriate exchange, given the circumstances.

"Abdullah speaks very little English," said Aziz. "He's been sent here by
the DICK to vet the Western recruit. If he approves of you, he will give
you the information on the Western target."

Great, thought Jameela. Trying to find Ibrahim was becoming more complicated by the minute, and she had to get the required intel from a guy who looked like he was sharpening his teeth with his tongue.

Aziz pulled out a piece of paper. "This question was formulated by the upper echelons of the DICK to determine if you are a true, authentic Western woman." Aziz put on reading glasses. "In season four of *The Real Housewives of New Jersey,* Melissa Gorga was accused of hiding her stripper past —"

"By Kim D. Everyone knows that. And when her sister-in-law Teresa Giudice didn't have her back, family drama hit the fan."

Aziz translated the answer into Arabic to Abdullah, who nodded.

"That is the correct answer," Aziz said.

Abdullah looked like his skin was glowing.

"Really, that's the question that determines if I'm for real?"

"Yes, the DICK are looking for the type of Western woman who has arcane knowledge of such matters. It says something about the vacuousness of her personality."

Jameela pulled Aziz aside so they were not within Abdullah's earshot, even though she knew his understanding of English was patchy. She whispered savagely in Aziz's ear. "Now that Mr. Drool approves of me, he tells me the plan, I tell you about it, I go home, hopefully tonight, and you can go about your day screwing up someone else's life."

"Partly correct."

"What?"

"They will tell you part of the plan. They feel that if they reveal the whole plan —"

"You might betray them. I don't blame them. I should never have trusted you either."

"And there's been a minor complication."

Jameela's heart sank.

Abdullah walked up to the two of them and spoke to Aziz in Arabic while continuing to stare at her as if she were a prime rib steak. Aziz seemed pleased at the utterances.

"He likes you," said Aziz.

"Well-done?"

"No, he'd like to marry you. He doesn't have much money, but he can offer you seniority over his other wives."

Jameela couldn't believe her ears.

"I already have a husband!" Jameela screamed. "The deal was I'd learn about their plot against a Western target, not marry Arab Aquaman."

"He will not make us privy to the plot unless he has some sort of commitment from you."

"Commitment? To carry out the plot maybe, I could understand, but marriage? How much sense does that make?"

"We never dreamed of getting cooperation from someone so high up in the DICK. He suspected right away that I was planting you as our spy, but after seeing your photograph, he decided he wanted you as his wife."

"You showed him my picture?"

"From your passport. Believe me, I wasn't impressed by the photo either, but the heart wants what it wants." Aziz continued, "Abdullah is what we call a soft DICK. He's worried Talal is becoming more erratic."

"Who is Talal?"

"The hardest DICK of all, as they say. He leads the group. Abdullah says Talal is becoming more turbulent and making decisions to kill people in brutal and inhumane ways. He says he didn't sign up for this. We have a chance to point Abdullah in another direction. But he won't give us the information without a price. You. This is a coup! Do you accept?" asked Aziz, who was the most excited she'd ever seen him.

"I do not accept!" yelled Jameela. "What the hell's going on? Are you getting money for selling me? Is this what the whole trip was about?"

She knew Aziz had never seemed trustworthy, but this seemed extreme, even for him. She wasn't sure if she was having a panic attack. Did those come with an intense need to throttle someone? No, it wasn't fear coursing through her, it was pure rage. Her fury seemed to have an interesting effect on Abdullah, who became more energetic. In a stream of rapid-fire Arabic, he gesticulated wildly to Aziz.

"Okay, he's agreed to give up his other wives if that will make you happy. After the wedding, he will put you up in his apartment in Dubai so you can shop for handbags all day. He knows women in the West aren't used to sharing a man."

Jameela forced herself to calm down. She needed a clear head to find a way out of this nightmare. And getting upset was only making Bigfoot more enamored with her. "Yeah, well, women in the West aren't used to husband-swapping either. Well, most of us. Did you tell him I was already married?"

"Of course not, he might back down. It's poor form to try to steal another man's wife."

"Then why are we doing this?"

"Because he knows about the bomb plot. He's in their trusted circle," said Aziz.

"I'm not marrying him to get intel for you. You're insane. You marry him if you want."

Abdullah rubbed his chin and paced the room.

"It was not my intention for you to become his wife. But we must follow this through — otherwise he will not give you the information. If Pakistan is known for anything besides terrorism, it's how to organize a wedding in less than twenty-four hours. After the consummation, Abdullah will give you the plan, I'll arrange for you to be whisked home, and I'll ask my operatives to bring back your imam. The Americans will be pleased with Pakistan, and our military aid will be restored. What could go wrong?"

Was anything going right? "Your mission involves more than what was agreed upon. I'm not marrying him!"

Aziz looked like he wanted to slap her. Abdullah spoke again.

"He's impressed with your spirit. As a result, he'll give you more concessions. What else do you desire? Diamonds, rubies, a block of gold?"

A block big enough to knock the two of them out. There was no point in getting hysterical. She'd better pull her act together, or she'd be trapped in a gold-plated castle in Dubai with pet cheetahs roaming the perimeter. It was time to take control of the situation.

"Since it's my marriage, I'm negotiating my own terms."

Jameela knew that in Islam, women were encouraged to stipulate their conditions before marriage. They could forbid polygamy or specify the number of children they wanted.

This caught Aziz off guard. "You can't change the rules of the game," he told her sternly.

"*You* are constantly changing the rules of the game."

"Sex with him wouldn't be so bad. You could explain the circumstances to your old husband later; he would understand," replied Aziz, with an indifferent look in his eyes.

"I thought they liked young, nubile virgins," said Jameela.

"That's just a Western stereotype. And ... I may have exaggerated your skills ... once I learned of his interest in you."

Jameela couldn't believe what she was hearing.

"And your current behavior certainly isn't turning off his amour for you."

Abdullah seemed to be panting. He turned to Aziz again and spoke in rapid-fire Arabic.

"He wants to know your conditions for marriage," said Aziz, scowling.

Jameela's mind raced. The entire point of this trip was to bring Ibrahim back, but Aziz clearly had his own agenda. Even if she did succeed in getting the intel to Aziz, there was no way Tarzan would let her go home to Murray and Lee Lee. She wasn't sure she could trust Aziz to rescue her or get Ibrahim out of Syria. Maybe she was supposed to go to Syria herself and rescue Ibrahim? But how? If Ibrahim were here, he'd tell her to have faith and seek help in prayer. *Help me now, if You're listening*, screamed Jameela in her head. And then inspiration struck. "I want to see Talal." Even Abdullah seemed to understand her now. Both he and Aziz stood up.

"The leader of the DICK?" screamed Aziz, spittle flying. "No one has seen him in over five years. Some people aren't even sure he's alive. You're asking to see someone who is more elusive than even Osama bin Laden was in his day."

"Either I see him, or I'm not getting married to Mr. Wonderful over here," said Jameela, sitting down and pouring herself cold tea. It wasn't half bad, and her chocolate cookie survived the dunk. She sucked it with a slurping noise, her habit since childhood, savoring the melting chocolate chips. Abdullah eyed her as if she were doing a pole dance. Some people had fetishes, and she had accidentally discovered Abdullah's. She kept her eyes firmly above his neck, so the only bulging she did see was from the veins in Aziz's temples, which were turning purple with rage. She wasn't sure who would explode from unrequited feelings first. Both wanted her for different purposes.

She eyed the samosas sitting near the cookies, but she feared that would be the last straw for Abdullah, and she didn't trust Aziz to protect her. He would probably let Abdullah eat her alive for the sake of revenge at this point, so she sat absolutely still. She didn't have to wait for long. Abdullah spoke in his very limited English.

"I agree."

15

IBRAHIM'S LEGS WERE SHACKLED, AND HIS HANDS were cuffed behind his back. There was a canvas bag over his head, but it didn't block the sound of the plane's engine. The last few days had been a nightmare. He had been forced to leave a fake voice recording on his answering machine. The worst part was being unable to give notice to the board of the Islamic Association of Liverspot. *What they must think of me, just walking out on the job like that!* And tonight was pizza and sports night for the youth. It was only once a month, and he had been looking forward to it. He had been preparing a special talk on how to avoid distractions during prayers, such as thoughts of buying new running shoes, watching the latest movie, or his personal favorite, undignified thoughts about the opposite sex.

If he was having this problem, then surely those in his youth group must be, too. His recommendation was to think about chickens laying eggs when unsavory images entered one's mind. It was thematically on point, as eggs were a natural product of procreation. This image had helped him immensely over the years. He was sure the teenagers were going to love the suggestion, but now he would never find out. It was doubtful that he would survive the night. He had heard stories about being interrogated by Syrian intelligence. Everyone at Al-Azhar had. His one consolation was that he would finally see God.

"What are you thinking?" grunted a strange voice from nearby. Ibrahim had thought he'd never hear a human voice again. Was it the angel of death? He didn't think so. He wasn't dead yet. Plus, the angel of death couldn't possibly have an American accent. It must be one of his captors. How does one answer the person with the ability to inflict further pain? His arms and legs were badly cramped already. He couldn't risk more discomfort.

"I was thinking, *It is a lovely day.*"

There was a pause. "Well, not for you," said the voice, sounding a little confused.

"I do admit, I have had better," said Ibrahim. "How are you?" He didn't want to seem impolite. A hand smelling of diesel removed the sack from his head. It took his pupils a few minutes to adjust to the light. He was shackled to a seat on some sort of small military transport plane. His seat faced the center of the plane and across from him, there was another row of seats similar to his, each with a small round window above it. His captor was pacing the corridor in between. It felt good to feel the movement of cool air on his face, and he didn't know when the hand would replace the sack, so he breathed deeply.

"Don't get too used to it, pal, you're only getting a few minutes before you go under again," said his captor.

"It is fine. I am grateful for the ease of breath and the small amount of light. I am reminded of the mercies of God: light and air. It is so easy to take them for granted."

He heard a snort. "You're pretty philosophical for a terrorist."

Ibrahim turned to the voice, but the man's camouflage helmet, which matched the rest of his gear, cast a vertical shadow across his face. Finally, his accuser sat down; his face had black eyebrows that were knitted in anger, large brown eyes, and an unhappy nose and mouth.

"I hope you die wherever it is they're sending you," said Angry Face.

His certainly wasn't a nice face. "I am sure I will die in the most horrible way one can imagine," said Ibrahim in a soft voice.

"You deserve everything you're gonna get."

"I helped a homeless man by inviting him to my apartment and preparing breakfast for him. I may have played too much *Angry Birds* with him. As a result, I prayed Maghrib late," said Ibrahim. "But God is merciful and forgives such tardy behavior."

"That's not what it says in your file," said Angry Face.

"I have a file? The résumé that I sent to the Liverspot Mosque? I may have exaggerated my knowledge of the classical forms of Qur'an recitation. I feel that three are sufficient for general —"

"It says here you masterminded the Yemeni airstrike in 2014. Over two hundred people were killed. Half of them were children. You're a sick, sick bastard."

Ibrahim recalled the incident. He was writing his final exams at Al-Azhar when the news reached Egypt. His favorite niece had been in the targeted school when the bombs struck.

"My niece Feroza died in that school," he said, remembering her blue-green eyes. "She was only twelve."

"You killed your own relative?" said Angry Face.

"She wanted to be a veterinarian when she grew up. Her father let her watch the family's camel deliver its offspring when she was only ten." The framed photograph of her smiling face, while she held a newborn calf, was on the side table in his apartment. He could feel the tears falling down his face, but his hands were still shackled so he couldn't brush them away.

Angry Face seemed confused and stood up. "Then why did you do it?"

Now it was Ibrahim's turn to get angry. He didn't lose his temper often, but accusations of killing his own brother's child were too much.

"I went to Yemen to visit my brother when Feroza was born. I became an uncle for the first time. It was my idea to name her Feroza, because her eyes were the color of turquoise. Why would I kill one of the most precious people in my life? I loved her like she was my own daughter!"

Angry Face suddenly started pacing again. "But you were in Yemen when the attack occurred. You are in this photo." He pulled out a grainy photo of a bearded man near the school that he showed Ibrahim.

"I was in Cairo, writing my exam in a room with one hundred other people during the attack," said Ibrahim. "I remember, because many of the students were so distraught when the news came that they could not finish writing their exams, so we were allowed to take a break outside for half an hour to recover. There are many witnesses who could place me in Egypt that day. Did you question any of my colleagues regarding my whereabouts?"

Angry Face stopped pacing, sat on a chair, and seemed to disappear for a few minutes. Finally, he yanked off the helmet releasing a ponytail of dark brown hair.

"You are a woman," said Ibrahim, before he could stop himself. That seemed to pull Angry Face out of her trance.

"Got a problem with that?" said Female Angry Face.

"No, I assumed only men were easily misled by false data, but women are more cautious and thus make fewer mistakes. At least that is what my mother told me."

Her face flinched. "Flattery isn't getting you anywhere, asshole. Can you confirm if you were at the coordinates you claim during the attack in Yemen?"

"I am in a picture Google Street View took that day," said Ibrahim, remembering an incident from the past. "My colleagues at Al-Azhar made a very big deal about it, because there was concern that I cheated on my exam. I was caught talking to a food vendor during a break."

"Did the vendor hand out answers to exam questions?"

"He was the local expert in the Hanafi doctrine, and there were some challenging questions on the exam regarding that school of thought."

"So, you got answers from him?"

"No, a falafel sandwich. But it was still suspicious. I was put on probation until he could be questioned. He had moved away to Sharm el-Sheikh by the time the picture was uploaded. I still remember the coordinates for the photo. I memorized it for the investigation that followed."

Female Angry Face typed as he recited the numbers, and then stared at the photo.

"Your face is blurred," she said. She seemed almost relieved not to believe him.

"Google provided them with the raw footage for the investigation. But I'm still wearing the same shoes." Ibrahim used to be embarrassed he couldn't afford more clothing. He consoled himself with knowing that his clothes were always clean and pressed. His mother had purchased a special pair of Egyptian running shoes for him as a gift for completing his studies. They were fakes of the original, and had white uppers with a reverse Nike symbol stitched in Day-Glo orange. It turned out they were rare because of the mistake. And convenient for him.

Female Angry Face looked at the markings on the sides of his shoes. They were a match.

"Where are we going?" he asked, knowing the answer to that question.

Female Angry Face didn't respond. She seemed deep in thought. And now unhappy, as well as angry. She typed something into what looked like an iPhone, but bigger and more industrial. Finally, she turned to him.

"We have a problem," she said.

That seemed like an understatement to Ibrahim, given his circumstances, but he felt this wasn't worth mentioning.

"Are the torture devices not working properly?" he asked, thinking this showed empathy for his accuser and might soften her toward his case. He was wrong.

"Do you think this is funny?" said Female Angry Face.

"No," replied Ibrahim, "I'm feeling unsettled since I'm going to be tortured in a diabolical fashion. But I am trying to remain calm as there will be much opportunity for distress later."

The plane began its descent. Female Angry Face sat opposite him and put on her seat belt.

"I'm not supposed to tell you this, but there seems to be some discrepancy with the intelligence reports I was given —"

"Who gave you the intelligence?"

"It doesn't matter —"

"It does matter. My life is about to be taken in the most horrible way possible, so I feel that it is my right to know."

"One of your classmates at Al-Azhar listed you as a member of DICK."

"It is common for people to give names when they are being tortured. I am sure I may give a few names for a chance at respite when I am being burned alive."

Female Angry Face looked a little pensive. "There's been a mistake, but I've relayed this information to my colleagues in the CIA. We, on occasion, do make mistakes."

Ibrahim felt sorry for the woman. She seemed genuinely distressed. He wanted to comfort her. "It is fine, it is the will of God, and we must accept our fate." But, strangely, this seemed to enrage her.

"That's the stupidest thing I've ever heard."

"It's a Muslim belief."

"It is not. I'm Muslim, and you're supposed to fight injustice, not sit there like a dummy and take it."

Ibrahim wasn't sure what shocked him more, the fact that she was a

Muslim, or that she was accusing him of sitting and taking the abuse he had so far received. It certainly had not been voluntary.

"You are a Muslim?"

"Yes, my name's Special Agent Amina Abdelnoor. I'm with the CIA. And you, my friend, have just become a valuable asset to our work."

"But you thought I was a terrorist."

"Yes, we did."

He wondered why they didn't think to double-check, but Ibrahim knew that blaming the CIA while he was on an American plane was a bit foolhardy.

"So now I can go home? I missed my youth halaqa, but I think the two-for-one pizza deal is still on until the end of the month. And before I go, I could help clean your airplane as a token of my thanks. Do you have any Windex?" It was killing Ibrahim to see the brown smudges on the white plastic walls and the carpet infused with dirt. Now that his eyes had adjusted, he was overwhelmed by the filthiness. What he would give for a bottle of bleach.

"You're funny," said Amina, with a bemused expression.

"I do not mean to be. I find a clean environment soothing. It has been a difficult few days."

"Yeah, sorry about that," said Amina, who looked contrite for the first time. "I could use your help."

Amina seemed excited by this new idea, but Ibrahim was worried it might jeopardize his pizza discount.

"Help you do what?"

"Haven't you ever wanted adventure in your life? To be a hero and save the day?"

"I have only wanted to serve God by teaching people about Her," said Ibrahim.

"You mean Him," said Amina.

"No, God is without gender, so there is no reason to assume a male. Women are equal to men, so it opens one's mind to think of God as a woman."

"Wow, I never expected an imam to think like that," she said.

"What do you think imams are like?"

"I think they're sexist jerks who think women are subservient to them."

"This is a trait not exclusive to imams. I believe many men of various ethnicities and religions share it. I am not one of those men. I fend for myself completely," said Ibrahim. "Is there a place to wash my clothes and bathe?"

The grime of the last two days was starting to weigh heavily on Ibrahim. Now that his fingernails were not in imminent danger of removal, he wanted to clean them and take a shower.

"We're on a plane, so, no. Plus, where you're going, showering may still be out of the question."

Ibrahim didn't like the sound of that. He just wanted to go home. Al-Azhar had never prepared him for this type of adventure. They said the most exciting thing would be mediating between warring spouses, or drug-addicted teenagers and their parents. Or talking someone out of getting a tattoo. He secretly liked tattoos and didn't think God would have an issue with him getting one. Sunnis felt it changed God's creation, but as Shia scholars pointed out, there were many ways in which we have already altered God's creation. That made sense to him. He spent many nights trying to decide what design he would pick. Perhaps a star or an octopus — he was fascinated by octopi. They could escape from the smallest of holes, unlike him.

"Ibrahim, you're in a special position," said Amina, staring at her phone.

"It does not feel that way."

"My supervisor wants to let you know that the Americans will pardon you on one condition."

"But I don't need to be pardoned. I have done nothing wrong."

Amina looked exasperated. Ibrahim decided to appease her.

"I understand," he said. "If the Americans feel you have done something wrong, then you have to pretend as though they are correct, accept their forgiveness for your fictitious crime, and move on."

"Yes, thank you for understanding. I have a new mission."

Ibrahim did not like the sound of that, but he felt it too impolite to decline immediately. And he was getting the sense that his opinion was of little interest to this determined woman.

"Which is?"

"Find the head of DICK."

Ibrahim's body involuntarily twitched. He did not want to find him or be anywhere near him. This could not be his destiny.

"Talal Abu-Khattab?" said Ibrahim. "But no one even knows if he is alive. Some say he is a made-up nom de guerre."

"He exists. We have intelligence on him."

"Like you had intelligence on me."

"Okay, I admit that was a total screwup. But we've been working on a plan, and you'd be perfect for it."

Ibrahim felt certain he was not perfect for it. He was on a plane, and escape was impossible. He'd have to listen to this woman's plan, placate her, and figure out how to get back home. How many prayers had he missed? Guidance from his creator was what he needed. And a chance to thank Her for saving him from torture. But he was curious.

"What is your plan to bring down Talal?" he asked.

"To infiltrate Raqqa, DICK's capital in Syria."

"And how will you do that?"

"We are going to pretend to be a married couple who have defected from the West to join DICK."

Marriage! Finally! This wasn't so bad. He could always try and dissuade her from this particularly poor plan later on, but he'd finally have a wife.

"But I will have to introduce you to my aunt first. My mother, may God shower her with mercy and blessings, passed away last year —"

"Whoa, whoa, who said anything about marriage?"

"You did."

"I said *pretend* to be married. DICK loves Western defectors; they feel it sticks it to the man. The two of us would be perfect for a pretend marriage."

"But that means we would have to live together."

"Yes, you're getting it now."

"I cannot do it, and you cannot compel me to do it."

"Why the sudden bashfulness?"

"Because I may succumb to my impulses if we are in such close quarters, and I do not want to break any rules of chastity." The idea was worse than getting tortured.

"You're not a virgin, are you?"

"Of course I am!" replied Ibrahim. He couldn't have been more insulted if someone had accused him of murder. "Prophet Yusuf is my role model."

"Oh, I know that story," said Amina. "That's the one where the prophet's super hot and some chick tries to get it on with him, and he swats her away."

Ibrahim decided to ignore how she summarily dismissed one of the most significant stories in the Qur'an, a story that had taught him patience and forbearance. A story that had given him spiritual direction, had answered all his existential questions, and forever changed the direction of his life.

"Yes, that is the one," he said. He could tell that she noticed the unhappiness in his tone.

"It was my favorite story growing up, too," she said. "I loved the part when he dreamed that the sun and moon were his parents."

"So, you have a good knowledge of Islam?" said Ibrahim, his tone more surprised than he intended. He hoped she didn't feel insulted.

"Oh yeah, weekend classes, evening classes. My father hired tutors to help with my Qur'anic recitation. I spent all my holidays and free time learning about Islam."

Ibrahim tried to hide his amazement.

"You seem . . . different to me than the religious women I have been accustomed to meeting."

"You mean I should be quiet and docile?"

"No, many religious women are quite authoritative. I mean you seem to have a negative attitude about faith. It doesn't give you a sense of peace. If I may be more direct, faith seems to irritate you and make you disagreeable."

"Well, if you had the same upbringing I had, you'd understand."

"Was your father unkind?"

"My father is Talal Abu-Khattab."

Ibrahim, Isha Prayer, 10:30 p.m., Oct. 6

Dear Lord,

Thank You for releasing me from my shackles. My legs were starting to cramp. And I am eternally grateful for the alcohol wipes in the first aid kit. Even though it is not the same as bathing, I was able to pass the wipes over my body. The process was slow and tedious and resulted in my smelling like a hospital, but I am not complaining. And it seems that I am to be married. This is the answer to my most earnest prayer. My only concern is the choice of bride.

This is not a complaint about physical attributes — she has an attractive face — and although I did not look below her neck for the sake of propriety, I am certain she has no physical anomaly, and even if she does, I will overcome my feelings by being patient, as is recommended in the Qur'an. I am rambling in this prayer because I am too shy to get to the point.

Amina is the daughter of the most dangerous, evil, and merciless man I have ever heard of. He was legend during my time at Al-Azhar. People spoke about him as if speaking about the devil himself. And in Your infinite mercy and wisdom, You have chosen his daughter as my new wife. I was hoping for a simple woman from the same village as myself, but instead, my future wife is also a trained CIA agent who is efficient in assassination and various torture techniques. These could be useful skills when teaching weekend Islamic school in the mosque, minus the assassinations, although I can think of a parent or two who would not be that brokenhearted, but I digress.

She wants to capture her father and bring him to justice, although an efficient beheading may also satisfy her too. There have been successful marriages built on less ambiguous goals than bringing down a homicidal maniac intent on the destruction of humanity, so I have great hope for a blissful future together. But I confess that there is a part of me that is a little afraid of the future. I expected my days to be spent in quiet contemplation of the unseen realm and teaching miserable teenagers how to read the Qur'an, but suddenly I feel as if You've put me in another person's life altogether. It's as if I was in the movie *Bambi,* and now I'm in *The Fast and the Furious.*

It does feel good to talk to You in this way. I know the answer already: put my trust in You, have patience, and pray for strength and guidance. And so I will. But can I ask one thing? When it comes to my wedding night, could You help me be creative?

16

IT WAS EIGHT A.M. AND LEE LEE SAT WITH HER FATHER in a conference room with black walls, black carpet, and a black table. The whole place smelled like plastic and rubber. They could probably perform surgeries here in their downtime, thought Lee Lee, as they waited for CIA agents to appear. She had packed homemade trail mix and pushed a large baggie full of various nuts and colorful M&M's toward her sick-looking father. Murray had brought his knitting, but it sat abandoned on the table.

The door opened, and two agents in black suits entered. "Hi, I'm Special Agent Woolly, and this is my associate, Agent Simon," said the large man, who had red hair and skin so pale Lee Lee worried he might sunburn from the fluorescent bulbs overhead. His eyes were also the color of blue Play-Doh, which she'd loved as a child. He made her feel relaxed right away. His partner was a thin woman who looked like Olive Oyl, a character Murray had introduced her to when she didn't want to eat her spinach. Murray loved watching old-timey cartoons with Lee Lee, who also had an encyclopedic knowledge of '80s music.

"Oh look, food! That's so great. I didn't have time for breakfast today," said Agent Woolly.

Lee Lee pushed the bag toward the agent, who took a huge fistful. Agent Olive Oyl declined and sat motionless beside her animated partner.

"I love trail mix — it's comfort food that's good for you," said Agent Woolly. "Reminds me of when I used to go hiking."

Watching him devour the trail mix gave Lee Lee time to collect her thoughts. "My mother's not a terrorist, at least not in the conventional sense," she said.

"Lee Lee!" said Murray.

"They know what I mean."

Agent Woolly was momentarily distracted, as though he had just realized this meeting had a purpose beyond snacking. "I know this must be hard for you, young lady, but your mother's aligned herself with some questionable people, and we have to examine her motives."

"My wife thought the imam had been unfairly deported because of his knowledge of DICK. She was trying to get him back," said Murray.

"Yes, Ibrahim Sultan is in custody with the CIA interrogation team," said Agent Olive Oyl, looking at Murray. "He's been cooperating, which is good, but that doesn't mean your wife is innocent."

"Look, she was under a lot of stress. Her book launch didn't go well, and she was having some sort of spiritual crisis," said Murray. "There has to be a way to get her back, and then you can ask her yourself."

"Well, we did have one idea," said Agent Woolly.

"What?" asked Lee Lee, gripping the edge of the table tightly.

"We rarely get people back . . . alive during situations like these," said Agent Woolly.

Murray started to sway in his chair. Lee Lee held his arm to steady him. She couldn't believe what she'd just heard. The idea that she might never see her mother again made her stomach feel hollow. It was true that they weren't close; her mother had difficulty bonding with people, bonding with her. But her mother was in trouble for trying to help Brother Ibrahim, and now Lee Lee felt guilty for believing her mother was shallow and didn't care about anyone.

"But lately, we've had some success when family members travel to their loved ones and make an appeal in person," continued Agent Olive Oyl, staring at Lee Lee intently. "Seeing a family member jolts them into coming home."

"I'll go," said Murray, squeezing his lavender ball of wool. "It's my fault. None of this would have happened if I had taken her seriously when she asked for help."

Agent Woolly seemed pleased with this answer, but Lee Lee could sense that Agent Olive Oyl wasn't happy.

"Sometimes husbands are the reason women leave and join DICK," said Olive Oyl gently.

"We had ... *have* a great marriage," insisted Murray. "I could have been more understanding, but what husband couldn't be?"

Agent Woolly seemed to agree.

"What about me?" blurted out Lee Lee.

Agent Olive Oyl nodded and smiled.

"Out of the question," said Murray. "It's not safe. There's a war going on out there."

"Exactly," said Lee Lee. "If I go, Mom will be panicked and want to come home with me right away."

"I agree with your father," said Agent Woolly. "It's too much of a risk."

Agent Olive Oyl looked enthusiastic, but if Lee Lee was reading the situation right, she was the subordinate, and the final decision wasn't hers to make. White men still trumped white women. And there were two white men that Lee Lee needed to defeat.

The key to all dealmaking, she knew, was to overwhelm the olfactory system. Growing up with a Pakistani grandmother, Lee Lee had learned about food and its effects on human beings. Sitting in the kitchen watching her nani cook, hearing the hiss of food hitting hot oil, and smelling the wafting scent of fried onion or rose syrup were seared into her memory. She remembered being fed mashed-up roti dipped in sugar by Nusrat as she learned words in Urdu. Lee Lee was the bridge between two worlds, helping her parents and grandparents stay connected. Now she was going to use culinary coercion to save her mother.

Lee Lee slowly reached into her backpack to retrieve an oblong plastic container with a blue lid. It contained pieces of carrot cake topped with fluffy tufts of gooey cream cheese icing. Lee Lee hoped Agent Woolly loved carrot cake as she opened the lid slowly — like the last unwrapped Christmas present — and the reveal had the desired effect. Agent Woolly inhaled the heady scent of vanilla and looked like he'd been hypnotized.

"I would follow CIA protocol for safety," said Lee Lee, letting her index finger scoop up the icing that had oozed onto the inside of the container. She put her finger into her mouth and slowly pulled it out. Agent

Woolly watched the whole performance with a look of desperation in his eyes.

"Carrot cake is your favorite," said Agent Olive Oyl, in a soft voice that was surprisingly seductive.

Lee Lee wondered if brainwashing was part of Olive Oyl's training. "I added walnuts," she said helpfully, pointing to the brown flecks. She was careful to make sure the container was far from Agent Woolly's grasp.

"Well, DICK loves Western schoolgirls as recruits," said Agent Woolly to the cake. "Otherwise, they may suspect you're a spy."

"We could arrange for safe transfer to the Turkish border," said Agent Olive Oyl. "Once you're in, find your mom and convince her to come back. And gather intel for us. We've never had an agent in Raqqa before."

"I won't have it," yelled Murray, slamming down his fist, causing the knitting needles to go flying and breaking Agent Woolly's trance. "You're recruiting my daughter to be a spy for you!"

"We could arrange for both of you to travel," said Agent Olive Oyl reassuringly. "It isn't unheard of for a parent to accompany their child. It's rare, but it could work."

Lee Lee needed to seal the deal. She pulled out a white paper napkin, gently plucked out a piece of carrot cake, and placed it on top of the napkin. She slid the confection closer to Agent Woolly, making sure it still wasn't within his range. His forehead was beaded with sweat.

"Agent Simon, could you make all the arrangements immediately?" asked Lee Lee, before her father or Agent Woolly could find the strength to protest.

"Of course, I'll arrange for the transfer this evening," answered Agent Olive Oyl, smiling.

"This evening?" asked Murray. "Are you insane? Think about what you're doing!"

"This is the only way to get your wife back alive," said Agent Olive Oyl. "The average life expectancy in the hands of DICK is . . . very short. I don't think we have much of a choice."

Murray slumped over, defeated. Lee Lee just needed to win over Agent Woolly now.

A piece of carrot cake hovered between Agent Woolly and what appeared to be his quickly extinguishing ability to think critically. Lee Lee remembered a packet of liquid caramel in her bag. It was meant to be poured over cut apples. She pulled it out, tore at the plastic corner with her teeth, and made a slow zigzag pattern on the cake. The light shone on the viscous liquid, illuminating it like gold.

Agent Woolly could take no more. "I authorize the transfer of two assets at nineteen hundred hours. Can you handle the details, Agent Simon?" he asked Olive Oyl, as Lee Lee pushed the cake toward his waiting fingers. He picked up the piece and swallowed it in one bite.

"Pure heaven," he mumbled.

Lee Lee had no idea what the next twenty-four to forty-eight hours would hold, but at least she wouldn't have to take her physics exam.

17

AZIZ SAT IN HIS BUNGALOW KITCHEN LOOKING LIKE HE
had just eaten a lemon. He was drinking a glass of falooda. Jameela
knew that rosewater sherbet drink from childhood. Every Ramadan,
iftar — the breaking of the day's fast — included a jug of milk flavored
with sweet rose syrup, vanilla ice cream, and sweet basil seeds. The
seeds had been soaked overnight in water, which caused them to plump
up into gelatinous balls. She used to call them eyeballs and loved the
way they felt in her mouth. She began to feel nostalgic about the past.
She poured herself a glass. The pink liquid slipped down her throat, taking the heat with it. It was like drinking a bouquet of roses.

"Something wrong?" asked Jameela, as she munched on the gelatinous seeds. Aziz ignored her. He was concentrating on a piece of paper. Jameela wondered if he was attempting to incinerate it with his
eyes.

"I've just received a disturbing intelligence report from the DICK."

Jameela froze.

"Is it about Ibrahim? Is he dead?"

"No, the last we heard he was in Raqqa. It's about Abdullah. The DICK
believes he's gone soft. They've told him that if you don't carry out the
attack, you'll be killed."

Jameela spat out the seeds. "Wait a minute, I wasn't supposed to kill
anyone or be killed. That wasn't part of our deal."

"Abdullah asked permission for you to meet Talal. That screamed assassin. So now they've told him that if you don't carry out the plot first to prove your loyalty, you'll die."

The horror of what Aziz said made her feel cold. There was a black cashmere shawl draped across the chair she was sitting on. She wrapped it around herself to calm her racing thoughts. She was a lot of horrible things — selfish, bitter, angry — but she wasn't a murderer. Nothing on earth could justify killing people.

"Well, that's a big problem, because I'm not killing anyone," said Jameela.

"If you want, I will send you home now, since carrying out the plot was not what we agreed."

Jameela saw a flicker of concern in Aziz's face. His plans were going AWOL, and for the first time, he wasn't in control. Welcome to the club.

"What happens if I go home now?"

"Abdullah will be recalled, and it'll take months for me to get someone that high up again."

"And Ibrahim will still be out there."

"Your imam will likely die in a few days."

It was hopeless. Nothing ever worked out for her. Her career was stalled, she had a crappy relationship with her daughter, not to mention she had gotten an innocent imam on torture row. She was spiraling. When Jamal was alive and heard her ranting about how life sucked, he'd stop her: *You're whining again. Remember, wine is haram.* It was their code. Using the Arabic word *haram*, which meant "forbidden," and the theological ruling that all intoxicants were forbidden in Islam, he was mixing his metaphors because it made her laugh as a child. But it always worked, and she would stop her self-flagellation. He would finish with his favorite verse in the Qur'an, *Call upon me and I will respond.*

She looked up and whispered, "You better not let me down twice," and wiped away tears with the black shawl. She turned to Aziz. "We're going to outwit these morons at their own game."

"Why the sudden confidence?"

"No choice. I'm Ibrahim's only hope. You don't even know where he is, so let's let DICK believe that I'm going to carry out the plot."

"You think you can fool them?"

"I didn't watch every season of RuPaul's *Drag Race* without learning a few things."

Aziz perked up. "I didn't understand a word of what you just said, but you've given me a sense of optimism."

Jameela sighed. "I wish the Middle East could keep it together. What's wrong with your leaders?"

"We've had some trouble keeping our leaders from —"

"Dying?" Jameela sat down and surveyed the table. "Probably from heart attacks. All this deep-fried food helped."

"Our leaders never manage to make it to the clogged-artery stage." Aziz poured himself some more falooda. "When they do something that upsets the Americans, like invading Kuwait in 1990, the Americans eliminate the offender with bombs, thus not giving arteries enough time to harden."

Jameela knew this sort of story from her father. Whenever the CIA didn't want a head of state in power, they orchestrated a coup and installed a puppet. Iran was the most famous case.

There was just enough falooda for a final glass. Jameela decided she deserved it and wanted to keep this moment of peace a little longer, since it might be her last, so she feigned ignorance to keep Aziz talking. "Saddam survived the first Gulf War in 1991 and got a second chance. Why did he blow it?"

Aziz wrinkled his nose at the fragrant drink in his hand.

"Because in 2003, Bush Junior decided to do what his father couldn't in 1991, get rid of Saddam once and for all. He claimed Iraq had weapons of mass destruction that never existed and bombed the country to smithereens. Saddam went into hiding, and there was a brief moment when Iraq could have embraced democracy, but then Paul Bremer —"

"Who's that?" asked Jameela, through a mouthful of gelatinous seeds. She felt five years old again.

"The head of the Coalition Provisional Authority, the CPA. They were responsible for overseeing Iraq's transformation from an authoritarian state to a democracy," said Aziz. "He decided that anyone associated with Saddam's Baath party would lose their pensions and couldn't help rebuild the country. But everyone of consequence had to be part of the Baath party to show loyalty to Saddam. How many military men do you think that affected?"

"Ten thousand?" Jameela realized she could eat more pakoras if she drank falooda to wash them down.

"Two hundred and fifty thousand. Think of it: hundreds of thousands of angry men with access to weapons, all out of work because of the stupidity of the Americans. Classic colonial arrogance ultimately destabilized Iraq and created a power vacuum in the region. The DICK swelled and rose to prominence."

"So, DICK is the Americans' fault, too. You'd think they would learn after all their foreign policy screwups." Jameela plunked her hand into a bowl of fennel seeds meant for chewing. It aided digestion, and she was starting to feel the effects of the large meal. "Once I know the target, how will I get the information to you?"

"You don't."

"Why?"

"You asked to meet Talal, and Abdullah has agreed. You are going to do what I haven't been able to do on my own for years. You have manipulated a meeting using your feminine wiles. If I tell the Americans about the plot, they will stop you, and it's much more important for you to reach Talal. Think of the greater good."

"What greater good?"

"You have a chance to kill Talal."

"How on earth would I be able to kill him?" asked Jameela, because she hadn't planned any further than delaying her marriage to Abdullah and finding Ibrahim.

Aziz placed a small hypodermic needle in her hand.

"Get close enough to him, plunge this into his arm, or anywhere, really. It will kill him instantly."

"You're asking me to assassinate Talal Abu-Khattab?"

"If you had a chance to kill Hitler, would you?"

"That's not a fair question," said Jameela, whose stomach was starting to make unhappy sounds.

"You kill Talal, Pakistan will take part of the credit and absolve ourselves of the bin Laden scandal, and the Americans will finally trust us again. It's what you Westerners call a win-win."

"Yeah, I'm not really feeling it," said Jameela. What she was feeling was nausea. It may not have been a good idea to drink so much falooda. The milk churned around her insides, along with thoughts that she was about to become an assassin. Jameela ran to the washroom and threw up.

Jameela, Fajr Prayer, 5:15 a.m., Oct. 8

Okay, there have been a few extra developments that I didn't foresee in the *GO* plan. You want me to go to Syria and find Ibrahim myself? Fine, I'll do that, but You better have my back. And everything else in between. Also, kill Talal? Isn't that murder? Which You frown upon. I don't want to kill anyone, so please don't make me. I just want to get to Syria fast. I'm going to put my trust in You, like Brother Ibrahim said to do. And I'm going to stop whining. As Jamal always used to say, *Wine is haram.*

And what's with the big, hairy, horny man who wants to have his way with me — why couldn't this have happened in my twenties when I was single? You wait until I'm almost forty and married before You send a sick, love-crazed lunatic my way.

I have to admit, though, it is kind of flattering at my age. Not that I'm planning on sleeping with him. Please make that impossible. I'm pretty sure there's a story in the Qur'an about adultery being sinful.

So, let's recap: no murder, no bombs, and no sex with a Neanderthal. Got that?

18

JAMEELA AND AZIZ LEFT THE BUNGALOW. A SMALL truck was waiting for them. Like the miniature version she saw on Aunty Parveen's bookshelf, this one was decorated in astonishingly vivid hues of lime green and fuchsia. "It's beautiful," said Jameela.

"It'll blend in, so we won't be noticed," said Aziz.

The airport was in a frenzy. People pushed trolleys full of overstuffed suitcases lashed with twine. Babies and little children rode on top of the trolleys, having the time of their lives. Abdullah was easy to spot. He stood out from the crowd with his towering frame, camel-colored hair, closely trimmed beard, and military-issue clothes. Jameela half expected him to have a bouquet of daisies for her. Instead, he was carrying a beige distressed-leather handbag. Aziz and Abdullah spoke briefly before Abdullah turned around to give her a lustful glance.

Aziz explained to Jameela, "This is your carry-on. You have a connecting flight to Damascus through Frankfurt. Instructions are coming later."

"Is Frankfurt the target?"

"Yes."

"Is Abdullah coming with me?" asked Jameela, noting that Abdullah would not make eye contact with her. Despite her bizarre circumstances, she had grown fond of his attentiveness toward her.

"No, the DICK's plan is for you to carry out the plot alone to prove your allegiance, and only after succeeding will you be allowed to meet

Abdullah in Raqqa. An introduction to Talal has been brokered as your marriage gift, followed by a small, intimate, and quick wedding," said Aziz, looking as uneasy as she'd ever seen him. "I'm not sure what the rest of the plan is."

She had no idea either. It was like walking into an abyss. But somehow that relaxed her. "Neither do I."

Aziz became the color of mulberry. "I cannot tell if you are mocking me."

"I'm telling you to have faith."

"Look where's it's gotten you so far."

Fair comment. Her life did seem to be going on a scale from one to Edward Snowden. But he was relaxing in Russia, not trying to outwit an apocalyptically obsessed group. She tried to find some positive in a bleak situation.

"I know where Ibrahim is. And I'd rather be here trying to save him than sitting in Liverspot, North Dakota, doing nothing." This was the furthest she'd ever gone out on a limb for anyone. Hopefully her limbs would remain attached to her.

Aziz sighed. "There is a man in this airport who will be following you and watching you. If you don't carry out this mission" — he pointed to the handbag — "you will be killed. As much as I do not like you, I don't want your life to end." Aziz handed Jameela a passport.

It was still American, dark blue with gold lettering. But new and stiff. She opened it to her picture and the name Ghazala Rahman.

"Can you do one thing for me?" asked Jameela. "If things ... don't work out, please find my husband and tell him the truth. I don't want him to believe I abandoned him and became a terrorist. And tell my daughter I'm sorry I wasn't the mother I should have been. She deserved more."

Aziz looked at her with a softness that she didn't think was possible.

"Murray's loved me like no one ever ..." Her throat constricted, and she couldn't get the words out.

Aziz looked at the ground for a few moments before looking at her again. "I will find him, Mrs. Jameela, and restore your reputation. Despite your stupidity, you are the bravest person I have ever had the misfortune to meet."

Jameela was surprised by the compliment and decided not to push her luck. There was no line at the security checkpoint so she took off her shoes and new handbag, placed them in the gray plastic bin, and watched it move down the conveyor belt. Jameela held her breath as it went through the X-ray. The security personnel seemed unbothered by both and ushered her through. After gathering her belongings, she continued on to the lounge.

As Jameela sat waiting for her plane to board, she looked at the handbag, which was plain and wouldn't attract attention. She got up casually and made her way to the prayer room down the hall. The door read FE-MALES ONLY. Normally, she'd be angry that men and women couldn't pray in the same room, as they had for centuries before Saudi Arabia's puritan views started dominating Muslim countries, but today, she was grateful for the privacy.

The room was dimly lit and simply furnished with prayer rugs scattered about. More importantly, no one was in there. Jameela's hands shook as she opened the zipper of the handbag and looked inside. It was dark and mostly empty. A man had clearly packed it. There were some large sanitary napkins, a lipstick, mascara, garish pink blush, and some cologne, all still in their packages. Jameela opened the bottle of golden-hued liquid — Escape for Women, by Calvin Klein. She sprayed herself. Not bad. *Focus.* There was a small black device that looked like an old-fashioned cell phone. It had a small antenna and was fully charged; no wonder security didn't pick it up as a threat.

Were there explosives inside it? Suddenly, it lit up and started to vibrate. Jameela's heart plunged, and she dropped the thing on the carpet. Was it going to explode? But it just moved around like a legless ant, willing her to answer it. She did.

"Hello?"

There was stony silence on the other end.

"Hello?" asked Jameela again.

"Is this Jameela Green?" asked an annoyed voice. It was male and had a slightly British-inflected accent.

"Yes."

"When you land at the Frankfurt airport, put this phone in the bag and leave it in the women's washroom in the Lufthansa First Class Lounge."

Not in a million years, she thought.

"So, I just leave it?"

"Yes."

"What happens when I leave it?" There was silence on the other end. "Does it crawl away, hoping to find its better-looking cousin?"

"It explodes."

"With laughter?"

"This is not funny."

No kidding.

"I don't get it. Doesn't it have to have some sort of explosive substance, liquid or powder or something? How does it blow up, exactly? How did I just get through security with this thing?"

"I have the second device. Once it is attached to the phone you hold, it turns into a bomb. I will not give you more details than that."

So, she had an accomplice who would help kill hundreds of innocent people in Frankfurt.

"Before I do this, I want to know one thing."

"You're not in a position to make demands," said the irate voice.

"Please, I'm worried about a friend. His name is Ibrahim Sultan. You've done your research about me, so you probably have information about him too. Do you know where he is?"

"We might," responded the voice, giving Jameela the confidence she needed.

"Tell me where he is, or I don't leave this place."

There was some static and muffled voices on the other side. After a few minutes, the voice came back, more strained and angry.

"The CIA took him to an American base outside Raqqa. That's all we know right now."

Jameela's pulse raced. Finally, some concrete information about Ibrahim. She had to get to Syria right away. A woman came into the lounge to pray. She removed her niqab, along with her black robe, as she prepared to do her ablutions in the nearby wudu area.

"I'm not going to kill people so you can bring about your End of Days obsession," Jameela whispered. "If you really want to see a dystopian future, watch *The Walking Dead*. But I prefer *Zombieland*. Way more fun."

"I am in this airport. If you do not board this flight, I will kill you."

Jameela looked at the fake passport in her hand. He, whoever he was, knew what she looked like. Jameela watched the woman in the ablutions area calmly washing her arms. Before she had time to turn around, Jameela grabbed her niqab and robe and put them on. She made sure the handbag was safely under the folds of the fabric before stepping out of the prayer room and into a sea of people, several of whom were dressed identically to her. Her flight was boarding, but everyone in the line seemed calm. She walked into the ticket issue office. There was a young woman at the desk, dressed in Western clothes, with her glossy black hair held in a high ponytail. A name tag said HUMNA. She started to speak to Jameela in Urdu, but Jameela's command of her mother's native tongue was tenuous at best.

"I'd like to exchange this Frankfurt ticket to Damascus instead," she said, handing her boarding pass to the woman.

The woman was taken aback by Jameela's request.

"I can get you on the next flight to Damascus, but it's restricted to diplomats because, um, there's a civil war, so commercial aviation is limited."

"That's inconvenient," muttered Jameela.

"Yes, well, do you have business in Syria that is making this trip . . . urgent?"

Jameela could detect a suspicious tone in the young woman's voice and noticed her reaching under her desk, where she was certain there was a panic button. Jameela leaned in conspiratorially.

"Okay, I'll let you in on a secret. You have to promise not to tell anyone."

The woman's hand froze, and she looked at Jameela's face with anticipation.

"I'm with Anonymous, the American hacktivist group."

"The hacktivist group? That's incredible. What are you doing here?"

"I've been working with Pakistani intelligence on developing a prototype for . . . remote neural control. That's a fancy word for brain wave manipulation. We're going to use it bring down DICK operatives in Damascus, but they sent me to Karachi first to . . . to pick up this outfit because it has . . . a hidden built-in prototype. Who would suspect a niqabi?" Jameela couldn't believe what she was saying. Out of the corner of her eye, she saw a distraught woman coming out of the women's prayer room, looking mortified and trying to cover her face with her shawl. Jameela felt a pang of guilt, but there was very likely a highly trained assassin trying to kill her and she had to escape armed only with arcane knowledge from hours of Netflix. If she got out of this situation, she'd write a letter to the president of the streaming service and thank him.

Jameela could see a thin man in a short gray Nehru jacket, with hair slicked back, looking intently at the lineup of people as they started boarding the plane. It had to be him.

"The prototype makes people angry and prone to violence, so we have to keep it out of the wrong hands until we reboot it."

"Like the Burka Avenger," said Humna, and her eyes widened. "My little sister watches it." Jameela remembered the popular Pakistani superhero show with a young girl who disguised herself with a burqa and fought villains who wouldn't let girls read or get immunized. And she had just found a bona fide fan. Thank God, because she needed someone gullible right now.

"Yes, well, I've been working with Pakistani intelligence to fix the neuro-electromagnetic frequencies, but there are still some technical difficulties. Brain waves are not easy to manipulate." Ugh. Could she not have come up with something more plausible?

The young woman looked very solemn. "Fascinating. Can I see it work?"

Oh God. "Okay, but because the electrical frequencies are overcalibrated, the subject becomes prone to violence."

Jameela lifted up a finger and pointed at the distraught-looking Pakistani woman who was trying to tear eyeholes in a plastic grocery bag as she pulled it over her face. She caught Jameela's eye and recognized her clothes at once. She came running toward the ticket booth.

"I'm sending signals to the auditory cortex of that woman's ear, bypassing her inhibitory reflexes. She'll respond to the stimuli by becoming enraged," said Jameela. "You better lock that door, or she'll come in and kill me. We're still working out the bugs of the . . . Burqa Brain Waver."

Humna quickly locked the bolt before the woman came flying toward them, the grocery bag rustling over her head. She banged on the door, pointing to Jameela and screaming in Urdu that she wanted her niqab back. Humna called security, and two men in military uniforms removed the frenzied woman.

"This burqa is a very dangerous weapon if it gets into the wrong hands," explained Jameela. "There are people in this airport who want to steal it. You've got to get me out of here."

From the corner of her eye, Jameela noticed that the Frankfurt passengers had boarded. The man with the short Nehru jacket had turned to the commotion in the ticket booth.

"Hurry, there's a man coming," said Jameela, panicked. Nehru Man must have seen the handbag, which was sitting on the counter. Humna concentrated on her computer and after a few seconds of furious clacking of the computer keys, rerouted her.

"Is it the burqa that's making this man crazy, too?" Humna yanked the boarding pass out of the printer.

"No, he's a DICK agent who's been sent to kill me and bring the burqa back," said Jameela. "DICK doesn't want us to fix the Burqa Brain Waver. They can use it to make their members even more violent. Not that they need it."

Nehru Man made great strides toward the booth, tried the door, and found it locked.

Humna jumped to her feet. "I'll keep him here while you leave." This was clearly the most exciting thing that had ever happened to her. Mind-controlling burqas did not appear every day.

"But how do I get out of here?"

"There's a way out back. Hurry, your flight is boarding. You can just make it," said Humna pushing the boarding pass into Jameela's sweaty hands.

She turned to see Nehru Man pull a hammer out of his jacket and start breaking the lock. He seemed to be prepared for all problems. Humna had pressed the panic button, and the same two security men who had removed the niqabi woman returned in time to catch Nehru Man entering the booth. He spoke rapidly to the officials, who seemed to believe him, but then Humna came up with an idea of her own — likely inspired by her favorite childhood Bollywood shows.

"That man has been stalking me for weeks," she said, as she squeezed out some tears. "I turned down his marriage proposal, but he cannot accept my decision. I am a good woman. Please don't let that man besmirch me."

The security officers looked at Mr. Nehru in a new light. Pakistan's national security could not compete with Humna's virginity. And Mr.

Nehru was doing himself no favors by swearing at Humna and telling her all the horrible things he was going to do to her.

Jameela sprinted toward her gate, approaching two flight attendants who were annoyed at her sudden, last-minute appearance. She boarded the plane, found her seat, and relaxed for the first time since entering the airport. Jameela closed her eyes. She loved airplanes. The feeling of being pressed against the seat during takeoff was her favorite thing growing up. Her mother believed that prayers to God were answered during this moment, so she asked God to keep Ibrahim safe before she drifted off. A sudden movement awakened her. She opened her eyes, saw the handbag balancing precariously on her lap and Mr. Nehru sitting beside her.

"I believe this is yours."

Jameela, Zuhr Prayer, 1:48 p.m., Oct. 8

What the hell? You were supposed to get me *out* of Mr. Nehru's clutches, not into them. And he has some sort of doomsday device in this hideous handbag. You can tell men organized this terrorist plot. A woman would have picked a decent purse — an Hermès or a Fendi; hell, even a Louis Vuitton. Don't give me the silent treatment right now. I'm not ready to die yet. I have to see Lee Lee and Murray and explain what happened. And Ibrahim's probably on a rack somewhere, being stretched to oblivion. My work here is not done.

And I will not be buried with ghastly unshaven legs.

19

"ARE YOU IN A TRANCE?" ASKED MR. NEHRU, WITH A slightly British-accented voice, which Jameela recognized from the phone call earlier.

He was in his late fifties and looked rugged, like a skinnier version of Benicio Del Toro.

The back of Jameela's throat was dry from having her mouth open for so long. She forced herself to swallow. "I was praying you would disappear."

"Sorry to disappoint; you have caused me considerable inconvenience. But I admire your methods. Using that woman as a delaying tactic was impressive. Unfortunately, her husband showed up with her lunch and told the authorities about his wife's active imagination."

"Are you going to kill me?"

"You're a terrible conversationalist. Let's get some orange juice first, shall we?" he said, yawning. "But yes, I'm going to kill you."

Jameela's head throbbed. How could she escape this man while confined on a plane?

"And then what? You're going to take that cell phone doohickey contraption and use it to kill innocent people? What did they do to you?"

Mr. Nehru sighed as he stared at his seat's screen and scrolled through the selection of films. He examined the choices with the focus of a dermatologist examining a patient for cancerous moles.

"It's a four-hour flight, so I'm going to wait until the end, but if you don't stop talking, I'm going to be tempted to shut you up now. Permanently."

Jameela had no doubt that he'd kill her just to watch *The Hangover Part II* in peace. She stared at the screen. Maybe if she could get him to watch a movie, he'd fall asleep and she could get away.

"Wow, they have the *Odd Couple*," said Jameela. "Walter Matthau with a mustache looks just like a young Saddam Hussein."

Mr. Nehru went pale. His breathing became labored.

"What did you say?"

"I said Walter Matthau looks like a younger Saddam Hussein."

He gripped Jameela's arm.

"Don't ever say that name to me again."

"What did Walter Matthau ever do to you?"

"Not him."

The fingers tightened around her arm. Maybe she could convince the crew her husband was abusing her. If she started screaming, they'd land the plane, and the police would take him away. But her scream sounded like a hissing cat. No one would take it seriously. The flight attendant would probably just give her a cough drop. Hatred for Saddam Hussein was her only clue into his psyche. Thank God for her father and his endless diatribes about Muslim politics. They might save her life.

"Saddam Hussein had a lot of similarities to Osama bin Laden. Both guys were CIA assets. But both relationships ended badly. After Iraq invaded Kuwait, the Americans launched Operation Desert Storm in 1991, but President Bush wasn't able to overthrow Saddam."

Mr. Nehru released his grip. Jameela noticed his eyes were no longer dark with contempt. She had said the right words. Clearly, history was his thing. She rubbed her arm to bring the blood back. She had to keep him talking.

"You have some historical knowledge of the Middle East." Mr. Nehru eyed her with more interest. Finally, a positive change in his emotional state. Maybe she could win him over.

"America's second invasion of Iraq in 2003 was just as illegal as Iraq's invasion of Kuwait in 1990, but no one talks about that."

Jameela felt like Scheherazade from *One Thousand and One Nights*. If she could keep spinning Middle Eastern history, she'd be allowed to live. A flight attendant came by, and Jameela asked for an orange juice. She was going to need energy to keep him entertained.

"Were you in Iraq at that time? Were you one of Saddam's bullies? A military advisor?" asked Jameela.

Mr. Nehru bared his teeth. "It's important to first find out who you are talking to before making such accusations."

Tactical error, thought Jameela as her heart raced. She inhaled and held her breath for two seconds, just like Murray had taught her to do. She let it out slowly.

"Sorry," she said, taking a gulp of juice. "I think we got off on the wrong foot, with you telling me I had to be killed and then me getting all upset about it. Let's start again. My name is Jameela, and I'm a writer. What do you do, besides . . . assassinations? Is that a hobby or more of a full-time thing?" She looked past him see if the aisle behind him was clear.

He leaned his head back on the headrest. "I used to be head of pediatric oncology in the biggest teaching hospital in Baghdad."

Not the answer Jameela was expecting.

"Don't look so surprised. Iraq used to be one of the most modern countries in the world," he said rubbing his eyes, as if the memories were too much. "But during the first Gulf War, the Americans didn't just hit military targets, they bombed Iraq's entire infrastructure to smithereens — sewage treatment plants, electrical plants, bridges — in violation of the UN resolutions."

While his eyes were closed, Jameela scanned the rest of the plane.

"Why?" asked Jameela, in a bid to show her sympathy.

He opened his eyes. "To spread terror, demoralize Iraqi civilians, and lead them to pressure their leaders to surrender."

"The US hoped Iraqis would revolt and overthrow Saddam?" Jameela could see a washroom twenty feet away.

"Yes, but it didn't work. They were too traumatized to overthrow Saddam, and he wasn't the type of man to back down."

A food cart was blocking the way; she'd have to buy time. "I read about the crippling sanctions the Americans and British imposed on Iraq."

"Correct, they dominated the UN Sanctions Committee, and for twelve years ordinary Iraqis couldn't get basic medical treatment like chemotherapy drugs or painkillers."

Jameela put her orange juice down and looked at Mr. Nehru, whose eyes were shining. "I had to treat patients with nothing more than a bottle of aspirin. Children died from cancers that were easily curable."

Jameela thought of the day she had brought Lee Lee home from the hospital after giving birth and how protecting her had been an overwhelming instinct. She touched Mr. Nehru's arm. "That must have been awful," she said.

"Not even chlorine was allowed. The drinking water became contaminated. Denis Halliday, the coordinator of humanitarian relief to Iraq, resigned. He felt the UN was applying a policy that 'satisfies the definition of genocide.' Hundreds of thousands died from diarrhea caused by gastroenteritis. Babies, children, my own daughter . . ."

Mr. Nehru suddenly became quiet, and Jameela understood why this was so personal.

Mr. Nehru stared at the screen, lost in thought. Jameela needed to escape soon.

"Killing me won't bring back those children," she said in a soft voice. "Or your — "

Nehru snapped out of his trance.

"Of course not. Do I look stupid to you? The bomb you were supposed to detonate was going to kill the British minister who has the blood of Iraqi children on his hands."

"But that war's two decades old. Why now?"

Mr. Nehru touched his pocket. "When the DICK asked me to choose a target, I finally had my chance for revenge, but you betrayed us, and for that you will die."

So much for bonding over human misery. Mr. Nehru was still focused on his goal, and Jameela had only delayed him long enough to review her history lessons. "Are you going to kill me now?" asked Jameela, while surreptitiously looking around for some sort of weapon but only finding magazines in the seat pocket.

"If they can't wake you up for dinner, they'll figure out you're dead and arrest me," said Mr. Nehru, as he pulled expensive-looking earphones from his jacket pocket, stuffed them in his ears, and plugged in the cord. "I'm going to wait until we land." And then he pressed PLAY.

Jameela didn't doubt that Mr. Nehru was going to kill her, but his unflappable attitude was irritating. If she could get away from him, maybe sit somewhere else. There was a middle seat open a few rows up. Would he kill her if she had seatmates as witnesses? Maybe he'd kill them too. He seemed to be nodding off. Jameela waited until she heard a light snoring. She unbuckled and quietly stood up.

"Where do you think you're going?" Mr. Nehru looked at her suspiciously.

Jameela jumped but tried to act natural.

"Sit down this instant."

"I'm going to pee," she said. "We're still allowed to do that, right?"

"I'm coming with you," he said.

"No, you're not." Jameela moved past him and started down the aisle. She could hear him unbuckling and following her. There weren't a lot of places to hide on a plane, and they still had an hour and a half of flight time left. They reached the washroom door together.

"I'm sorry, but only one passenger at a time," said a flight attendant, stopping Mr. Nehru. *Tasneem* was stitched on her lapel. "We've had some unfortunate accidents when couples decide to have 'special time' and turbulence hits."

"My wife requires some assistance in the lavatory," said Mr. Nehru. "I assure you, we are not engaging in any hanky-panky. She has severe anxiety, and the toilet flush could induce a terror response."

Jameela wasn't sure what irritated her more, being murdered on a plane or being referred to as his wife. But now she knew he planned on killing her in the lavatory.

"But, honey, we've talked about this," Jameela said to Mr. Nehru sweetly. "I only had a panic attack once when I flushed the toilet."

"They are loud," said Tasneem, sympathetically.

"I'm a really nervous person, but my husband bought me the most advanced noise-canceling earphones to use whenever I'm in an airplane toilet. Now I don't hear anything."

Jameela reached into Mr. Nehru's jacket and pulled out the earphones.

"But I still need to be in there with you, darling," he said.

"But why?" asked Tasneem.

It was a fair point.

"Because she also suffers from claustrophobia. Having me with her helps her concentrate."

"Wouldn't having you in there make it more claustrophobic?" asked Tasneem.

Jameela was worried Mr. Nehru was going to kill Tasneem for talking too much. "We've spent weeks preparing for this exact moment, haven't we?" offered Jameela. "What was the point of me peeing in a simulated airplane washroom, spending five thousand dollars on cognitive behavior aromatherapy? We could have spent the money on a new stainless-steel refrigerator-freezer combo."

"They have fake airplane washrooms?" asked Tasneem.

"Oh, yes," said Jameela, trying to keep her poker face as she spun around, opened the door, slipped inside, and bolted the lock behind her. She could hear the flight attendant talking to Mr. Nehru.

"You are such a devoted husband," the woman said.

"I don't like leaving her alone. Planes make her extremely nervous. I'm going to sedate her when we're back in our seats."

So that was how he was going to kill her.

"Buttercup, Daisy Petals," said Mr. Nehru, in a sweet voice. "Are you okay?"

"Coming!" said Jameela. She flushed the toilet, opened the door, and started screaming. "The therapy didn't work!"

Even Mr. Nehru was caught off guard. She took advantage of this momentary lapse and started running. She saw the food cart up ahead blocking the aisle. She dived sideways, clambered over several passengers, and kept going.

"Someone stop my wife! She's having a panic attack and needs her drugs!" yelled Mr. Nehru as he chased her.

She turned around and saw a hypodermic needle in his hand. Jameela thought quickly. Maybe if she was calm again, she could convince everyone she didn't need meds. Escape plans are hard to come by in hermetically sealed planes. There was an empty row in the middle aisle, so she crossed over and headed back to her seat. Mr. Nehru came jogging to her and slid beside her. He was out of breath and appeared to be very angry. Tasneem was by his side.

"Can I do anything to help?" she asked.

"No, my wife will be fine just after I give her the needle. It calms her down instantly. But she will be asleep for the rest of the flight," said Mr. Nehru.

"I'm calm now, honey, I don't need the needle. I have some pills in my bag. I'll take those instead."

Jameela started rummaging in her bag.

"No, no, my pet, this sedative works much faster than your pills."

"He's right. You'll feel much better after a short nap," Tasneem said reassuringly before walking away. "Who knew airplane toilets could be so traumatic?"

Mr. Nehru grabbed Jameela's left arm and tried to push up her sleeve. Jameela tried twisting away, but Nehru managed to get the needle into her arm as Jameela sprayed cologne in his face. His hand jerked away to wipe his eyes and was about to return to push the plunger, when he suddenly looked at her, confused. There was a syringe, already stuck in his leg.

Jameela pulled it out, along with the one in her arm and stowed them in her bag.

"Aziz gave it to me to assassinate Talal Abu-Khattab. But he wasn't trying to kill me. First come, first served."

"You're naive," he sputtered. "You may live in peace, but it's an illusion."

"Maybe, but I have a family that's waiting for me. And they're very real."

But Mr. Nehru didn't hear her. He was struggling to breathe as he clutched at his throat and tried to open his collar. Bubbles started forming at the corners of his mouth.

Jameela couldn't believe none of the other passengers noticed their tussle, but they had both been discreet as assassinations go. *I'm good at this,* thought Jameela sadly.

"I know you went through unbelievable tragedy during the invasions of Iraq. And you have every right to be angry. But inflicting terror on innocent people is wrong. I'm really sorry I had to do this." Jameela pulled down his tray table just in time for his head to land with a thud.

"Is your husband okay?" asked a flight attendant, handing out coffees from a cart.

"He's exhausted, poor guy. Too much stress dealing with my issues."

"Such a good husband."

"You have no idea. But once he sleeps, he's really hard to wake up. I'm going to let him snooze for a while."

"Okay, but we'll be landing soon, so his tray table will have to be up."

That meant she would have to touch him. She had never touched a corpse before. But then, she had never killed someone before, either. Was murder a gateway to other immoral behavior? Was there anything worse than murder? *No, this was self-defense,* she thought. *Don't lose it now, it's only just beginning.*

Jameela waited until the flight attendant left before lifting the armrest between her and Mr. Nehru. She got out of her seat and pushed him toward the window seat. Heads were heavier than one would think. His slumped against the airplane wall, looking very pale. Jameela took out her blush compact from the doomsday handbag and powdered Mr. Nehru to give him a healthy glow.

The plane started its descent. Blood was seeping out of a tiny hole in her blouse. She picked up the bottle of cologne, Escape for Women, off the floor. *Thanks, Calvin.* She was lucky that she'd sprayed Nehru in the eyes before he had time to push the plunger, or she'd be the dead one. Jameela stared at the growing red bloom to distract her from Nehru, dead beside her. *I had to kill him,* she told herself. *If I die, Ibrahim will die. I lost Jamal, but I can't lose Ibrahim, too.* She felt a tiny bit better, but it bothered her how easy it was to take someone's life. Something protruded out of Mr. Nehru's vest pocket and Jameela gently removed a photograph of Mr. Nehru holding the hand of a smiling child. Her finger traced the small face, which had the same dark eyes as her father. "I'm sorry I had to kill your father, but you're together now." The sudden jolt of tires on the ground caught her off guard and snapped her to attention. She replaced the photograph. As soon as the seat belt light went out, Jameela grabbed the handbag and quickly moved down the aisle.

The airport was deserted, its stores closed. Jameela knew it was only a matter of time before someone discovered her dead "husband," so she hurried as fast as she could without drawing attention to herself.

Jameela stepped outside of the airport into the stifling heat. All the passengers had someone waiting for them in vehicles, most of which had blacked-out windows. She needed one of those to take her to Raqqa fast, where Ibrahim had been taken. Buses idled nearby with elderly people shuffling in and out. She looked at the closest one. It read *Raqqa.* She asked an old man standing nearby how to buy a ticket. But he only spoke Arabic.

"If you go to Raqqa, it's a one-way trip," said a voice behind her in English. She turned to see a bus driver with a crutch, leaning against a pillar, smoking a cigarette. "No one young is allowed out."

"They let you out."

"I was chosen to drive this bus because my leg was damaged during an attack. They had to amputate it, so I'm not useful to the DICK as a soldier."

An elderly man holding a cigarette came to the bus driver and spoke in Arabic, but Jameela could only make out the name Bilal. Bilal the bus driver gave him a light, and the man walked away.

"Bilal," said Jameela, "I need to find a friend who went to Raqqa. I'm worried that DICK may be after him."

Bilal regarded her closely. "Then you'd be better off checking the ditches for bodies."

"No, he's alive. I just know it."

"I can take you as far as Raqqa, but as soon we arrive, they'll arrest you because you're a single woman traveling without a male escort."

"I just need to get there."

"The bus is loading now. We leave in twenty minutes. But remember, you're going to the most dangerous place on earth."

20

JAMEELA SAT ON THE RIGHT SIDE OF THE BUS. EVERY-
one who got in fell into one of two groups: elderly people clutching each
other or young people with machine guns strapped around their chests.
She had to assume they were fighters for DICK. Outside, a young woman
started running toward them. The bus driver closed the door. All eyes
swiveled as she pounded on the door until the driver opened it. A mini
tornado entered, bringing in its wake the scent of fruit-flavored bubble gum. She scanned the bus with sparkly turquoise-rimmed eyes, obviously looking for a place to sit. The men didn't seem to be radiating
warmth, and the elderly clutched themselves harder, so when she saw
Jameela, she looked elated and came to sit down beside her.

"Asalaamu alaikum, I'm Reem from Birmingham," she said, putting a
pink suitcase emblazoned with the Hello Kitty logo under her seat. She
was wearing a black abaya over galaxy-themed yoga pants and white
high-tops with lime-green laces. She couldn't have been much older
than Lee Lee. Thinking about her daughter made Jameela's heart hurt.
What must Lee Lee be wondering now? A mother who didn't love her
enough to explain why she left? And Nusrat must be beside herself with
worry. She had already lost one child, and now to have another one go
missing . . . Jameela had to stop dwelling on the thought.

"Wa alaikum asalaam," said Jameela.

"I thought I was going to miss the bus," said Reem in a British accent.

"That would have been a disaster." She was behaving as if she were going to a sleepover.

Bilal turned around and gave curt instructions for when they reached Raqqa. Women had to wear abayas and cover their faces, men should have full beards and trimmed mustaches, no cell phones with pictures, no music, no cigarettes. He looked at them grimly and repeated what he had told Jameela: this was a one-way trip, and he wouldn't be bringing anyone back. There was silence from the passengers, and then the diesel engine roared.

Reem opened her bulging backpack. "It was so stressful finding the bus station, and the bus manager tried to talk me out of going. I have a fast metabolism, so I get hungry quickly. What's your favorite kind of crisp?"

"Sour cream and onion," said Jameela, suddenly feeling as if she were in a movie theatre getting ready to watch the latest Bridget Jones film, instead of sitting on a bus full of men who looked like they were heading to an open carry convention in Alabama.

"Oh, I don't have crisps in that flavor, but I have popcorn."

"That'll do," said Jameela. Reem passed her a bag, and Jameela ripped it open and shoved a fistful straight into her mouth. As the chemical flavors dissolved on her tongue, Jameela realized how famished she was.

"Wow, you're really hungry," said Reem, watching Jameela devour the entire bag of popcorn in minutes. She passed her an orange flavored soda pop in a small plastic bottle which Jameela finished in three large gulps. Lee Lee had purged the house of unhealthy foods so Murray wouldn't be tempted. It had been a while since she'd had a junk food binge.

"I've had a long day," said Jameela. "What else do you got?"

Reem pulled out a selection of chocolate bars. Jameela chose the Cadbury Flake and took a bite, savoring the creamy layers. She justified the bag of peanut-covered M&Ms, since at least those had protein. Assassinations take a lot out of you, she thought, as she crunched up all the wrappers and placed them into a plastic bag attached to the end of the seat. She was starting to feel better.

"My husband, or I guess my fiancé, told me to bring a lot of snacks for the journey. He said there wouldn't be much food along the way," said Reem as she passed Jameela a second bottle.

"Smart man," said Jameela, opening the bottle and taking a swig. "Convenience stores are hard to come by in a war zone." She stared at the girl's glittery leather bracelets and smiley-face plastic ring. Reem was similar to Lee Lee in her eclectic choices of jewelry and dress. "You look a little young to be married. Shouldn't you be in high school?"

"Secondary school? Yeah, but I dropped out, I wanted to do something different with my life," said Reem, blushing. "Become a mother."

"So . . . what does your mom say about your new plans?" asked Jameela, in as casual a tone as possible. She opened a bag of Cheezies and pretended they were carrot sticks.

"She died two years ago," said Reem quietly.

"I'm sorry," said Jameela. "But doesn't your father want to meet your man, make sure he's good enough for you?"

Reem grew animated again. "Oh, he doesn't care. He remarried. He's too busy with his new family. I told him I needed money for a field trip, and he gave it to me without even asking where I was going. His new wife'll probably be glad I'm gone."

Jameela had read stories in the *New York Times* about young people with troubled home lives leaving the US and UK to join DICK. Or men like Mr. Nehru, who felt all their options had been taken by the Americans and were hell-bent on vengeance. Young women, too, wanted to join DICK and become wives, but they tended to be immature girls hoping for a romantic adventure in the deserts of Arabia. Their husbands never lived long, but new ones always showed up on their doorsteps. After a few months of this, the brides wised up and tried to return home. Like their husbands, they were disposable items in DICK's endless war to win territory and influence.

"When I was your age, I felt like running away, too," said Jameela, looking at the young woman with maternal affection.

"But you can still join DICK; they take grandmothers. You could fold laundry or something."

Jameela ignored the slight. "Oh, I'm joining up, all right. And I'm getting married."

Why she added the last part, she wasn't sure. It wasn't like she needed to compete, but she still regretted not having a picture of Abdullah. They could have giggled over which one was cuter. But it did the trick. Reem was impressed.

"Ooh, we could have a double wedding!" she squealed. "My fiancé would totally love it. He grew up in France but couldn't find a job."

"Sure, that sounds like a great idea. But doesn't DICK frown upon lavish weddings?"

"Well, they do, but we could still ask to get married together and give out treats to everyone," said Reem. "I packed a whole suitcase full of makeup because I know that's hard to get there. I could totally give you a makeover and get rid of those dark circles. We need to neutralize with a bit of orange base, and then put the concealer on top. That's the secret."

Jameela couldn't believe it. If she'd known she would be traveling to a war zone, she would have packed a bulletproof vest for protection; but this young woman had packed waterproof mascara. That would be useful during waterboarding, thought Jameela.

"So how did your fiancé convince you to join him?"

"I was really sad after my mother died and made some friends online. They sent me presents — chocolates and cards. They're the first ones who made me feel loved since . . ." She stopped speaking for a few minutes while her eyes filled.

Reem wiped away a tear and quickly pulled out a heart-shaped Valentine's Day card. Inside were signatures in fluorescent hues of purple and lilac with messages like *Can't wait for you to come.*

She has no idea where she's really going, thought Jameela. "Did anyone tell you what life is going to be like there?"

"Yeah, we get to live in our own homes, there's no rent, and DICK pays our husbands, so we can have the perfect life. Do you want a halal marshmallow?"

A knight in shining armor had rescued Reem from a dull and sad life in Birmingham.

"My friends introduced me to Umar, and we started Skyping. He says life is amazing. They get weapons and train in the desert."

"Wow," said Jameela. "It's like one long camping trip."

"It's going to be so much fun," squealed Reem.

Jameela felt that if someone had promised her a life full of adventure, friends, and a hunky husband during her high school years, she'd have packed her bags and left pronto. Luckily, the only group recruiting at the time was the chess club, and those guys weren't that sexy.

Without warning, the bus shuddered to a stop. Two men in black robes boarded; they had long beards and were holding Kalashnikovs. They spoke to Bilal, and he pointed at Jameela. Even Reem, the eternal optimist, seemed apprehensive.

"Are you Jameela Green?" asked the larger man.

"Depends on who wants to know."

"Did you kill this man?" said Red Beard, producing a picture of Mr. Nehru from his better days. Jameela looked at a young, hopeful man standing beside a pretty woman with two young children at their sides. She recognized one of the children.

"I remember sitting beside this man on the plane," said Jameela, looking at the big man's automatic rifle. Men and their toys. "He was feeling a little unwell. Did something happen to him?"

"If you had thirteen milligrams of succinylcholine injected into your thigh, you wouldn't feel well either. It paralyzes the larynx and causes the person to choke on their own saliva," said Black Beard.

Jameela thought the young man's detailed explanation of the drug was impressive. "Pharmacy should be your new calling. You're wasting your time firing bullets into the air. If there's ever a bullet shortage, you'll be sorry for all the senseless waste."

Black Beard looked perplexed at the verbiage. "I was studying to be a pharmacist—"

His friend butted him with his elbow. "Where did you get this drug? It's used for assassinations."

"Why are you assuming I killed him? There must have been over a hundred other people . . . suspects . . . on the plane." *Damn it,* thought Jameela. She couldn't believe how stupid she'd been for not throwing away the needle, but there had been a lot going on. In retrospect, she should have tossed it with the orange juice cup and napkins. Next time. There wouldn't be a next time if she couldn't pull it together. She tried to kick her handbag further under the seat in front, but the strap was tangled around her foot, which was making her angrier. And anger made her more prone to sarcasm. "He wouldn't stop complaining about the pulp in the orange juice. I'm sure one of the flight attendants snapped and killed him to shut him up."

"Search her!" commanded Red Beard.

Black Beard strode toward her. "Out," he yelled at an almost paralyzed Reem, who practically fell out of her seat. It was no use; the bag was attached to Jameela's ankle like a clinging lemur. Black Beard saw it almost immediately and untangled it. As he searched the interior, Jameela worried that he might accidentally inject himself with the unused needle, which wasn't going to make her look any less suspicious. Warning him to be careful was also pointless. He found it and held it up to Black Beard, who looked like his purpose for existing had finally come true.

"Oh, that," said Jameela. "I carry it around in my purse for self-defense. Some women carry pepper spray or a rape whistle. I prefer injectable poison when a man attacks me. Save another woman from the same grief."

This caught them off guard.

"That man was supposed to detonate a bomb in Germany. You were supposed to help him."

Jameela nodded helpfully. "Yes, but it was hard to help him when he died so inconveniently?" She needed to stop being so flippant, but the seriousness of the situation was causing her to become defensive.

The men looked momentarily stymied but pressed her again.

"You are the murderer," said Black Beard.

"That's a little harsh," said Jameela.

"We believe you have been sent to kill Talal Abu-Khattab, and that you killed this man when he thwarted you."

Reem gasped. The rest of the passengers had been straining to understand their conversation, and there was a hushed reaction at the mention of the DICK head.

Jameela was impressed by how fast they had figured her out. Talal's people weren't entirely dimwitted. Now the entire bus was looking at Jameela in horror. Reem hugged her bag of Doritos.

"You are on your way to Raqqa to fulfill your plan," accused the big man.

"Actually, I'm heading to Raqqa for some sun and sand. I hear it's got a Vegas vibe to it, what with all the matrimonial exuberance. You'd make a great Elvis, you've definitely got the hair, even if it's mostly on your face."

"Jameela Green, for the crime of murder and attempted assassination, you are now sentenced to execution by beheading."

Jameela wished she had a better filter. Her sarcasm had only enraged them further. But it was how she dealt with fear and anxiety, her defense mechanism when she was emotionally overwhelmed. She turned to an ashen-faced Reem.

"I think the double wedding's off."

21

IBRAHIM'S BODY STRAINED AGAINST THE SEAT BELT AS the plane's wheels bounced and skidded on the tarmac. These last few hours had been the most difficult in his life since his mother had died. The CIA had devised a cover for him and Amina as a radicalized married couple who had joined the DICK. They had managed to take his few photos on Facebook, add commentary, and now he was a terrorist. Amina said it was important to build credibility in case their cover was investigated by the DICK.

"How're you doing?" asked Amina as she unbuckled her seat belt.

"My stomach has calmed down, thank you for asking," said Ibrahim rubbing the blue prayer beads in his inside jacket pocket.

"Okay, so we've been over the plan several times, but you're sure you understand it?"

"We have landed on the outskirts of Raqqa, and from here we will walk into the city where you have a contact to shelter us," he replied.

"Good, you've been paying attention."

"Are you not worried that Talal will recognize you as his daughter?"

Amina breathed deeply. "Baba and I have been apart for a long time. I doubt he'd recognize me now. My parents sent me to America when I was fourteen years old, and they haven't seen me since."

"Why would they send you away for so long?"

"They didn't intend to. In 2003, the Americans had just invaded Iraq and were bombing the hell out of it. My parents were caught in the insurgency. They sent me to stay with relatives in the US for safety. My father got sent to Abu Ghraib and later to Camp Bucca."

Ibrahim remembered those camps. Photos of Americans electrocuting prisoners and raping women were published in the international press.

"It was during that time that he began organizing DICK. He felt that Iraq was never going to be free of American interference."

"You sound like you have some sympathy for him," said Ibrahim.

"I have sympathy for his grievances, yes. The injustices were very real. But when the oppressed becomes the oppressor, there is no excuse," said Amina.

Ibrahim was conflicted. He felt a solidarity with Amina that bordered on affection. But her callousness toward her father bothered him. It put up a shield in his heart.

"How will we be given an audience with him?"

"Well, that's the question no one's been able to answer. There isn't a lot of information about him anymore. Some people say he's not even alive, but I know he is."

"Do you feel it in your bones ... as people in the West are fond of saying?"

Amina looked at him in a way that unnerved him.

"No, our satellite got a picture of him a month ago when he was outside for a few seconds. He's not like bin Laden, who made videotapes like he was at Disneyland and wanted to show off."

This piece of news surprised Ibrahim. Talal didn't seem real anymore, more like a legend. People were so afraid of Talal that larger armies put down their weapons when he entered a town rather than risk the possibility of losing the battle and facing his wrath. "I did not think he would risk emerging."

"Yeah, we were a little surprised, too, but there are extenuating circumstances. He's been diagnosed with bone cancer."

Ibrahim was startled. Even bloodthirsty terrorists got sick. "I am sorry to hear that."

"Don't be. He's kidnapped several cancer specialists to treat him, which is how we got a picture. Raqqa isn't the best place for him to be living right now — not when he needs a transplant."

Ibrahim remembered a sermon he had delivered several months

back about the importance of donating blood and blood stem cells because there was a shortage of matches in multiracial ethnicities. He was
proud of himself for organizing a blood drive in the mosque. The board
was a little wary at first, but he convinced them that, as Muslims, they
needed to participate in the wider community and be a source of ben-
efit for everyone.

"There is a very low chance that children match their parents," said
Ibrahim quietly.

"I match," said Amina. "The CIA has his DNA."

"You are his only chance at survival?"

"That's how I'm going to smoke him out," said Amina, looking out the
window at the tarmac dissolving into the desert. "He'll want to meet me,
because he knows I can save his life. Then I'll kill him."

Amina, Maghrib Prayer, 5:43pm Oct. 8

Thank You for sending Ibrahim to me. Thinking about my parents makes me crazy, and his weirdness has a calming effect. I can't wait to see the look in my father's eyes when he finds out his only daughter joined the CIA to capture him. Even the CIA couldn't believe it.

You know why I hate him so much. I had to change schools three times after people found out who I was. Finding dead animals in my locker, bullies chasing me home, getting rocks thrown at my window. My entire life was ruined because of him.

I know Ibrahim doesn't approve of revenge, but DICK wants to kill people like him. They believe he's too wishy-washy, with his belief in peace and social justice. So really, killing my dad is about preventing religious persecution. Plus, he deserves to die for not letting me watch Britney Spears videos.

A win-win for all of us.

22

LEE LEE AND MURRAY STOOD IN A HOT, SANDY PARKING lot. Agent Simon, or Agent Olive Oyl, as Lee Lee preferred to call her, was standing beside them in a black abaya and robe. Lee Lee was wearing a simple striped, beige shalwar chemise with a light gray hijab. Dressing like locals was supposed to make sure they didn't draw attention. After traveling overnight by military transport to Turkey's border, a bus was going to take them to Raqqa, where they would meet the militants.

"Any minute now," said Agent Olive Oyl, looking at her military-issue watch.

"Are you sure this is safe?" asked Murray, growing pink in the sun. He was about to pass out from both heat and stress.

Agent Olive Oyl regarded him. "Well, we're about to join DICK, a group not known for its bake sales."

"I'm sure it's fine, Dad," intercepted Lee Lee. "The US military's going to be monitoring us the whole time, and as soon as we find Mom, they have a detailed extraction plan." He was desperate to get Jameela back and knew she could die, which was why he reluctantly agreed to come here. But the danger of this plan was becoming more and more apparent as they got closer to the destination, and Lee Lee was worried her father would pull out of the whole thing.

"So, explain to me again how this is all going to work?" asked Murray, now looking like a lobster in a pot. Lee Lee straightened his sunhat and passed him a bottle of cucumber-infused water. Earlier on their trip, she had placated him with different types of high-fiber sugary snacks to lull him into submission.

"Once both of you arrive in Raqqa, ask the locals if anyone new has arrived. Use the information to find Jameela and then escape," said Agent Olive Oyl calmly, as if sending them on a shopping trip for milk and eggs. "We'll have a team waiting right here. Nothing will go wrong."

"Everything could go wrong, especially with a cockamamie scheme like that," said Murray, sweat dripping down his face. "Lee Lee could be forced into marrying a militant, or I could get shipped off to fight and never come back."

"We'll have to work quickly," admitted Agent Olive Oyl. "There are risks no matter what you do in life, even tying your shoelaces."

Lee Lee winced. Agent Olive Oyl was not good at reassuring her father. She pulled out a tub of sugared mango slices, but Murray's gesticulating hands hit the tub, and the fruit pieces went flying like shrapnel.

"Tying your shoelaces! Are you crazy? You don't get shot dead when you bend down to tie your shoelaces unless you're stupid enough to join DICK!"

Agent Olive Oyl was about to rebut when a dusty yellow vehicle appeared around the corner. Lee Lee was relieved to see the busload of terrorists, since it ended this painful conversation. Agent Olive Oyl went over to speak to one of the men. They seemed to argue about something for quite some time. She came back looking flustered.

"We have a problem," she said.

"You think?" shouted Murray, a piece of mango trembling on the brim of his hat.

"They've just discovered a plot to assassinate Talal, so they're no longer accepting groups of recruits."

"It's the terrorists who have the most common sense. What does this say about the rest of us?"

Agent Olive Oyl mopped up some sweat from her upper lip with the edge of her sleeve. "They no longer trust North American men. They're only accepting young women unaccompanied by male guardians."

"Well, good. I knew this plan was crazy before we even started. We're going home. Come on, Lee Lee."

Murray turned to his daughter, but it was too late. She waved at him from the window of the bus, which was already pulling away.

"Lee Lee!" screamed Murray. He tried to run, but two men from the CIA held him back. Lee Lee cried silently, watching him struggle with them. She had made this plan with Agent Olive Oyl while Murray had been sleeping. DICK never allowed fathers to accompany daughters; there was too much risk that they would change their minds and go home. Only single girls were allowed, but Agent Olive Oyl couldn't get Lee Lee across the Turkish border without her father present because the government had cracked down on Western girls recruited by DICK. All unaccompanied girls were being detained in the Istanbul airport for questioning. Agent Olive Oyl was so desperate for a secret agent that she had broken agency rules to get Lee Lee inside the most secretive city in the world.

Now, Lee Lee would have to rescue her mother on her own. Guilt coursed through her. Instead of supporting her mother, she'd called her superficial, materialistic, and a bunch of other terrible things. Lee Lee had to come back with her mother, or she didn't want to come back at all.

Lee Lee, Isha Prayer, 9:06 p.m., Oct. 8

I'm really, really scared. I've never done anything like this before. Dad's going to be super mad, but this was the only way to get Mom back. Please take care of him, and make sure he eats steel-cut oats for breakfast. The fast-cooking kind are okay, too, because even I get tired of stirring that pot for three hours.

And let Emily know that I'm sorry for not going to her birthday party. Jane and Tinku are gonna be so mad. I was supposed to help decorate the cake as a surprise. We were gonna do a *Frozen* theme, and I already made the icicles out of melted Life Savers and had sugar fondant for the snowflakes and everything. I'll explain it to them when I get back.

I've been to all of Brother Ibrahim's youth halaqas at the mosque, so I know the advice he would give me. I'm going to be brave, pray a lot, and put all my trust in You. That's really hard to do right now, but I'll try. Please make me strong like my mother. I miss her so much.

23

MURRAY LAY AWAKE IN HIS BED IN LIVERSPOT. THERE were five empty bags of Milk Duds in the trash can, weighed down by his knitting needles and unfinished scarf. The Turkish government didn't take kindly to people trying to make contact with DICK on their borders and had deported him. The CIA escorted him home first class and apologized for their subterfuge, but a chance to have an agent inside DICK was too good to pass up. And since Lee Lee was so willing to go, she was the obvious choice.

Murray had returned to an empty house, canceled his patients for the foreseeable future, and packed his things. The next day, he was going to fly to New York to stay with his in-laws. How he would explain Lee Lee's disappearance to his mother-in-law, he didn't know. But he had to tell Nusrat in person. His in-laws would be apoplectic with rage — not only was their daughter missing, but so was their only grandchild. Still, he couldn't bear to stay in this house alone.

His cell phone rang. Murray glanced at the clock which glowed 12:07 a.m.

"Hello?"

"How can you be calm at a time like this, You Idiot?"

Murray's heart sank. It was Nusrat. "I'm coming to see you tomorrow."

"With Lee Lee? Put her on the phone. I want to know how's she's doing."

"There's a problem."

"Of course, there's a problem. Maleeha's mother is missing. Now put my granddaughter on the phone."

"I can't. That's why I'm coming to Brooklyn. To tell you in person."

"Tell me now, or by the will of God, my hand will come through this telephone and rip your testicles off."

Murray believed that if rage could pass through radio waves, his gonads would be gone by now. "Lee Lee joined DICK to save her mother. I tried to stop her, but the CIA was in on it."

There was a pause on the other line.

"My only grandchild is gone too," whispered Nusrat.

Murray wished she would scream at him. The shock had numbed her normal ferocity.

"I'm sorry, I still can't figure out how it happened."

"You let it happen! That's how it happened. You were supposed to keep them safe, You Idiot!"

She was back, thought Murray. It gave him some comfort.

After hurling more insults at him, Nusrat eventually became exhausted, got his flight information, and hung up.

Murray looked over and saw his wedding photo on the side table. He was smiling in his black sherwani. He was thinner and had more hair in those days. Jameela, dressed in a red langa decorated with gold embroidery and imitation rubies and diamonds, was gripping his arm for dear life. He had thought that day would never arrive.

Spurred by Jameela's hatred for her faith, he had taken a history class about the Ottomans, who had an empire that rivaled that of the Romans in its breadth, power, and influence. In 1492, the Catholic Reconquista of Spain targeted the Jews who had lived in the Muslim-ruled land for millennia. They were given three choices: conversion, death, or exile. While Europe was setting up pogroms against the community, the Sultan Beyezit II sent ships to the Iberian coastline to rescue the Jewish refugees and bring them to his empire, where they practiced their faith without fear of persecution. Murray knew it was wrong to romanticize slavery, but when he learned that the majority of Sultans who ruled the Ottoman empire were the sons of Christian-born slaves, it surprised him. He'd expected a bloodthirsty history, and some of it was, but there was also a tolerant, pluralistic Muslim history that he never knew existed.

Inspired, he took a trip to Istanbul, heard the azan from the public minarets, watched as people flocked to pray in mosques built centuries ago. People welcomed him into cafés, plied him with kebabs and Turkish coffee while bonding with him about their hopes for the future. He felt a strong longing to be part of this large, enveloping world. Not long after, he attended Friday prayers at NYU. When everyone left, he turned to the young Saudi student, Bashar, who had given the sermon, and asked to become Muslim. Bashar, who seemed unsurprised, took Murray's shahada, a declaration of faith, in front of a few remaining students. Bashar taught him the basics of prayer and advised him to go slow. Murray loved the solace of speaking to God several times a day, the sense of communal comfort he got every Ramadan when he broke his fast with hundreds of other students. He had found his people. Jameela's family was so different from what he was used to. Everyone expressed emotion like it was going out of style. Not like his quiet and impassive parents, who only seemed to get excited when they discovered a new cheese at the local deli.

They weren't a religious family, but their reaction to his conversion was acute embarrassment. His parents were part of the country-club set: golf every weekend and summers in their cottage. "Murray, we don't marry 'other' people," his mother said when she learned of the engagement. Both sets of parents looked glum on their wedding day. And after 9/11, Murray's relationship with his parents became more strained. Lee Lee was the glue that held both family strands together.

Taking Lee Lee to the Liverspot mosque and learning to read the Arabic alphabet with her was a joyful experience for them both. He offered free dental care to refugees and, unlike Jameela, made friends quickly. He was on the board of the mosque and gave the occasional sermon until they hired Ibrahim.

After years of marriage, Murray realized that he would never be able to replace Jamal, no matter how much he supported his wife. She was going to have to find her own way to peace, like he had. But the growing gulf between Jameela and Lee Lee worried him. He had hoped that letting Lee Lee take control of his diet would help her feel like there was some semblance of normalcy in their lives and she wouldn't be as hard on her mother. The two of them couldn't go on like they were much longer. And now he'd lost them both.

The pressure in his sinuses hurt from crying for so long, but after blowing his nose with the last tissue in the box, he got up. As he looked at his red, splotchy, bloated face in the bathroom mirror, he knew only one thing gave him comfort and strength. Murray performed his ablutions in the sink, laid his prayer mat beside his bed, and begged God for the safe return of his family.

24

JAMEELA SAT WITH ROPE AROUND HER BODY SECURING her to the chair. The men had brought her here a few hours ago, and her arms were beginning to cramp. As the pain increased, she distracted herself by examining the room. The walls were dune-colored, interspersed with broken patches of stucco. The only window let in a shaft of light between its dirty, torn curtains, but it was nailed shut and couldn't be opened. There was a table and some chairs. In one corner she could see a camera on a tripod, set up to point at another corner of the room where a dirty white sheet hung as a backdrop. On either side of the sheet stood two DICK flags with their dark-green background and simple Arabic script.

This is the room where they're going to behead me, and probably livestream it, thought Jameela. Mark Zuckerberg didn't realize how important Facebook Live and Instagram were for terrorists of every hue. The videos were never taken down in time to prevent a few thousand people from watching. What would her last words be? Murray and Lee Lee deserved an apology for her self-centeredness. Lee Lee had wanted to go on a trip to Japan in ninth grade, but they didn't because Jameela couldn't stomach working with the other parents for six months doing fundraising activities. And how many dental association parties did she miss because she didn't like Murray's colleagues?

She was lost in these thoughts when the door opened and Abdullah, her long-suffering fiancé, walked in with a young man who looked like

Zayn Malik. Abdullah had sprouted a few more gray hairs since she'd last seen him in Karachi, but his eyes had the same yearning.

"I'm Abdullah's bodyguard," said Zayn in a working-class British accent. "He's very upset that they've tied you up."

"Can he make them let me go?"

"You've caused him a great deal of trouble. Talal thinks that you were trying to assassinate him. So he's having to be very careful about your security."

"Talal? The head of DICK?" asked Jameela. "So he really does exist."

"Of course he does. How else do you think the DICK functions?"

"I figured someone with balls was running the show."

"I assure you, their balls would be cut off immediately if they tried to impersonate Talal. He is the true head."

"Good to know," replied Jameela. She willed herself to behave; she'd already gotten herself into a bigger mess with her mouth.

"Why didn't you follow through with the plan, as directed?" asked Zayn.

"I didn't want to kill hundreds of people for no reason."

Abdullah and the bodyguard conferred.

"Abdullah has delayed your execution by convincing the inner circle that you couldn't carry out the attack because Western mosques teach a wimpy version of Islam."

"You teach murder and call it Islam." Jameela realized that these men were trying to help her, but it was no use; her mouth had its own will, and she couldn't trust anyone now.

Zayn looked at her. "If Talal didn't feel he owed Abdullah a debt for saving his life back in Camp Bucca, you would be dead by now."

"That man in the plane was coming on to me," protested Jameela. She knew that Abdullah would be unhappy with this news. "When I told him where to go, he decided to kill me. I did what I had to do."

When Zayn relayed this information to Abdullah in Arabic, he fluffed up in jealousy.

Zayn patted Abdullah's shoulder in consolation. "It doesn't matter now. Talal has set your execution for seven p.m. tomorrow. We are making the arrangements. You will be given a script to read before your beheading."

Jameela felt light-headed and swayed forward in her chair and was grateful to be tied to it. Her family had to know her regrets before she died. She should have suffered with those goody-goody parents so Lee Lee could have gone to Japan, and worn her best ball gown to the annual Sparkling Smile gala. "I don't need a script. I need to tell a few things to my family."

"No, you will apologize for your disloyalty to the DICK and encourage others to follow orders."

The nerve of this idiot. "And if I don't read the message?"

"They will make you."

Jameela laughed. "How? They're gonna kill me anyway. They don't exactly have leverage."

Zayn opened the door. Lee Lee walked in.

25

JAMEELA STARED AT LEE LEE AND FELT A SENSE OF LOVE followed by confusion. Reality sank in. *Not here, not here. Anywhere but here.* She could see the joy and terror flash across her daughter's face. Lee Lee ran over to Jameela and hugged her awkwardly since her arms were still tied. Warmth coursed through her as she felt Lee Lee's slender frame press into hers. *When was the last time she'd hugged Lee Lee?* That was a disturbing thought.

Zayn quickly pulled them apart. "She's here as an inducement for you to comply."

"How on earth did you get here, Lee Lee?"

"Dad and I flew to Turkey, and then I ditched him, got on a bus, and crossed the border into Syria. When they were herding us into groups, I told them I was your daughter —"

"And we took care of the rest," said Zayn.

"Where's your father now?"

"Back in Liverspot, probably with his head in a bag of Ho Hos."

Jameela looked imploringly at Zayn. "What are you going to do with her?"

"She'll be married to one of our men," said Zayn, smoothing down his beard self-consciously.

"She's only fifteen years old," said Jameela. "Find someone your own age, you maniac."

"Mom, don't argue with them, they'll kill you," said Lee Lee, looking around the room for the first time.

Jameela looked Zayn in the eye. "Fine, I'll say what you want, but you have to promise me you'll send my daughter home."

"No one is being sent home," said Zayn. "At least not alive."

"So, if I don't say what you want, you'll kill me and kill her, and if I say what you want, you'll kill me and then marry her off to one of your goons. Those don't sound like great options."

"One of those options keeps your daughter alive," said Zayn. "And I don't consider myself a goon." Jameela thought he looked hurt.

"If this is my last night with my daughter, can I at least spend it with her?" asked Jameela. "We've been apart for a while." She needed to buy herself some time to figure out how to save herself and Lee Lee.

"What do you mean, 'last night'?" asked Lee Lee.

Lee Lee was frightened, and Jameela wanted to rake her fingers through her hair and hold her close.

"Your mother disobeyed a direct order and killed one of our operatives," explained Zayn. "She's scheduled to be beheaded tomorrow after she delivers a message about the perils of disloyalty."

Lee Lee's lips trembled.

"I'll do what you want. Please, could you untie my hands so I can hold my daughter?"

Zayn undid her knots, and Jameela grabbed Lee Lee tightly, determined to help her daughter through this. "Don't cry, Lee Lee," said Jameela, feeling like this was the perfect time to cry. "Remember when you tried to get Dad to eat his broccoli by boiling it, mushing it up, and adding it to his coffee?"

"He choked and told me he couldn't drink coffee again for two weeks without feeling nauseous," Lee Lee said. They both laughed at the memory.

"Did I ruin your childhood?" asked Jameela, abruptly ending their laughter.

"I had a great childhood. But you have to have faith, Mom," said Lee Lee, staring intently at her. "Everything's going to be okay."

Neither global warming nor terrorists could faze Lee Lee. How her daughter had become so optimistic and strong was beyond her. She was definitely her father's daughter. And her brother's niece. Thank God her own genes were recessive.

"It's been a long time since we've talked," said Jameela, regretting the time they'd never have. "Nothing like a beheading to make you remember what's important."

Zayn watched them closely. "My mother and I used to make French toast together every Sunday in Portsmouth," he said with a melancholy air. "We used to eat it with blueberry syrup and whipped cream. She still sends me letters, even though I never reply." Zayn turned to Abdullah and relayed their conversation in Arabic. Abdullah looked sad and said a few words.

"He says his mother is no longer alive, but he misses her whenever he makes hummus."

"Mothers are the most important people in the whole world," said Lee Lee. "I'm sorry I was so mean to you, Mom."

Jameela saw a tear in Zayn's eye.

"I'm sure that Talal wouldn't mind if we let the two of you spend a few hours together," he said. "I should have said goodbye to my mum before I left, but she would have tried to stop me."

"I'd appreciate it," said Jameela. "Will we be able to be alone?"

"No, you may try and escape."

He wasn't completely daft. "We need privacy."

"Yes, of course, but a woman will guard you."

"Who?"

At that moment, the door opened and a tall, older woman wearing a dark gray abaya entered. She looked a little like Charlotte Rampling, with her hooded eyes and severe expression.

The men seemed surprised by her entrance and started to salute. She put a hand up to still them.

"Gentlemen, at ease." Her voice was deep and regal. She slowly walked around the room like a lion examining its prey.

"The DICK has never executed a woman before, so I thought I'd come and see her for myself." She looked Jameela up and down for a full ten seconds.

"You're disappointed, aren't you?" said Jameela, reading the woman's thoughts.

"Yes," said the woman. "You seem . . . inconsequential."

Jameela laughed at the description. "I am. I should be at home selling insurance to my canola farmers, or picking Froot Loops off the floor."

Charlotte Rampling sighed, adjusted her abaya, and sat down.

"I want to be alone with this woman and her daughter. Find something more useful to do. Go out on the streets and measure some beards or robes. Surely somebody is letting their ankle show and deserves to be flogged."

"But our orders . . ."

"You'll leave, or there'll be new orders, and you won't like them," she snapped. "Your ugly heads won't look any better on spikes."

"Yes, ma'am," said Zayn, his eyes down. He pulled Abdullah with him.

"He wanted to marry you," said the woman, watching Abdullah's sorrowful expression.

This was news to Lee Lee. "What?" she cried. "Does Dad know about this?"

"Of course not," scoffed Jameela.

"That's not why you left, is it? Because there was another man?" Lee Lee looked scandalized.

"Yeah, I was trolling OkCupid, and found a religious extremist who looks like an orc and has four wives already, and thought, 'That's the man for me!'"

Charlotte tilted back her head and laughed hysterically. When she was done, she wiped her cheeks and looked at the two of them with kinder eyes.

"It's been a long time since I've laughed like that. These men are so serious with their constant talk of war and Armageddon. Sometimes I think I'm in an episode of *Game of Thrones*. I've never met more ridiculous people in my life."

Lee Lee and Jameela looked at each other.

"Who are you?" asked Lee Lee.

"My name is Nusayba Kareem. I'm Talal's wife."

"As in Talal, the head of DICK?" asked Jameela.

"The biggest DICK, as they say."

"So, you can save my mother?" Lee Lee asked, her face alight with hope.

"I'm the one who decided your mother should die."

Jameela, Isha Prayer, 11:47 p.m., Oct. 10

What the fudge monkeys is going on here? How could You let Lee Lee out of Liverspot? This is pure insanity, even for You. Lee Lee can't get hurt. She's totally innocent in all this, and now she's in Nusayba's clutches because of me.

What a total bitch. She thinks she can kill me on her own schedule. Aren't You supposed to rain hail, eggs, or bowling balls on people like her? It seems like she wears the pants under all the robes in this terrorist organization. I blame Sheryl Sandberg. It's good to see women in power, but she may have taken the advice to "lean in" too far.

I would have a nervous breakdown, but I can't afford to right now, because I'm about to be executed, and Lee Lee needs me. And Murray is going to kill me for getting Lee Lee into this mess. But I guess DICK will beat him to it. Oh, Murray, how could I do this to you? You're probably worried sick about us.

Okay, listen carefully. Lee Lee loves You. And You take care of people who love You. I'm expendable, but she's one of Yours, so don't let her go down with this crazy, terrorist ship.

Lee Lee, Isha Prayer, 11:47 p.m., Oct. 10

Thank You for letting me find my mom. She totally freaked out when she saw me, but she's calmer now. I know she's worried about my safety, but I'm glad I came. Turns out she was right about Brother Ibrahim getting deported. But the weirder part is that Mom cared enough to do something about it. She's really changed.

Dad always told me to be patient with her. He said she'd talk about losing her brother when she was ready. I always prayed that we could hang out together more. And now it's come true!

Please don't her die. Please help us find Brother Ibrahim and return home safely. We're in a really bad place with scary people who do scary things. I know this sounds crazy, but this is the most fun I've ever had with my mom. I want to keep having this much fun but at home.

26

TO PREVENT DETECTION, IBRAHIM AND AMINA HAD
been dropped off on the outskirts of the city, which meant walking for
what seemed like days in the desert, trying to reach Raqqa. They only
traveled by night, sleeping in a beige tent during the day.

"Is this hardship necessary?" asked Ibrahim, as he surveyed the vast
sand dunes. There was little vegetation in sight, mostly rocks and small
hilly areas.

"They'd kill us on sight," she said. "Spies have infiltrated Raqqa lately,
and DICK is getting jumpy and demanding proof of loyalty."

"What kind of proof?"

"They ask you to kill people as a sign of devotion."

This sounded like something the DICK would do. From what he'd
read and heard, their original vision of a caliphate, an oasis of humanity,
living up to the ideals of the prophet, had morphed into an authoritarian cult that demanded utter loyalty to its commander.

"I see buildings up ahead," said Amina. Ibrahim saw them too, squat
structures that blended in with the sand. It saddened him to reach
Raqqa. He had enjoyed his time in the desert with Amina, insisting on
sleeping outside the tent, promising to keep a sand-colored blanket over
him the entire time so he wouldn't be seen. As they walked during the
night, they talked about their childhoods and their hopes for the future.
He had never had a chance to speak to a woman in such an informal setting before and had been careful to keep his behavior professional and

above reproach. He was also careful to let Amina dress in the privacy of the tent and perform any other tasks without ever having to worry that he was watching. He had a secret plan. He was going to win Amina over by proving to her that he was worthy of being her husband. There was a saying in Islam: to really know someone, you must travel with them; in their case, travel and infiltrate a homicidal movement.

While Amina plotted their route, Ibrahim cleaned, organized, and prepped their travel supplies for the day. She seemed to appreciate his work. He even managed to kill animals and cook them on the propane stove. His efforts had provided them with fresh food, which was useful, because Amina's dried rations were running out after traveling now for two days. After a few hours of walking, they took a break to eat.

"How did you learn to do that?" asked Amina, as she watched Ibrahim skin a rabbit.

"When I was a child, we would have to catch our food sometimes to help us get by when money was short," he replied.

"Wow, we just went to the grocery store to get our food," said Amina, watching Ibrahim with admiration as he dissected the rabbit with an army knife.

"There was no grocery store where we lived," said Ibrahim. "Villagers sold different types of food in stalls during the week, and sometimes we traded food. We owned a buffalo, and we exchanged milk for eggs."

Ibrahim could tell that his stories fascinated Amina. In the city, he felt out of place, but here, in the desert, they were in his territory. Between his knowledge of the desert and Amina's high-tech gear, it felt like paradise. He could do this forever. The desert was harsh, and you had to look hard to find its beauty, but Ibrahim knew its face well. The shifting sand dunes during windstorms reminded him of the ocean. The nights were cool, and there was no better place on earth to see the stars. But he knew their time alone was coming to an end. They finished eating and started walking again.

"How did you become separated from your parents?" asked Ibrahim.

"When the second Gulf War started, my mother stayed in Syria to help my father lead a revolution against Assad, but things got out of hand. I grew up in California and joined the CIA after college," explained Amina.

"What did your mother think about you joining the American military?"

"Well, at first she thought that I would be a great mole for my father, but after a while, she figured out I wasn't joining to help him defeat the West. You could say we're estranged."

"When was the last time you saw her?"

"I haven't seen her since I left in 2003 when I was fourteen."

"Who raised you in America?"

"Relatives of my mother. They helped me see that my parents weren't just fighting Assad but were becoming consumed by their need for power."

Ibrahim could understand what Amina meant. The global war hadn't ended terrorism; it had increased it a hundred times.

"Killing your father won't destroy the DICK," said Ibrahim. "Did killing Osama bin Laden end terrorism? No, an uglier monster sprouted from his neck."

"Because of his obsession, I lost my family. I was raised by relatives who didn't want me. Kids in my school hated me when they found out I was Muslim. I just wanted a mother who loved me, like everyone else. But she abandoned me."

Ibrahim hadn't anticipated how growing up alone would affect Amina's emotional state, but before he could comfort her, they had reached the city. Tiny square buildings in pink, beige, and yellow stucco simmered in the distance. They walked on the side of a highway that led into Raqqa. Cars and motorcycles were raising dust as they sped past. Soon they neared cross streets and passageways teeming with people. The hum of life surprised him. The DICK had managed to take over a society and apply their puritanical values to it, but it was still functioning. Amina and Ibrahim joined the pedestrians, their supplies hidden carefully in bulging grocery bags. They had buried what they didn't need before entering.

Ibrahim could see the stress on the faces of the men and women. The DICK morality officers walked around with rifles slung over their arms. The women, in black abayas, covered their faces so completely, it was a miracle they weren't tripping over their own feet. Some of them also carried AK-47s. Everyone kept to themselves and moved hurriedly, as if to finish tasks and get home to safety. Morality police were notorious about pulling people over and asking questions.

"Where are we going?" asked Ibrahim.

"I have an aunt who lives here. We'll go to her apartment."

"Do you trust her?" Ibrahim knew that people often double-crossed each other to stay alive.

"Yes," said Amina. "I've known her since I was five."

As they turned a corner, a black sedan drove toward them. A man rolled down his window and stared at Amina. Ibrahim's blood froze.

"You!" the man shouted in Arabic, pointing his finger at Amina. Ibrahim could tell by her stiffened posture that she was scared. She walked robotically up to him.

"I can see your face — it's not covered properly. What do you think you're doing walking around like that?"

Amina tried to cover her face, but her scarf was too short, and she couldn't quite manage. The man had started to open his car door when Ibrahim stepped in front of him.

"This is my wife. How dare you stare at her in this manner?"

"But she's not covered properly," the man protested angrily. "We have rules here."

"She's covered enough, and you should lower your gaze. The prophet never harassed women in the street. And your own clothes aren't proper. I can see your knees. I'm reporting you to the morality police for violating the rules of shariah. What is your name?"

The man quickly shut the car door, started his engine, and drove away.

"You shouldn't have done that," said Amina, looking around nervously. People had stopped to stare at them.

"I dislike men like that. They think that God gives them authority over women. There is no single story of the prophet or his companions ever treating women in this manner. These men just want to abuse women and call it religion." But Ibrahim knew she was right.

"Look, I appreciate what you're trying to do. That was truly an act of bravery, but our goal here is to blend in and not be noticed. We may have blown our cover."

Ibrahim accepted the gentle chastening, but she had been impressed. He bowed his head, and they hurried through the streets. They entered an apartment building and walked to a dirty white door on the main floor. Amina knocked in what Ibrahim realized was a coded pattern. After a few seconds, the door opened slightly, revealing an elderly woman dressed in a dark blue robe. She ushered them in.

"Welcome, welcome," she said in Arabic, checking the hallway to make sure none of the neighbors had noticed her new visitors. "I am Sahar, Amina's aunt," she said, introducing herself to Ibrahim. She ushered them into a small, cramped living room with peeling, ivy-patterned wallpaper. They sat on a plush couch with brightly colored teal and orange cushions. She served them sweet, hot tea in glass cups with gold rims.

She turned to Amina. "The situation is deteriorating very quickly," she said, offering them pieces of baklava. The light, airy pastry layered with crushed walnuts melted in Ibrahim's grateful mouth. He felt right at home. This tiny apartment reminded him of the house where he'd grown up in Egypt, and this woman reminded him of his mother.

"How have they treated you?" asked Ibrahim. He worried for her safety.

"Even though I don't get along with my sister, Amina's mother, we are still family, and the DICK respects that."

There was a knock on the door.

"Everyone, stay calm," said Sahar. "There are rumors of spies, so people are on edge."

"And we're assassins, so they're right to be nervous," said Amina. Ibrahim noted the "we," which warmed his heart, but also made him wonder if he was being manipulated.

"Should we hide?" asked Ibrahim.

"That will make the situation worse," said Sahar. "If someone has reported you, they will search the apartment and find you. I will say you are my guests. The best thing to do is stay calm."

Sahar went to the door. Two men in fatigues with AK-47s around their shoulders and black and white keffiyehs covering their faces stood there silently.

"Welcome, welcome," said Sahar, leading them into the living room where Amina and Ibrahim sat very still.

"Amina, Ibrahim, these are my neighbors from two doors down. They visit me to make sure I'm safe."

Ibrahim noticed Sahar twisting the end of her headscarf around her finger. The young men shook Ibrahim's hand and put their hands over their hearts when they got to Amina.

"Please sit and have tea with us." Sahar brought out another tray of cookies. One of the men kept staring at Ibrahim. As the men unwound their face coverings, Ibrahim recognized him. It was Barkley.

27

"DO YOU HAVE A PLACE I CAN PRAY ZUHR, KHALA SA-
har? I have a terrible habit of waiting for the last minute," said Barkley.

"Of course, you may use my bedroom. The prayer mat is already out."

"Can I join you? I, too, have been tardy, and must perform my salat,"
said Ibrahim, standing up.

"Would you like to join us, Taha?"

Taha was eyeing baklava and various cookies, while adding spoonfuls
of sugar to his tea.

"No, no, you go ahead, I prayed already."

Barkley and Ibrahim avoided eye contact, and they both moved
slowly to Sahar's bedroom, where they shut the door quietly.

Ibrahim was about to talk when Barkley put his finger to his mouth.

"We have to whisper so Taha doesn't get suspicious. What are you doing here, man?"

"It is a long story, and I do not believe we have much time to catch up."

"No, our job is to go from house to house and report any unusual
guests. And you don't wanna know what they do with them."

"We are in trouble."

"They keep a tab on Khala Sahar, because she's a DICK relative, so
we're gonna have to report you guys."

"But how will we make it out before you report us?"

"The guy's a bottomless pit, so I'll try and stall him at the kebab shop.
But you two have to vamoose."

The word brought pain to Ibrahim's heart. Even though it had only been a few days, that word seemed like from another lifetime.

They stared at each other for a moment. Ibrahim could see the dark circles under Barkley's eyes. He'd lost weight and seemed less like his gregarious self. He seemed . . . smaller. Ibrahim embraced Barkley, who started to weep silently.

"They make me kill people," he whispered into Ibrahim's ear.

"I forgive you for stealing the two thousand dollars from my home. I will not leave here without you, Brother Barkley. I promise you that."

"I'm sorry for betraying you. You have every right to say 'I told you so.'"

Ibrahim believed he did, too, but saying so would be a display of arrogance.

"My pretend wife belongs to the CIA's special forces. She has an extraction team ready to get us out."

Barkley looked ecstatic. "When?"

"After my pretend wife assassinates Talal Abu-Khattab, who also is her father."

Ibrahim could not find the English word to identify the look on Barkley's face. "You look surprised," he said at last.

"That's the head DICK's daughter out there? Wow, Ibby, you really know how to pick 'em."

"Yes, but she will not call the extraction team until her mission is complete."

"And you're gonna help her?"

"I feel I must. I believe she is suffering from emotional distress from being apart from her parents and doesn't understand how difficult her goal is. I can help her navigate in this part of the world. She has been gone a long time."

Ibrahim felt a strange sense of pride. It was a feeling he had never had at the mosque. He was finally doing something more meaningful than being the victim of spitballs.

"Ibby, I'm in, too. That bastard deserves to die." Barkley scribbled something down. "Here's my cell phone number. If you can get ahold of a phone, call me and I'll help you, but right now, I gotta buy you time to escape."

As they entered the living room, they could see that Taha had finished all the dessert and was looking a little restless.

"Finally. What were you guys reciting, Surah al-Baqarah? We gotta report Khala Sahar's new guests to headquarters immediately."

"Of course. We'll try that new kebab place later. Yusuf said their meat is like butter, practically melts in your mouth, and something about a secret sauce . . . It's on the way, but we shouldn't risk it."

Taha looked conflicted. "If it's on the way, we can grab a bite quickly. I can feel my blood sugar starting to drop. Why don't you go ahead and file the report, and I'll get us some food?"

"That sounds like a plan, dude."

Taha bolted out the door. Barkley waited until he was out of earshot.

"I'll give you guys a half-hour head start. Run!"

28

JAMEELA STOOD UP FOR THE FIRST TIME IN HOURS. Zayn had agreed to untie her at Nusayba's request, though he gave her a dirty look.

"You people are minimalists," said Jameela, looking around the room. There was an old, dilapidated office chair with suspicious stains on the back. It was better not to think about it.

"Interior décor is a little hard to come by these days, due to the blockades, sanctions, and whatnot," said Nusayba, who was stretched out on an army-issued cot. The cot reminded Jameela of the ones they lay on in high school while donating blood. She imagined that people did the same thing here for different reasons. "Men are obsessed with smuggling in guns and give little thought to life's other luxuries. I would kill for a good mascara."

Jameela believed her.

"Some women here think makeup is a Western plot to keep women psychologically imprisoned," Nusayba continued. "They don't realize they're already real prisoners here. You might as well look good while you're still alive, amirite?" She laughed. "Those simpletons think they're doing God's bidding, but they're really just a cheap janitorial service with benefits. As soon as one husband is blown up, they're given a new one. And they never protest, although it wouldn't matter if they did."

Jameela thought of Reem on the bus and wondered how things were going with her. Lee Lee exchanged glances with her mother. They were going to have to be very careful around Nusayba. She seemed unpredictable.

"I've got some in my bag," said Lee Lee. "Mascara, I mean. I read that makeup and tampons were the second most requested items by women here." She pulled out a pink tube still in its packaging and handed it to Nusayba, whose face lit up with jubilation.

Jameela was surprised. She thought a machete or an axe would be more up her alley.

"Thank you," gushed Nusayba, as she took the tube and unwrapped it. "We have so few indulgences here." She went to the chipped mirror hanging on the wall, took the wand out of the container, and then carefully applied a layer of mascara.

"What do you think?" she said. Her eyelashes drew more attention to her hazel eyes.

"Wow, your eyes look so beautiful," said Lee Lee.

Even Jameela had to admit she looked more striking.

Nusayba laughed. "I do look better. I tell you, this place just sucks the woman out of you."

"You're not really going to kill my mother, are you?"

"Of course. How do you think the DICK has been able to win so many battles? Our brutality and mercilessness have made men drop their guns and surrender when we enter their cities. We were outnumbered by the thousands in Mosul, but the Iraqi army just ran. Your mother will be the first woman executed for disobeying the commands of Talal. After that, there will be no more treachery."

Jameela's stomach dropped. She'd actually thought they were winning Nusayba over.

"You know what would make your eyelashes look even better?" asked Lee Lee.

"What?"

"An eyelash curler. Although technically, you should curl your lashes before you put on mascara. I've got one here in my bag."

Nusayba grabbed the eyelash curler out of Lee Lee's hand and turned back to the mirror. She started to crimp her eyelashes. "You're right! I used to do that back in —"

Jameela heard a *thwak*, and Nusayba fell to the ground.

Lee Lee was standing over her with a small fire extinguisher.

Jameela looked at her, stunned. "Are fire extinguishers the third most requested item in Raqqa?"

"I found it on the bus when I got on. I put it in my backpack after they checked for contraband. I thought it might come in handy."

"That's my girl." Jameela suddenly felt maternal pride. If her daughter could outsmart a terrorist, how bad a mother could she have been?

"Is everything okay in there?" asked Zayn from outside the door.

Jameela put a finger to her lips to silence Lee Lee. "Yes," she called, "we're just having a hijab-free moment, giving our hair a chance to breathe." Zayn wouldn't dare enter the room knowing they weren't covered. She could practically hear him squirming outside.

"Is that true, Khala Nusayba?" asked Zayn. So clever, thought Jameela, to get verification from the ice queen herself.

"Her face is covered in a mud mask I brought from home," said Lee Lee. "She can't talk right now, or it'll crack."

"I'm getting a female to verify your story," said Zayn. The sound of his footsteps grew fainter.

"We don't have a lot of time," said Jameela. She opened the door and looked up and down the hallway of what she realized was an apartment building. It was empty, but she could hear Zayn knocking on doors around the corner, yelling for the woman of the house. The neighbors would be reluctant to hand over their female relatives. Who knew what would happen once they left the safety of their homes? When she heard a man arguing that his wife wasn't well enough to come outside, Jameela grabbed Lee Lee, and they crept down the corridor in the opposite direction. They were almost around the corner when Zayn returned with a frightened woman in tow.

"Come back, or you'll be beheaded," he yelled. The woman broke free from his grasp and ran back to her apartment.

"You'll behead us anyway," yelled Jameela, as they reached the end of the hallway and yanked at the stairwell door. It was heavier than she thought. She turned and saw Zayn running, his semiautomatic aimed at them. Lee Lee riffled through her backpack.

"We gotta go, MacGyver!" screamed Jameela as she tried to grab Lee Lee, but it was too late. Zayn had reached them. Lee Lee pulled out an aerosol can and sprayed a blast of noxious chemicals into his face. Zayn screamed and collapsed in a heap, firing his gun randomly at the stucco ceiling. Pieces of plaster rained down as Jameela finally got the door open far enough for her and Lee Lee to slip through.

"Wasp spray," gasped Lee Lee as they ran down the stairs. "It's got longer reach than pepper or bear spray." She took a deep breath. "For use on rapists and thugs."

Jameela didn't have time to be impressed; Abdullah lumbered after them at a surprising speed. He looked angry. Jameela and Lee Lee ran down two more flights of stairs and reached the ground floor and opened the door. This time, Lee Lee pulled a small bottle of oil from her backpack and poured it over the door handle. "It'll buy us a few seconds," she said.

As they ran along the hallway toward the main entrance, they could hear Abdullah behind them, struggling to open the stairwell door, then kicking and punching it.

"Lee Lee, look!" screamed Jameela pointing to heavy glass doors.

They were almost at the building exit when they heard an apartment door open, and they turned around and saw Ibrahim. They all looked at each other in disbelief and amazement. He quickly pulled them into the apartment.

But before Jameela could get over her shock at seeing Ibrahim, Lee Lee ran back outside.

"Where are you going?" yelled Jameela. She watched as Lee Lee opened the main entrance door and then ran back into the apartment.

"He'll think we went outside," Lee Lee panted, shutting and locking the apartment door behind her quietly.

They froze and waited. Seconds later, Jameela heard bullets fly as Abdullah shot the stairwell door handle and kicked the door open.

Jameela looked through the peephole and saw him staring at the swinging main entrance door. He cursed in Arabic and ran out into the street.

29

"I CANNOT BELIEVE YOU CAME ALL THIS WAY TO FIND me," said Ibrahim, more ecstatic than Jameela had ever seen him.

"It was my fault you got taken," said Jameela. "I couldn't just leave you."

"Technically, it was the fault of the American CIA. Their enthusiasm for extrajudicial torture is unfortunate. But it is so good to see you again. I feel like hugging you," said Ibrahim, looking like he was about to burst.

Jameela stepped up to Ibrahim and hugged him. She picked up Ibrahim's limp arms and put them around her shoulders.

"God isn't that rigid," she said, and stood there awkwardly until she could feel Ibrahim hugging her back.

"You are correct, God is not that rigid. Although, it is not part of the customs where I come from, to hug a woman." He let go of Jameela and stepped back a respectful distance.

"It's a long story, but I came to find my mother," said Lee Lee before Ibrahim could ask her. They all heard someone clearing her throat. Jameela caught a woman watching them out of the corner of her eye and detected a sliver of jealousy. She seemed unhappy to be taking a back seat to this boisterous reunion.

"I have exciting news," Ibrahim said. "I have met a CIA agent who realized the truth of my innocence, and instead of sending me to be tortured, we came together to Raqqa. She is pretending to be my wife."

Ibrahim introduced the two of them to Amina.

"I thought you didn't have female friends," said Amina in a casual tone.

"I do not, except for Sister Jameela, who is my first female friend. We have gone on several adventures already."

"I'm married," said Jameela raising her eyebrows. "And this is my daughter, Lee Lee." Jameela brought her forward to shake Amina's hand. "Ibrahim is helping me be a better person."

"Your husband and daughter can't do that?" asked Amina.

It was a valid point. "They've tried, but so far only Ibrahim has been successful. I'm sure you've noticed that he's . . . different."

"He's unlike most men," admitted Amina.

"The most terrible thing about this place is the lack of proper cleaning products," said Ibrahim as he rubbed a gray smudge on the wall with his sleeve.

"That's definitely the worst thing about this place," said Jameela, smiling. Ibrahim was himself, so at least she didn't have to feel guilty for any immediate psychological damage caused by his arrest and deportation.

An older woman in an abaya greeted Jameela and spoke in formal English.

"I am Amina's aunt, Sahar. It is a pleasure to have you in my home. You may stay as long as you want. My house has never been cleaner."

That jolted Ibrahim. "We must leave this place. Our presence will have been reported by now."

"How did you get here?" asked Lee Lee.

"We walked through the desert."

"Perfect. Less yapping and more moving," said Jameela as she pushed Ibrahim toward the door. "We've gotta leave this city right now. Lead us."

"I cannot leave Raqqa." Ibrahim looked at his feet.

"Why not?" said Lee Lee, looking upset.

"I did not mention that my pretend wife is the daughter of Talal, and her secret mission is to assassinate him."

Jameela stared at him. "Jesus, Ibrahim, that's more than a minor problem. That's suicide, which is haram, so let's go."

"I cannot leave her."

"Yes, you can." Jameela turned to look at Amina. "You look like someone who can take care of herself. Kill Talal, and meet us in any civilized place of your choosing. Let's go, Ibrahim. We can get out however you and your pretend wife came in."

"And Barkley is also here and needs our help. He gave me his cell number."

"Barkley's here?" Jameela couldn't believe it. That idiot had made it after all.

"Yes, and he also does not want to stay."

"No kidding. Listen, Ibrahim, it's too bad he's having buyer's remorse, but we can't save him. Let's go!" Jameela could feel panic surge through her. She started to push Ibrahim again.

"Sister Jameela," said Ibrahim, holding his ground, "you have to have faith in God. She will protect us in our time of need."

"Faith will protect us? Look where it's gotten us so far. We couldn't be in worse shape if we were about to be dropped into a vat of acid!" yelled Jameela.

"But God has found a way to bring us all together and support one another. Is that not a beautiful sign of Her protection?" Ibrahim implored.

"We are surrounded by men who sling AK-47s over their shoulders like they're bags of onions. Why don't we just go outside and put our necks on the chopping block to save everyone the trouble?"

"Mom, you're getting hysterical again," said Lee Lee, moving Jameela toward a chair. "Brother Ibrahim has a point. We can't leave Barkley here to be killed. Then we're just as guilty."

Jameela couldn't believe what she was hearing. Was she the only reasonable person here? "Lee Lee, please. I couldn't live with myself if you died here. We have to get to safety now. There may never be another chance like this."

"Your mother's right," said Amina. "Everyone should leave. I can take care of myself and my aunt. You guys are only going to get in my way."

"I don't think you could have managed to get here without my help," protested Ibrahim, which was the most immodest behavior Jameela had ever witnessed in him.

Amina leveled her eyes at him. "You're overestimating your importance."

"I think I am not," said Ibrahim. "You would have died of thirst and hunger if I hadn't killed those animals and found alternate sources of water."

"I would have survived on my rations. Having you around only put more pressure on my supplies."

"Then why did you bring me? You could have dropped me off in a country that would not have pulled out my fingernails once the CIA realized their mistake."

Amina looked uncomfortable. "I thought I needed help with translation. My Arabic is a bit rusty."

Sahar looked at Amina. "Why are you fighting with such a good man?"

"Because he thinks that I need him, and I don't need anyone."

"You are speaking like this because of your parents, Amina," said Sahar. "They hurt you, but this is a good man who wants to help you. Let him. You are not the only one who has suffered because of your parents. Look around."

Ibrahim's head was moving back and forth watching the women argue. Little beads of sweat formed on his brow.

Jameela stepped in front of him. "Could we at least continue our discussion in the safety of a Starbucks or Falafel Hut?"

The door burst open, and a red-eyed Zayn strode in with three other men.

"You will die today, Jameela Green. And this time, I will make sure that I kill you myself."

Ibrahim, Zuhr Prayer, 1:38 p.m., Oct. 11

My Lord, I seek Your forgiveness. I allowed my pride to get in the way of my feelings. To be honest, I'm not sure what just happened to me. I was trying to let Amina know how much she mattered to me. I even removed the tiny bones from the rabbit, so she would not inadvertently choke. But it is obvious that her feelings for me do not match my own for her. I can see now why people choose arranged marriages; they are much less complicated. As a result of the time wasted by our argument, we were caught. They found us because Barkley's friend reported suspicious guests to the high command. Thank You for not allowing Barkley to be revealed as our friend. I have been put in a room with a guard, but when my meals come, Barkley has notes inserted into my falafel before they are fried to let me know what is happening. Please do not let the others suffer on my account. Take my life, because I am not worthy.

30

JAMEELA WOKE UP TIRED AND GROGGY. THE ENTIRE
night had been spent traveling to a different location in a truck while
wearing a blindfold. She could hear a lot of angry men and the occasional woman yelling instructions. Clearly their escape, or near escape, had caused a lot of unhappiness in the leadership of DICK. She
was brusquely removed from the vehicle and ushered into a new location. Someone removed her blindfold and untied her hands. While her
eyes grew accustomed to the dim light, she focused on the sounds of
tanks and army fire outside and the smell of diesel. She was sitting beside someone. "Lee Lee is that you?"

"No, it's me," said Amina.

This was a surprise. But where was Lee Lee? Jameela willed herself
not to think the worst. She must be close by.

"Where are we?"

"In a military bunker of some sort," said Amina, who also looked like
she'd had a bad night. The walls were made of corrugated steel with no
windows. A small utilitarian kitchen was in the back with a tiny washroom, but the ground was just sand.

The door opened, and Nusayba appeared with a black eye and bruis-
ing on the side of her head. But her eyelashes were prominently curled
and blackened. She surveyed them for a few moments, clearly savoring
their new imprisonment.

"Where's my daughter?" Jameela tried to keep her voice from shaking.

"I have Lee Lee. A remarkable child, but I'm keeping her apart from you as an inducement not to escape again or I'll have her killed. And if she tries to escape, I'll have you killed . . . earlier. And as an extra precaution, we've moved to a more secure location in the desert. If you're stupid enough to try and escape, thirst will kill you before I can."

Jameela's heart squeezed. *Don't panic,* she told herself. *Focus, have faith, you'll get through this.* She forced herself to think about the positive: they were all alive, and Amina was an undercover CIA operative sent here on a secret mission, so the American military knew about their existence. Someone would rescue them. She looked at Nusayba, who had propped up a portable mirror and was applying fake eyelashes. Lee Lee's knapsack had been a veritable Sephora for Nusayba, providing her with a pastime more absorbing than killing.

"Don't worry, I'm not angry at you for trying to escape. It was actually quite admirable," said Nusayba, looking like she had attached daddy longlegs spiders to her eyes. "And now I have two women to execute."

Jameela noticed Amina watching her mother with an intensity that unsettled her. Ibrahim had told her a bit about their relationship, how they had been separated for a long time, but Amina didn't look like she was ready for a mother-daughter mani-pedi.

Nusayba continued, "I know you won't try to break free this time, so I didn't bother with ropes. And I have your husband," she said to Amina.

It took a second for Jameela to register that Nusayba meant Ibrahim. Their ruse had worked. She wondered if Nusayba recognized Amina as her daughter. It didn't seem like it.

"Please don't hurt him, I'll do whatever you want," Amina said.

She was pretending to be a doting wife and using Ibrahim to get to these people, but she didn't care if he lived or died. How could Jameela judge her when she too had used Ibrahim, trying to help him get her book to number one? She had forgotten about that in the blur of the last few days. For years, it had been the only thing she obsessed over. But now she had more pressing things to think about.

Nusayba interrupted her thoughts. "So, we'll be livestreaming your executions. The videos will be used to recruit more soldiers to the

DICK. I'll have to think of something creative this time. Even I'm getting bored of the same old beheading scenarios."

"If you really want it to go viral, can I make a suggestion?" Jameela asked.

Nusayba looked at her with interest.

"We can do a version of the Great Bake Off. I'll make my famous carrot cake," said Jameela. "You taste it, and then chop my head off for adding too much sugar."

Nusayba gave a loud, throaty laugh. "I will miss not having you around. Maybe I'll keep your head on a stick to remind me of the good times. But you have a point," said Nusayba. "The men always want to add orphans and sick people in wheelchairs for gravitas, but we need to add a bit of levity. I will consider the idea, but right now, you both need to take baths and get cleaned up for the execution. You smell like camels." She gestured toward a door that had some robes hanging from a hook. "There are some fresh clothes." Then she walked out of the bunker.

Jameela turned to look at Amina. "You don't really want to escape, do you?"

"As I told you before, I have things to do."

Jameela rolled her eyes. "I know, I know. You've got to murder your father."

"And my mother too. I don't like her."

"Anyone else? A creepy uncle who pinched your bum when you were little?"

"He got blown up in '99."

Jameela breathed deeply. She could have won Bad Mother of the Year, possibly of the decade, but she must have done something right. Lee Lee tried save her, and now she was being held hostage in the desert. At least in a city you could find shelter; here they were at the mercy of DICK. They couldn't just run away without water and provisions. Jameela had no idea how to save her or anyone else, much less herself. She would need Amina's help.

"If I help you kill Talal, will you help me leave with Ibrahim, Lee Lee, and Barkley?"

"Yes, but I don't know how much help you'll be. You seem kind of useless."

"You'd be surprised," said Jameela, a little insulted. She had managed to kill Mr. Nehru easily enough. That had to count for something.

"All your assets are being held for ransom. You've got no allies on the inside, and no military training. You're deadweight."

That stung. It was true that giving out insurance advice to farmers didn't require the ability to kill — the insurance companies always sent out adjusters if they felt a claim was too high. She should have concentrated on kickboxing fitness classes instead of tai chi, but her muscles were sore from sitting and typing so much, so stretching had seemed like the best option.

Please, God, help me.

There was a knock on the door.

"Come in, we're in the mood for guests right now," said Jameela.

The door opened, and Abdullah stood in the doorway with a tray of tea and a plate of chocolate digestives. His muscles bulged under his gray spandex T-shirt.

"Wow, it's DICK's number two. And our intel was right, he's a beast." said Amina taking in his bulk.

"He's also my fiancé," said Jameela, with the satisfaction of finally having something over Amina. It worked; Amina looked impressed and confused.

"How is that possible?"

"It's complicated." Jameela took the tray from Abdullah. "Darling, I thought you'd never come."

Jameela, Asr Prayer, 6:38 p.m., Oct. 12

Thank God for men and their sex drives. They're so predictable. Well, no one could have predicted that this walking gorilla would have a sexual kink involving eating cookies with tea. I should thank You for that. I know it could have been much, much worse. Anyway, he'll do anything to marry me, and he probably wants a bride with a head attached. His loyalties seem a little conflicted. I really better not have to have sex with him. Murray wouldn't understand.

Oh, Murray. How could I have done this to him? And I can't leave until I help Ms. Looney Tunes kill her father. I assume You won't punish me with hellfire and brimstone for being involved in another death. Remember, the last one was self-defense and this one is the only way to free Lee Lee and Ibrahim. Sometimes you have to lose some to win some.

What *is* brimstone, anyway?

Ibrahim, Asr Prayer, 6:17 p.m., Oct. 12

Dear Lord,

Thank You for keeping us alive so far. It is a true miracle while living in the grips of the DICK. The man whom Sister Jameela refers to as Zayn was very angry when he found us. He clearly has orders not to kill us yet, or we would be buried with our heads beside our feet by now. On the positive side, I would finally get to meet You. It was my hope that I'd die pleasantly in my sleep, as opposed to being hacked to death by an axe, so I am grateful that wasn't Your plan for ending my life. But whatever Your plan is, I accept it.

And Lee Lee is full of wonderful knowledge about food. She taught me that if you combine different grains and legumes, you create "whole foods," which makes up for not eating meat. Brother Zayn has a gluten allergy, and Lee Lee is instructing the kitchen staff in how to prepare meals that will not hurt his stomach. Apparently the "fools" in the kitchen don't know what a gluten allergy is, so they were making food that would eventually kill him. In fact, he did wonder if that was their intention.

But now that the kitchen staff has been instructed on gluten-free substitutes, Zayn is able to eat a more varied diet. For this, he is so thankful that he will not let anyone hurt Lee Lee. Everyone here seems very afraid of Brother Zayn due to his propensity to take a large sword and remove an appendage on a whim, so they listen to whatever he says. He is enjoying his gluten-free cookies and cakes so much that he has Lee Lee working in the kitchen full-time. Who knew that gluten-free "Mac 'n' Cheese" could bring a terrorist so much happiness? May Your blessings continue to shower on her in this world and the hereafter.

As a result of Zayn's good spirits, Lee Lee has extracted a promise from Zayn to not shoot me or remove any of my limbs. So now I, too, am in the kitchen making something referred to as "zoodles," which is a way of cutting up a vegetable called a zucchini to replace spaghetti. Zayn has become very fond of this food, and I am making it for him in large quantities. Apparently, Lee Lee feels that Zayn could lose some weight and reduce his cholesterol levels. The local doctor agrees, because the fighters' diets consist mainly of large quantities of meat, baklava, and tea with copious amounts of sugar, which has resulted in diabetes and weight gain.

Lee Lee has brought much happiness to the kitchen staff as well. Her skills have calmed many people, and they are taking her orders as if she is the new head chef; the old one lost his head recently when he didn't put enough garlic in the roasted lamb. Zayn will not speak to Lee Lee about her mother or Amina because he says these things are out of his hands. I have told Lee Lee to be patient and have faith. This is like the story of Moses's mother when she was forced to put him in a basket and then relinquish it to the stream; You have found us a safe place to live. For this, I thank You so much and am so grateful. I know You will take care of Sister Jameela and Sister Amina. I put my full trust in You always.

31

TO FULFILL HIS END OF THE MARITAL BARGAIN, ABDUL-lah had given Jameela a map to Talal's hideout on the edge of the city. Abdullah had smuggled it into the bunker where the women were staying. Jameela was a little disappointed. She thought Talal would be in a cave or an underground military installation.

"You have the second in command revealing my dad's whereabouts? Respect," said Amina.

Jameela was taken aback by the compliment. It was the first time Amina had acknowledged her usefulness.

"Our intel tells us that Abdullah is the popular one around here. The guys love him. My dad, not so much."

"That's a little weird, don't you think?" Jameela asked Amina after she came out of the shower wearing a light gray abaya. Jameela was already in her potato-colored one.

"Abdullah is all about hanging out with the men and finding out who they are. If the men get my dad's attention, it means they're bothering him and it's time to die."

They had been given small rations of food, mostly a selection of cheeses, nuts, hard-boiled eggs, hummus, and pita bread. It was like camping, but in a corrugated metal box.

"Do you think your mother knows where he is?" asked Jameela.

"I imagine they try and keep away from one another. They never got along, even before all of this."

"So, what's your plan to assassinate your . . . father?"

"You don't happen to have succinylcholine, preferably in injectable form?"

"Is that the one that causes instantaneous death by suffocation?"

"Yes."

"Sorry, I used my only needle on the last guy who tried to kill me. Come to think of it, I was supposed to kill your father with it."

Amina sat on a metal chair and dipped a piece of pita into the hummus. "Well, I'm really glad you didn't. I've been planning this for years." She munched slowly.

"Was it that horrible growing up?"

"Until I moved away, my father wouldn't even let me cut my hair. That's why they don't recognize me now. I look completely different. You could never understand."

Yes, I could, thought Jameela. Amina had basically lived Jameela's life right down to the dress code.

"You look confused," said Amina as she chewed on a cashew.

"I just thought you'd have more issues with Talal's participation in cultural genocide. You know, the rape of ethnic minorities. Wanton cruelty by beheading. Fueling the hatred of Muslims in the West."

"Yeah, I know I told Ibrahim those were the reasons I wanted to kill him," said Amina. "I didn't want him to think I was shallow, but as we get closer to my father, all my childhood memories are coming back. I'm getting angrier, and it's making me a little irrational about the small stuff, you know? I mean, he wouldn't even let me wear nail polish. I get to rid the world of its most sought-after terrorist *and* a super-strict father. Think of it as killing two birds with one sniper's rifle."

Amina's moral compass seemed to be in free fall, which was understandable given that her emotional triggers were all going off at once.

"Listen. I was beaten up every day on the way to school for looking like I just walked out of an Amish village, but *I* don't want to kill my parents," said Jameela.

"Did your parents abandon you?"

Jameela was quiet for a moment. "No. They were overinvolved in my life."

"Mine disappeared when I needed them most. They constantly wrote they were coming back, but they never did. The final letter said they had to sacrifice me for the greater good. I told them never to write me again."

"That's a terrible thing to tell a child," said Jameela.

"I used to hate how strict they were, but after a year, all I wanted was my dad to come home and tell me I couldn't talk to boys." She stared at the sandy floor. "There were no more rules, there was no more anything. My aunt, who never wanted me to begin with, wanted me even less as my father's notoriety grew. It wasn't enough that my parents deserted me, but my relatives hated having me around because of Talal. Eventually neighbors would find out and their house would get vandalized, so I moved out after I went to college. The CIA became my family. They understood how much I loathed my father and gave me a reason to live again."

"I can't relate to parental abandonment. Mine just interfered constantly. But can't you move past 'I have to kill my father'? Let a more impartial person do it, like the guy who took out Osama. He's probably got time on his hands. The CIA is just using you."

"Look, the plan is made. Once I kill my father, I'll dig up my buried supplies and phone my Navy SEAL team with my sat-phone, and I'll give them the coordinates of Talal's location from the map you just got from Mr. Lovesick. We'll be extracted by a Chinook CH-47 helicopter before you can say 'I do.'"

Jameela's frustration erupted. "We could leave right now, Amina! But you want to stay so you can murder your dad?"

"I spent my life waiting for this moment. I'm not going anywhere until—"

The door suddenly opened, and the Wicked Witch of the Middle East appeared.

"What is this commotion? The men are being distracted from their shooting practice."

"We wouldn't want that," said Jameela.

"There are many people here who disagree with me for letting you live this long, and I'm starting to think that they are right."

Nusayba cut a couple slices of cheese and made herself a little pita sandwich with olives.

"What were you two arguing about?"

"Who had the worst parents," said Amina. "Jameela thinks she had a rough childhood, but I think I had it a lot rougher."

Nusayba munched on her sandwich. She took another piece of pita and spooned out some hummus. "Mothers can never win. We have the worst job on earth. Everybody hates us: our children despise us for having rules, and our husbands blame us if they're disappointed with the kids. Why any woman still has children is beyond me."

"Are you disappointed you had children?" asked Amina coolly. Jameela couldn't believe Amina's mother didn't recognize her after all these years.

"I had to send my teenage daughter away to keep her safe." She shrugged. "We tried keeping in contact, but she stopped responding to our letters. This is what happens when you have children. They're ungrateful."

Amina examined her perfect cuticles. "Maybe she hates you because you weren't as committed to motherhood as you should have been."

Nusayba looked at Amina and threw her sandwich on the floor. The olives rolled away. Her eyes looked like they could swallow a person. "What would you know about raising children and the pain they cause?"

"I'm sure you deserve whatever pain your child caused you," replied Amina, returning the death stare with a matching one.

Jameela could feel the heat in the room rising as the two women stood up, glaring murderously at each other, nose to nose. She stepped between the two. "Okay, this conversation is obviously going nowhere good. I'm a mother and daughter, too, and it's hard for everyone."

Nusayba pushed Jameela aside roughly and confronted Amina with eyes radiating hatred. "How dare you accuse me of being a bad mother!" She pulled out a gun from her robes and started to aim.

"You never came back for me!" yelled Amina, oblivious of the gun, shoving her mother with two hands.

Nusayba's long dark lashes fluttered. A look of recognition flashed across her face — confusion, then perhaps joy — before she dropped to the ground.

Jameela, Maghrib Prayer, 8:29 p.m., Oct. 12

That was close. Way too close. I could see her pulling the trigger.

Thank You for making Nusayba faint. The men threw water on her, which brought her back to life. She started to scold Amina for not covering her hair properly and missing her prayers. They promptly got into a fight about who is the worst person. Finally, Amina blurted out that she was a match for Talal's bone marrow. Nusayba was all suspicious that Amina was a spy and wanted to kill her father, which is technically true, but what mother jumps to that conclusion so fast? Even the Kardashians have more tact.

I haven't heard from or seen Lee Lee in days. Please take care of her, she's strong, but I'm not, and I need the chance to be a better mother.

32

JAMEELA WAS IMPRESSED BY HOW CALM NUSAYBA AND Amina were after their fight. Nusayba had decided that Amina needed to be reunited with her father. All three of them piled into a military jeep that Abdullah drove through the desert, past sand dunes and farmers tending goats and sheep and entered the city. Eventually, they stopped in front of a small building that apparently functioned as both a terrorist hideout and butcher shop. Jameela, Nusayba, and Amina approached the building, the outside of which was adorned by drying animal carcasses hanging by hooks. Jameela thought the animals looked like they were doing headless handstands. *These people just don't like heads.* She had to admit, though, that the bodies acted as a very effective curtain, concealing the front window.

"It's weird that he's here, right?" asked Jameela.

"Well, this is the center of civilian life," said Amina. "It makes him harder to find and bomb. Plus, who bombs a butcher?"

Jameela knew this wasn't true — civilian sites were bombed all the time by both sides — but she figured this wasn't the time to argue. Amina was part of the American military and was as deluded about the CIA's morality as Abdullah and Zayn were about DICK's.

I let my personal grievances blind me from seeing the consequences of my actions. Her self-awareness caught her off guard. Now Amina was making the same mistakes she had. As they approached the front door of the butcher shop, armed guards emerged from either side to question

Nusayba, who, in typical fashion, barked at them until they relented and withdrew.

"Foolish men. If I wanted to kill Talal, I would have done it years ago."

Jameela had no doubt about this. As they entered the building, her eyes adjusted to the dim light. Young men sat around the large room, typing on laptops. Some were editing video footage, and others were on Twitter and Facebook. *This must be the nerve center of DICK's social media recruitment schemes,* thought Jameela as they passed by.

Nusayba led them upstairs into what must have been the butcher's home. The walls were turquoise and decorated with small yellow handprints. Jameela hoped the original family was safe somewhere far from here. As they turned down a hallway and entered the last room on the right, she assumed sinister music would start playing; instead, there was just the squeaking of the wooden floor and plaintive, lustful looks from Abdullah.

The room was dark, and the curtains were drawn. A man whose face was covered by an oxygen mask lay on an old military bed, dimly lit by a lamp clamped onto a nearby crate. It was Talal. Nusayba told them he was getting chemotherapy from the plastic bag hung from a makeshift IV pole made from a coatrack and hangers.

Jameela watched Amina carefully as she took in her father. Talal looked like a half-deflated Middle Eastern Santa Claus. His cheeks were sunken, and his face was wrinkled from fatigue as much as old age. Despite his dismal state, it was clear he still owned the room. He removed his oxygen mask and turned and looked at Amina with interest.

"You've come back home." He held out his hand as if to a lowly subject. Amina wavered for a second, and then took and kissed it.

Jameela feared for his life. She couldn't see any weapons on Amina. But she was a trained operative and would know how to conceal them. If Amina wished, she could plunge a knife into his heart at any moment. Or even a poisoned syringe. Cutting off his oxygen supply could also work. *Where were these ideas suddenly coming from?*

Amina was silent, so Talal spoke instead. "You've grown so much," said Talal. "And my sources tell me you're married."

"You'll love him, Baba. He's so kind and gentle. Not like you at all."

Talal flinched and regarded his daughter sternly. "You've always been unfair to me, Amina. And to your mother. Why do you hate us so much? We have done nothing but try to provide a good life for you."

Jameela could hear echoes of the conversations she'd had with her own parents. Parents that she would kill to see again — not kill if she saw them again.

"I want you to meet my new husband," said Amina, continuing to bait her father. "He's here, too."

"He is only alive because of me," Talal thundered. He coughed and replaced his oxygen mask.

"Yes, all life hangs in the balance because of you. God forbid we want to have a life that doesn't revolve around your precious needs."

Talal coughed again and beckoned one of his henchmen to go to the end of the room, where Jameela saw a door she hadn't noticed before.

Ibrahim stepped into the room. He took in Amina and Jameela, and his eyes lit up. "Sister Jameela, have you been kept well? I asked many times about your safety and that of Sister Amina."

Jameela could see that Amina did not appreciate playing second fiddle to her. She wished she could use telepathy to give Ibrahim some advice about women.

Talal removed his oxygen mask. "I had your husband sent to me so I could judge him for myself. So far, I'm not impressed. He talks incessantly and gives me a headache."

"I have implored your father to change his ways. To see that his organization has done nothing but destroy people's lives and the reputation of our precious faith," said Ibrahim. "He doesn't take my words seriously," he continued, looking at his shoes in defeat. "But they do have better cleaning supplies here." Ibrahim had a broom in his hands and was eyeing the dust bunnies under Talal's bed.

"And who is this friend of yours?" asked Talal, looking straight at Jameela.

Jameela felt tingles of fear run painfully through her body as he rested his dark eyes on her.

"She's —"

Both Ibrahim and Amina spoke at once. Ibrahim's face became red, and he gestured for Amina to continue.

"She's just written a book about her life," said Amina. "And she'd like it to go to number one on the *New York Times* bestseller list. She is trying to do good things so that God will answer her prayers."

Damn Ibrahim and his love-coddled brain! He'd told Amina everything about her; suddenly, she felt very exposed and shallow and ridiculous.

Talal regarded her with a different expression.

"I've had many discussions with God as well," he said. "I am also trying to do good in my own way, by bringing us justice. The Muslim world has been pummeled by the West for decades. Bombs dropped as punishment for weapons of mass destruction that never existed. Attempts to restructure our countries in their own image, while never allowing us to be the architects of our own lives. The Americans have only brought pain and humiliation to us."

It was hard to counter that argument.

"You think I'm a wicked monster," said Talal, gazing at her.

"I think you've got legitimate grievances," she responded carefully. "What you're saying about the Americans is true. They've done unspeakable harm to the Muslim world for decades. But how does terrorizing your own people and innocent non-Muslim civilians in the West solve anything?"

"It's time for the West to feel what we have felt. As for the Muslims who die, they are in my way. And I'm not listening to foolish pacifists" — Talal looked at Ibrahim — "who know nothing about the ways of the world and tell us to keep praying and be patient. The strongest force is with the one who stays alive the longest. There is nothing else."

"You will have to meet God eventually and account for all you've done!" said Ibrahim. "Do you have no fear in your heart for that day?"

From the corner of her eye, Jameela could see Amina reaching for a pen in her pocket. It probably had some sort high-velocity projectile device that would inject a pellet coated in poison into Talal's artery. Jameela knew his death would mean instant death for all of them in the room. Talal's henchmen would exact revenge immediately.

"I know exactly what I will tell my Lord when I meet Him," said Talal, defiantly.

"Meet Her, you mean," said Ibrahim.

Oh my God, thought Jameela. *Not now.*

"Referring to God as a woman?" shouted Talal. "What is this heresy?"

"My beloved feels that there's no shame in referring to our Lord as a woman, since there is no shame in being a woman," replied Amina with more excitement and glee than Jameela had ever seen in her before.

"Is this true?" demanded Talal.

"It is unusual, I admit." Ibrahim sounded like he was defending a PhD thesis in front of a dusty old university professor instead of someone who slaughtered people for enjoyment. "But theoretically, there should be no objection. We do not have to do things the way our forefathers have done them. Even the Qur'an talks about not blindly following the traditions of those who came before us."

"What are you saying? We can have women giving sermons, leading prayers, standing beside men during the prayers?"

"There is precedent in our faith," said Ibrahim, warming to his subject. "Women and men prayed side by side during the Hajj. The prophet never ordered that to stop, and he gave women the authority to lead men in prayer. Perhaps it's time for men to hear what women have to say—"

Talal shook his fist. "This man is not a suitable husband! His brain has been infected by a liberal, you-can-change-gender, LGBTQ-loving West. You will divorce him immediately."

"I'm going to have a thousand babies with him and let them pick their own pronouns, Baba!" shouted Amina. She put the poison pen back in her pocket.

Apparently, being married to a man her father despised was more satisfying to Amina than assassinating him. After all, if your father is dead, you can't make him watch his only daughter defy him and raise nonbinary babies with a male feminist. A fate worse than death.

As if on cue, Talal screamed, "Death to everyone!" His oxygen mask flew to the floor, and Ibrahim wiped it clean and handed it back to him.

Guards moved toward the three of them with what seemed like ominous intent, but then Nusayba emerged from the shadows and raised her hand for them to stop advancing. "Talal, Amina is a match for a bone marrow transplant. We have not been able to find anyone else. Because of her, you can live."

Jameela couldn't believe that Nusayba was trying to help him live. Their relationship confused her. She couldn't tell who was really in charge. It seemed that they needed each other to run DICK. A partnership that she almost envied. Jameela didn't support Murray half as much as Nusayba supported her husband. True, her support helped prop up a merciless regime, but it wouldn't kill Jameela to give Murray a shoulder rub and listen to him talk about his day at work.

Talal relaxed and lay back on his bed to consider his wife's advice. But then Ibrahim spoke up again.

"Only God gives life and death," he intoned.

Jameela knew a bad setup line when she heard one.

"Shall we test your theory?" asked Talal.

Jameela, Isha Prayer, 10:39 p.m., Oct. 16

Talal is keeping us alive because Amina is the only one who can give him a bone marrow transplant. But she'll only agree to it if Ibrahim is kept alive, and Ibrahim wants me and Lee Lee alive. We're playing dominos, with each one of our heads held in the balance.

For now.

Amina's agreed to receive injections to increase her white blood cell count. She's not divulging her plans about how she's going to kill her father to me; she wants to enjoy torturing him for a while first. Ibrahim told me that Lee Lee is safe, making gluten-free pizza pops for Zayn, who is apparently drunk on his newfound snacks.

I don't know how the prophets did it. When the Pharaoh was breathing down Moses's neck, You parted a sea for him. Please, part the desert for us, and let us walk out unmolested and free.

I would happily go back to selling insurance if it meant never seeing another AK-47.

33

THE SLAUGHTERHOUSE HAD BEEN SET UP AS A BLOOD transfusion unit. Nusayba was a registered nurse; Jameela thought it ironic that she had healed people before deciding to go the other way. Nusayba removed blood from one of Amina's arms and then it returned to her other arm after her stem cells were extracted. Jameela watched the whole process in fascination. Disinfectants had been brought in to decontaminate the room, and yards of plastic sheeting had been stapled up to make germ barriers. Talal was being kept in a germ-free facility in another room.

Amina said she wasn't going to send for an extraction team until she'd had her revenge, but Talal was only postponing the executions until after the transfusion. *When is she going to make the call,* Jameela worried, *after we are dead?*

"I believe certain promises were made," said a sarcastic voice, breaking Jameela's line of thought. She turned around to see Zayn standing just outside the doorway, eating a gluten-free churro. Beside him, Abdullah looked sweaty, as usual. He was carrying a tray of tea and cookies and motioned for Jameela to follow them to another room across the hall.

As they entered, Jameela noticed it was a child's bedroom. The ceiling had yellowed plastic decals of stars glued to it. They sat on small furniture. Abdullah teetered on the bed as he put the tray on a wooden desk where Jameela imagined a child made Play-Doh animals in another more carefree time. The tea set was a modest one: thick white ceramic cups with a simple white teapot, intended for utility, not elegance. Fine bone china would not have survived the tremors caused by rocket launchers.

"Your fiancé believes that he has waited long enough for his nuptials," said Zayn.

Jameela needed to buy time. She took one of the cookies, dunked it in her tea, and sucked on the thick biscuit. It was infused with almond essence, noted Jameela, as she watched the effect of her actions on Abdullah. "Isn't just hanging out with me enough?"

"He wants more, which requires a quick wedding." Zayn was not going to use the word *sex* in front of her.

Drinking tea and eating cookies naked didn't really appeal to Jameela. This was creepy enough with her clothes on. "I want a proper wedding," said Jameela. "With all the trimmings."

"We don't do weddings with all the trimmings. Plus, we blew up all the Hyatts," said Zayn, smirking. "We'll get an imam, and you two can sign papers in front of a few witnesses in this room. It can all be over in the next five minutes."

Jameela slowly ran her tongue across the ridges of the cookie. How she learned to be so seductive, she would never know. Maybe it was her conservative Muslim upbringing that encouraged her to use her imagination with the only options available to her. Her tactics seemed to be working. Beads of sweat developed on Abdullah's brow. His hands shook as he drank his cup of tea.

"Tell Abdullah I want a fancy wedding. A custom-made dress, a gluten-free, three-tier wedding cake, and all the Indian desserts that my mother used to make for me as a child. And I want Ibrahim to perform the ceremony."

Zayn stamped his foot in apparent fury. "How dare you make demands? You are an ant in a village. Don't forget your place." But Abdullah wanted to know what enraged him. After hearing the translation, Abdullah nodded vigorously.

"You win," said Zayn. "He'll give you the wedding of your dreams. I'm only going along with it because I've never eaten a gluten-free wedding cake before. Can it be strawberry? With whipped cream? It's my favorite, but my mother wouldn't let me eat cakes during family events because she didn't want my stomach to hurt."

Men. It was either their stomach or their loins. She was sure some wars could have been ended by dangling a giant shawarma in front of the troops.

"Strawberry shortcake it is. In fact, you can be Abdullah's best man and pick out all the dinner items as well the desserts for the menu."

Zayn's mood suddenly changed. He was ecstatic. "Gluten-free samosas and spinach-cheese pastries?"

"Yes, whatever your heart desires."

"Your daughter is going to be able to make all this food? She's pretty handy in the kitchen, but even I know these are tough foods to make."

"If you let her speak to my mother in Brooklyn, she can get some family recipes, which will help a lot."

Zayn paused, wary of a trap. "These calls will be short and to the point. She better not say anything to your mother that we don't like, or else."

"Lee Lee's a smart girl. She won't do anything that displeases you. Do you like cream puffs?"

Murray, Fajr Prayer, 6:39 a.m., Oct. 17

Thank You, God! Thank You! My mother-in-law got a call from Lee Lee, who said, and I quote, "Nani, Mom said to call and get our famous gluten-free samosa recipe." There's no such thing! That was the joke in my in-laws' home. How white people make up diseases to feel special! How gluten-free food is just first-world indulgence, like being vegan! Nusrat likes to say, "White people drop drones on innocent Muslims, but won't eat chicken."

Of course, the CIA had the phones tapped in case this would happen. I don't know Your plan for rescuing them, but what a relief to know they're safe and alive. And Lee Lee is cooking.

I'm sorry for doubting You, but that was the hardest test of my life. Until they're both back in my arms, I'm not going to feel complete relief, but I already feel calmer now, and I've started knitting again.

Jameela, Fajr Prayer, 5:47 am, Oct. 19

Getting married twice. This had better not get back to Murray, or he'll have a heart attack. Which may happen anyway, because Lee Lee isn't there to monitor his diet.

Who knew a wedding would be just the thing to distract DICK from their take-over-the-world-or-die-trying obsession?

The problem is, they don't do big weddings, because that takes time, energy, and money, all resources better spent on killing people. But thank You for tying Abdullah's libido to tea and cookies, and for giving Zayn a gluten allergy. And it seems all these brutes are dying for a party. They want a nice sit-down wedding, with napkins and cutlery, and some semblance of civility.

Abdullah has agreed to a gluten-free strawberry shortcake in the shape of a teapot, as long as I lick the cookies that surround it during the ceremony. And Lee Lee is in charge of all the cooking. She's told Zayn that she needs to talk to me about some special gluten-free recipes that I made at home. She's lying, of course. I never did any of the cooking. Murray was the cook in the family, until Lee Lee was old enough to know what antioxidants were and then she took over. I feel horrible. Lee Lee should be a regular teenager, out with friends, playing video games, worrying about what colleges to get into. Instead, she is literally feeding an entire camp of terrorists to save us.

Zayn watches us when we're together, so I make up crap advice like, "Make sure you overbeat the almond flour," which she knows to ignore. I massage my daughter's shoulders when she's tired. Zayn lets us watch Netflix if he's been given an extra helping of peanut butter and marsh-mallow cookies. We're only allowed to watch *The Good Place* because there's no swearing or nudity. Zayn feels that a show about heaven is Muslim-appropriate. Yesterday, Lee Lee put a henna mixture in an old icing bag and made intricate designs on my palms. I had no idea she was so artistic. Bonding with your daughter in a terrorist camp has been a gift I didn't anticipate.

I've asked for engraved invitations to be sent out to all the guests. They're taking their old leaflets advertising public beheadings and writing over them to announce the wedding date instead. They're low on good-quality paper stock due to sanctions, and they're trying to recycle. Kudos to them for looking after the environment.

I always wanted a pink wedding dress. My mother forced me to wear the hideous red one she wore for her own wedding. It was so garish, with gold ribbons all over it. I'm sure in its time it was quite fashionable, but for my wedding, it was wrong continent, wrong era. Now I get to pick my very own dress. At least terrorists can be counted on for giving a girl the wedding of her dreams.

34

JAMEELA STOOD ON AN OLD WOODEN CRATE. HER ARMS were outstretched as Rashad, the tailor, silently took measurements, being very careful not to touch her. His assistant, Ismail, wrote down the numbers that Rashad called out. Jameela realized her wedding dress was going to be sized too loosely, given how far Rashad's measuring tape was from her body. From their grim expressions, both Rashad and Ismail looked like they had been asked to deactivate a nuclear device instead of sew a wedding dress. Dealing with bombs was less dangerous than breasts.

"We're going for a baggy look, are we?" quipped Jameela. Rashad ignored her. He was dressed in a pale-blue cotton shalwar and leather sandals. His beard was scraggly, and his hair looked like a mop: a Middle Eastern Shaggy from *Scooby-Doo*. He was missing his right leg below the knee and was wearing a prosthetic, with a mismatched sandal attached to the plastic foot. In contrast, Ismail's beard was well manicured, and his face was round, like the rest of him. He came up to her shoulders. He reminded her of a miniature Ali Baba. Jameela was glad that this misfit pair hadn't been sent out to the front lines.

Dusty bolts of fabric lined the walls, from coarse khaki-colored denim and black industrial polyester to Day-Glo orange and yellow plastic sheeting. There were outlines of overalls cut out of construction paper hanging by clothespins nearby. A Vera Wang bridal studio this was not. It was a factory for industrial garments, mainly for construction and emergency personnel. A sign nailed at the top of the fabric shelves read KAREEM'S CLOTHES FOR EXPORT in faded red letters. On the cutting board lay large, heavy silver scissors, which Jameela noted could be used to plunge into someone's heart if necessary. She scolded herself; she had to stop thinking like this. What happened to the days when knives and forks were cutlery, instead of weapons to gouge out small organs?

At the far end of the room, Jameela spotted industrial sewing machines in gunmetal gray. Rashad pulled out pink fabric with a metallic sheen to it. It was obviously not intended for wedding dresses. She looked closely at the label, which read *ripstop nylon, fire retardant, tear resistant.* Well, at least she'd be able to eat as much as she wanted without splitting a seam.

"It's used to make parachutes," said Rashad. "It's the only pink fabric we have."

"But it has a gossamer quality to it, don't you think?" said Ismail, as he ran his hand down the fabric. He draped the material around him like a sari and did a pirouette. "When you twirl, you'll catch the light."

Jameela wondered if he was gay. She hoped not; this would not be the place to come out. "Yes, it has a certain je ne sais quoi," she agreed, feeling the grain of the fabric. It crinkled in her hands, and she could see tiny glimmering metallic squares along the surface. She hoped that these poor men could make her an acceptable wedding dress out of it; God knows what Abdullah would do to them if they didn't. They had the assignment from hell. And they'd thought they'd be fighting at the front when they joined up.

"So, you've had a lot of experience sewing wedding dresses?"

"I've sewn uniforms for welders," said Rashad. He thrust a grubby paper into her hands. On it was a sketch of the wedding dress. Jameela looked at it. A pair of pink plumber's overalls, complete with deep utility pockets, embellished with a hi-lo tulle skirt and a long head veil. It looked like Super Mario had crashed into Princess Peach.

"The extra-deep pockets on the outside were my idea," said Rashad, bashfully. "The men appreciate them for carrying their blowtorches."

Ismail clapped his hands delightedly. "The hi-lo was mine. I thought it would add more flair." The two men looked at her anxiously for approval. It was the most hideous thing she had ever seen.

"I — love it," gushed Jameela. "It's a cross between utilitarian and . . .

flamboyant. Perfect for dancing! Once photos get out, every bride will be wearing one. I could bring a blowtorch and fire my own crème brûlée."

"There's going to be dancing?" asked Rashad, slowly winding the tape measure.

"Of course. It's a wedding, after all."

"Could there be bhangra?" he asked, becoming more animated.

Jameela's family was from Punjab, and there had been a lot of traditional bhangra dancing at her wedding. It was a folk dance that resembled the Irish Riverdance in terms of high energy, but Murray, who was normally shy when it came to dancing, had her cousins choreograph a dance for him. He had astonished her by gyrating enthusiastically to the drumbeats. She knew he was doing it to please her parents, who felt that among their other shortfalls (like passing off boiled food as cuisine), white people had no rhythm. In the end, Murray's extra efforts on the dance floor worked. He had been a hit with the whole extended family.

"Depends on how talented you are," teased Jameela. "I know good bhangra when I see it."

It was obvious that Rashad wanted to show off his skills. He put a cassette in the stereo beside him and turned it on. Immediately, the room started to vibrate as bass thudded out of the subwoofer.

"We use the speakers to hear the azan better," explained Rashad, unconvincingly. He started to shimmy with one hand behind his head and another held out. He was quite good for someone with one leg. She wondered how long he'd wanted to do that.

Ismail looked at Rashad in astonishment. "That's not dancing, that's jumping around," he said. "Real dancing is erotic and sensual."

"You think you can do better?" said Rashad, looking insulted.

At this challenge, Ismail took a plumber's utility belt and tied it around his waist. Jameela recognized this move from all the women's belly dancing parties she'd attended, but usually, women tied colorful scarves around their hips. He turned off Rashad's music and put on his own tape. A slow, tempered beat filled the air, and Ismail began a gradual and erotic rolling of his pelvis.

Jameela had never seen a man belly dance before. He undulated better than any of the women she'd ever seen. Why was he wasting his talents in DICK when he could be hiring himself out at parties?

"That dance will put you to sleep," said Rashad. "You're hardly moving at all."

"And yours looks like an aerobics class for fat Americans," Ismail retorted.

"Tell you guys what," said Jameela. "Since I'm Punjabi, and Abdullah is Syrian, I think we should have both dances at the wedding. We'll have a dance-off."

The men seemed incredulous at this suggestion. "Can I get my friends to join me?" asked Rashad.

"The more the merrier."

"And no one will be . . . upset?" asked Ismail.

"We'll have a guillotine set up behind the hors d'oeuvres, and if anyone's dancing proves subpar —" Jameela banged her hand on the table.

The men jumped at the sudden thud, the blood draining from their faces.

"I'm kidding," said Jameela, feeling a little guilty at having scared them. "You guys can choreograph a whole Middle East versus South Asia extravaganza. It'll be fun."

Fun was not a word that was often used to describe DICK activities. The men looked at her like she was their terrorist fairy godmother, delivering all their hearts' desires.

And I'll have the costume to match soon.

The door opened, and Abdullah walked in. Jameela was relieved that he wasn't carrying another tray of tea and cookies. He looked distressed. From his rapid Arabic, she recognized the word *Talal*. Ismail translated, but Jameela already knew what Abdullah said. Talal wanted to see them. Ismail stopped the music and took off his utility belt.

"Excellent work," said Jameela, as she bid the men goodbye.

"We're going to trim your dress with industrial-strength zippers," said Ismail. "And we'll attach Velcro to your pockets and add metal safety harness clips for some extra sparkle."

"Even Cinderella couldn't ask for more."

The men beamed. They'd get to keep their heads for another day.

They walked outside, where the heat was high enough to cook a pancake on a car hood. There wasn't a single cloud in the sky. Jameela was able to get away without covering her face or wearing a black abaya because the morality police wouldn't dare to criticize her while she was with Abdullah. She was the prom queen walking with the prom king, which made up for the fact that her parents hadn't allowed her to go to the dance at her own high school graduation ceremony. They thought white people fornicated behind the garbage bins in the alley behind the school afterward. They weren't wrong.

Even Abdullah seemed a little imperious. People stared at them with curiosity. She could practically read everyone's minds. How did she nab the most popular guy here? By knowing how to suck tea out of a cookie. As Abdullah opened the door to the slaughterhouse, she gave his hand a squeeze. Abdullah's eyes widened with either excitement or fear. When they reached the door to the room where Talal was being housed, Jameela saw him through the plastic sheets taped up to the walls that separated him from everyone else. Abdullah and Talal looked at each other with distrust. The fighters were loyal to Abdullah, and Talal, along with Nusayba, were the strategic brains behind DICK. But neither man apparently liked the other.

Talal twitched in annoyance. "I have heard the two of you are planning quite an extravagant wedding."

"Well, Meghan and Harry won't be jealous, but it'll still be pretty swank."

"I have allowed my second in command what he so clearly desires, but on one condition."

Jameela noticed that Abdullah had stopped making eye contact with her. He looked at his shoes. How had she gotten away with so many of her crazy wedding plans for the last few hours? Clearly, Abdullah was doing a lot of mollifying behind her back and had struck a bargain.

Jameela noticed that Nusayba was sitting behind Talal on a chair, like a puppeteer.

"Before you marry Abdullah, I need you to prove your loyalty to my caliphate."

"Lie detector test?"

"I want you to kill someone."

Jesus! It was like being in Groundhog Day.

Jameela apologized to God for saying the name of Jesus in vain, even though Muslims didn't believe he was the son of God. It wasn't nice to bandy about the names of prophets like that.

"Did we not reach today's quota?" asked Jameela. "Could a goat count?"

"I feel that you are not to be trusted, but Abdullah is blinded by your womanly charms. Many men have been deceived by their feelings."

"I'm sure your feelings have never gotten in the way."

"They once did, but no more."

"Feelings are for the weak and spineless," said Nusayba, channeling Nosferatu.

Jameela's mind went back to her own mother. Nusrat was also unhappy with Jameela's choice of groom but had never insisted on a human sacrifice for the wedding to go forward.

There was no way Jameela was going to kill anyone. "I'm going with a vegan wedding theme, so no killing people during the ceremony."

"Tell her, Talal."

"We would like you to execute a woman live on Facebook tonight."

"Who?" asked Jameela, worrying that it might be Lee Lee. On cue, a woman was brought into the room with her hands tied behind her back. Her head was covered by a burlap sack.

Talal ordered the sack removed.

A frightened Courtney Leland blinked up at her.

Jameela, Zuhr Prayer, 1:48 p.m., Oct. 19

Courtney Leland is a scab that never goes away. Is she going to follow me into the grave, too? She's really scared, I'll give you that. She doesn't want to lose her head live on the internet, although it would fuel her book sales. But if she's not around to convert those sales into a red Ferrari, then what's the point?

Nusayba apparently hates happy endings, and she's convinced a beheading will destroy DICK's joyful wedding reverie. She caught Zayn trying to match the napkins to the ink color of the wedding invitations. People are forgetting DICK's mission is terrorizing humanity.

The end of Courtney Leland wouldn't be the worst thing in the world, although Jamal wouldn't approve of me thinking like that. But if I don't kill Courtney, Talal will have me killed, and then Lee Lee will be the same age I was when Jamal died. She'll never recover. I'm under the gun, or a large sword, here. I know what I have to do, and it's not because I hate Courtney, but because I know what it's like to be left alone in the world.

35

IBRAHIM PACED OUTSIDE THE SLAUGHTERHOUSE. Guards watched him carefully as he moved back and forth. He slowed his movements, so they wouldn't spook and inadvertently shoot him. He had convinced Talal to let Courtney write goodbye letters to her parents before killing her. This bought all of them some hours to think of a solution. Amina joined Ibrahim and stared at the guards pointing their guns at Ibrahim. The guards looked momentarily confused. Ibrahim knew they had orders not to shoot her, since Talal's life depended on her.

"Stop pointing those guns at him, or I'll take your eyes out with a corkscrew."

The guards immediately dropped their guns. Ibrahim had no doubt she would do it.

"Go inside and mop the floors; they're a disgrace," ordered Amina.

He couldn't argue with her. In fact, he wondered why he hadn't thought of that himself. Ibrahim began to follow them, but Amina held out her hand.

"Not you."

She looked at him with great concentration. Ibrahim felt nervous, watching Amina watching him. She was quivering with emotion. He was unused to a woman gazing at him so intently. In America, the few women who stared at him usually wanted to know where he bought his robe because it would make the perfect nightgown.

"What are you thinking right now?" she asked.

"At present, I am perplexed as to how the woman Courtney may be saved. I am asking God for help." Ibrahim believed that if you prayed for assistance, She always responded, perhaps not in the way you would have predicted or even anticipated, but one would never be abandoned.

"You're not worried about yourself?"

"God is All-Protecting. We must have faith, or what is the point of believing in the unseen?"

"You're killing me!"

"No, the guards may kill me if I move too quickly, but I am not a threat to you."

"You're exasperating in every way."

Ibrahim was used to this sentiment and could not argue. He had learned his lesson in humility and wasn't going to remind her of his usefulness. "You are correct. It is my goal to try to be more pleasant to be around."

"Which is why I want to marry you."

Ibrahim felt as if he'd been hit by a thunderbolt. He knew they had bonded over their journey to Raqqa, and back then the idea of Amina as his real wife would have overjoyed him, but lately, his head had started arguing with his heart. For the first time in Ibrahim's life, he had no words. After a minute of silence, he saw Amina's eyes fill up with tears. Death, disease, students shooting spitballs into the back of his head during prayer, these were things he could deal with. Anything but this display of emotion. Ibrahim made a silent prayer for help.

Jameela walked outside. "The guards seem a little upset inside. Something about not being janitors and the indignity of having their eyeballs removed by a corkscrew?"

"Sister Jameela, please help Sister Amina. I have upset her."

"What did you do?"

Jameela looked at Amina and was surprised to see her crying.

"She asked me to marry her, and I said nothing, and now she is greatly distressed."

"Okay, what's really going on? There's a war out there, Lee Lee is doing her best Jamie Oliver so she won't be killed, Courtney is about to be killed, and here you two decide to have a lovers' quarrel? Your timing is terrible!" yelled Jameela.

"Ibrahim won't answer my question," Amina said. She faced him again. "Will you marry me or not?"

"I feel that we must first find out . . . if we are compatible."

"Isn't that a Western concept? Did your parents know each other before they got married?"

"No, they did not and had a very happy and successful marriage. It's just that I worry that you —"

"May be prone to evil," said Jameela. "Sorry, but I have to call it like I see it. You just want to marry Ibrahim to stick it to your dad. And since you're planning on killing him, isn't your sole motivation for marrying Ibrahim . . . soon to be dead? So the question is why do you really want to marry Ibrahim?"

Amina kicked some sand with her boot.

"You got to marry a better person than yourself; I want the same thing."

"Why?" asked Jameela.

"I . . . I don't want to become like my mother or my father."

There was a look of pain in her face. But Ibrahim wasn't sure if that was enough for him. All his life, he'd believed that his requirements for finding a life partner were simple: he wanted a good and simple person. But he worried that Amina wasn't sure who she was right now. The concept of "finding oneself" suddenly made sense. He looked at Jameela for the words he couldn't convey.

"There are other men out there," said Jameela, in her pathetic attempt at soothing Amina. "He doesn't make a lot of money, and then there's the OCD with the cleaning. And he dresses like he's an extra from *The Handmaid's Tale*. Are you sure you've examined other options? No offense, Ibrahim."

"I am only offended a little bit."

"I don't want anyone else," said Amina. She twisted the end of the scarf around her finger. "I want to change. No one's ever made me feel this way before. And now he's having doubts. Why doesn't he want to marry me?"

"It's a fair question," said Jameela, looking at Ibrahim.

"I wish she was more like . . . you."

"Jesus, Mary, and Joseph!" yelled Jameela. "Why would you say such a thing?"

"You were willing to do a tangible good thing to find your way to God. That is a sign of someone who is sincere. Up to now, Sister Amina has just wanted to kill her parents, so I have no way of assessing her sincerity."

"If I do good things, you'll reconsider marrying me?" asked Amina.

"Of course," said Ibrahim.

Jameela heard screaming coming from upstairs. "Guys, let's put a pin in this conversation. I gotta go." She ran back into the slaughterhouse and up the stairs two at a time.

36

BARKLEY KEPT HIS GUN TRAINED ON JAMEELA AS SHE sat with a tearful Courtney Leland on her army cot in a tiny room that served as her holding cell. Jameela avoided looking at him so that no one would suspect they knew each other. "Of all the places on earth, why would you come to Syria?" she asked Courtney, who, despite the circumstances, still looked amazing. The waves in her long blond hair never seemed to be out of place.

Courtney dabbed the corners of her eyes. "When I heard on the news that you had joined DICK, I felt a little left out."

Unbelievable. "Left out of a murderous pileup of killers? What's wrong with you? Wait, did you say I was on the news?"

"DICK is the biggest news story in the world. This story could be your ticket to fame."

Jameela felt repulsed. "That's not why I'm here, Courtney. I'm not trying to get another book deal. I was searching for the imam of my mosque."

"But I couldn't take the chance that you'd one-up me with a story of being kidnapped by DICK."

It was the high school popularity contest all over again. But Courtney always won, so why would she risk her life?

"Courtney, this isn't a game. They're going to kill you. The DICK head's wife wants a Western woman dead on camera. You've fallen right into their hands at the worst possible moment."

"I know," Courtney wailed. "But the thought of you getting all this attention for being kidnapped by the vilest group on earth. I couldn't take it anymore. I got so jealous."

The pitch of Courtney's whiny voice made the idea of beheading her less distasteful. Jameela forced herself to focus on the situation at hand. "How did you get here?"

"It's pretty easy. You go online, say you want to join, and they send you all the directions. I just had to pay for the ticket."

If DICK ever decided to get out of the terror business, they could give Expedia a run for its money. But getting Courtney out of the room looked impossible, much less getting her out of Raqqa. Amina had told her that, without a transport vehicle and papers allowing safe passage through DICK territory, there was no way to escape the city.

"Listen, Courtney. They want me to kill you, live on Facebook. They say if I don't go through with the execution, they'll kill my daughter. I'm sorry."

"I'll give you whatever you want," begged Courtney, hoarsely. "My Louboutins, my green Kelly bag, my Prada raincoat . . . I've got money, lots and lots of money. Could I pay my way out, like a ransom?"

"There'll be no ransom this time," said Nusayba as she entered the room. "All I want is your head." Nusayba held Courtney's green Kelly bag and teetered in her snakeskin stilettos, which kept catching in her long hem.

"Who comes to a terrorist camp with high heels?" asked Jameela. The only use of heels that long and sharp was as weapons. In a pinch, one could always fling a shoe and take out an eye.

"I thought when I got rescued there'd be a camera crew."

Jameela had to give Courtney points for being prepared. If Jameela got rescued, she'd look like crap in all the photos, and Courtney, as usual, would make the cover of yet another magazine.

Nusayba examined the contents of the Kelly bag and plucked out an eyebrow pencil. "I'm bored by this conversation. I'm going to tell the men to start the execution." She turned and looked at Jameela. "If Talal didn't need Abdullah placated by this wedding, I'd have killed you by now, but when the wedding is over . . ." She ran her finger across her neck, and left the room. They could hear murmurs outside.

"What a bitch," exclaimed Courtney.

"You've no idea. I think she's the mastermind behind this whole operation."

Courtney took a deep breath. "Since I'm going to die, you should know, despite our differences, I've always been jealous of you."

Now Jameela knew how Ibrahim felt receiving news so astonishing it knocked the breath out of you. She sat back and tried to process what she'd just heard. Courtney had never been supportive or kind to her when they were in school together. In fact, she stole her greatest achievement, being the editor of the yearbook. And then she ruined her book launch by making it all about her.

"Then why are you always trying to one-up me?" asked Jameela.

"In high school, you had the loving brother who didn't know I existed. Then after college, you got the guy, the kid, the house, the life." Courtney picked at a flawless gel nail.

"How do you know all this stuff about me?"

"Your daughter's Instagram account, since you never update yours. Do you know how horrible it was to watch Murray obsess over you all those years in college?"

"You watched me?" Jameela was dimly aware of Courtney's presence during those years. She was always being followed by a throng of young men and seemed as inaccessible as ever.

"What do I have? A brilliant writing career, millions of dollars, and adoring fans everywhere. But every guy I like eventually leaves me for a younger, skinnier version. Murray seems to love you just the way you are: dumpy, with no sense of fashion. I'm friends with him on Facebook and he just posts photos of you and Lee Lee. You look awful in every one of them. Have you ever heard of concealer?"

Jameela had taken Murray's devotion to her for granted for a long time. He was her rock in both friendship and marriage. She had never considered that behind all Courtney's success and glitz was a very lonely woman. Why did it take a self-absorbed writer to show her what she'd had this entire time?

"No more talking," said the guard. He looked at Courtney. "Put on your orange jumpsuit."

"You've always looked good in orange," whispered Jameela.

"That's true," said Courtney, comforted. "Could you aim the sword to the right? It's always been my better side."

"Sure."

Jameela left the room and entered the large landing area where the men were setting up the camera in front of a white drop sheet. They were discussing various camera angles and lighting. Abdullah and Zayn approached Jameela.

"Abdullah wants to let you know that the wedding tent has been set up outside and one hundred and fifty-seven guests have confirmed their attendance."

"Really? This is what you want to talk to me about, just before you force me to behead my . . . friend?"

"More people wanted to come, but there wasn't a bigger tent in the city," said Zayn, misinterpreting her anger.

"I'm a little busy here!" Jameela hissed. "Could you please leave me alone? This is a very emotional time."

"We must sample different flavors of cake to determine the final choice. How long do you think you'll be?" said Zayn, tapping his foot impatiently.

It was no use. Zayn was in full-blown wedding fever.

"Is there a lemon summer berry or chocolate raspberry truffle sample to try?" said Jameela, attempting to buy time.

"I'm not sure, but those are excellent suggestions. I'll find out." He left with Abdullah.

The men setting up the camera indicated that they were ready for the event to begin. Jameela was asked to hack melons in half to make sure she knew how much pressure to apply. With Facebook Live, there were no takes, no edits, just action. One time to get it right. Jameela was about to kill her second person. Mr. Nehru had tried to kill her, but Courtney was different. This was harder to justify. Lee Lee wouldn't approve of killing Courtney in order to be saved, and she was right. But to lose Lee Lee? Jameela didn't know what to do. She looked up. *Help.*

Dressed in her orange jumpsuit, Courtney was brought onto the landing, with a burlap bag over her head, and forced into a chair.

Nusayba entered. She was wearing foundation too light for her skin tone, her eyebrows were thick like caterpillars, and the highlighter over her cheekbones shone garishly. But her lips were what stood out the most. They were lined with black lip liner and then filled in with glossy red lipstick. Her headscarf was hot pink with pearl-bead edging. She looked so dramatic, it was a shame that *Drag Race* didn't have categories for hijabis. Nusayba would have destroyed the competition, literally. Even the men stopped and gaped. Jameela worried for them. Staring at the head DICK's wife was probably forbidden, but her kaleidoscope of colors was so mesmerizing, it was hard to rip your eyes away from her. She took out Courtney's iPhone, its pink bling diamond-encrusted case glittering, and used the camera mode as a mirror, examining her face and removing some lipstick from her teeth. Satisfied, she stowed the phone.

"I will remove her head covering, and then you will remove her head from her body," said Nusayba.

That broke the spell.

Jameela raised her sword. She would make this as quick and merciful as possible.

Nusayba snatched the burlap sack and Jameela squeezed her eyes shut and brought down her sword.

Jameela heard a scream mid-arc and felt a shuddering jolt as Nusayba hit her in her ribs. Her sword clattered, bloodless, to the floor.

Her jaw dropped. Amina, not Courtney, was sitting in the chair.

Jameela, Asr Prayer, 5:59 p.m., Oct. 19

Well, thanks for waiting till the last minute. I could have killed Amina.

That girl is so ballsy. How could Amina be sure her mother wouldn't have let me kill her? She'd walked into Courtney's room wearing a niqab, switched their outfits, and had Barkley hide Courtney in a fuel transport truck and drive it to the border where a Navy SEAL team was waiting. Now our only means of escape is gone. Amina says there isn't another extraction team. Apparently, she was doing a good deed to get into Ibrahim's pants.

Ibrahim was indeed impressed, but no one could get into Ibrahim's pants without a marriage certificate, sealed, signed, and notarized, with at least one hundred witnesses to make sure he's not having sex before marriage — a fate worse than death. And he still wants Amina to spend more time praying and getting to know the real You. Plus, he's a little leery about the purity of her intentions — doing things to please a man versus God. Not sure if Amina has the stamina to see this whole spiritual thing through to Ibrahim's satisfaction, but we'll see how much infatuation can motivate someone.

So now, we're back to my current problem of the wedding night. Abdullah made the argument that I had every intention of killing Courtney, so my test is over, and the wedding is on. Nusayba wanted to substitute someone else for me to execute, but everyone is busy with the wedding, and there's no one to volunteer their head at the moment. I'm pretty sure Nusayba still doesn't trust me, but she's really distracted by all the frippery she found in Courtney's suitcase. She's trying to convince the local cobbler to make her a pair of high-heeled combat boots that will look like Manolo Blahniks.

So, thanks for saving Courtney, but now I have a bigger problem. Tomorrow night, I marry Sasquatch, and all the tea and cookies in the world won't save me after the ceremony. *I do not want to have sex with that man!*

Ibrahim, Asr Prayer, 5:56 p.m., Oct. 19

My Lord, I have a terrible dilemma. My pretend wife wants to be my real wife, but I'm not sure we are compatible.

She defied the CIA and changed her mind about killing her parents, and tried to prove her worth to me by rescuing the woman named Courtney by purposely putting herself in harm's way. It is true, she succeeded, but now we have lost our means of escape. I am grateful that an innocent woman's life was spared, but something is still bothering me. I feel that the intention behind Amina's actions is to please me and not You, and therefore I am vexed.

I will speak to another person regarding my dilemma. Perhaps Sister Jameela can provide me with help. She is busy with her own marriage preparation, which is also a worry. She has asked me to perform the ceremony, but I know that she is already married. The man she is marrying is the DICK's second in command and cannot be easily dissuaded. For some reason, he is attracted to Sister Jameela when she drinks tea with cookies. He reminds me of an uncle I had in Jordan who was enthralled with my Aunt Yasmeen's toes. Love is truly a mystery.

37

JAMEELA SURVEYED THE WEDDING TENT. IT WAS A VAST
white expanse in front of her. When she married Murray, she had hoped
for a tiny ceremony in the backyard with only close family and friends.
Her mother had worried that having a tiny wedding would give people
the impression Jameela had something to hide; she'd married a serial
killer or, worse, someone her mother didn't approve of—which was
true. But Nusrat had her reputation as a strict mother to uphold. She
wanted to make sure everyone knew her daughter had married a Muslim on her watch, even if he was a substandard white one. Anything less
would be blasphemy to her. Murray had convinced Jameela to hold the
wedding in the local mosque. It wasn't fancy enough for her mother, and
was too fancy for Jameela, but Murray had been thrilled to be married in
a Muslim house of worship.

Jameela had enjoyed her modest wedding, but a part of her wondered
what it would be like to be a Bridezilla—to have a crazy wedding with
all the trimmings. As she took in the enormous, pristine white tent, she
realized her fantasies were coming true today. Except for the Bridezilla
part; that role went to Zayn.

Men were busily putting up decorations. They were attaching mini
flashlights in green, blue, and red to the tentpoles with twist ties to create a fairy-lights effect. They covered tables with ratty barracks curtains,
and stuffed teacups full of desert flowers and dry shrubbery for table ar-

rangements. The decorations reminded Jameela of the Muslim camps she had attended as a child.

Her reverie was broken by the sound of automatic gunfire. One of the men shot an errant cat under the table he was setting. Okay, maybe that didn't happen at Camp Good Muslim.

She felt a well of happiness bubble up within her as Ibrahim loped toward her. His eternal optimism in humanity and the future was infectious.

"Sister Jameela, tell me about women. Why do they want men to love them so much? Why can't they be satisfied that God loves them instead?"

"Seriously, Ibrahim? Even you can't be that out of it. I'm pretty sure there's a verse in the Qur'an about it."

"God has created love and mercy between your hearts, verily in that are signs for those who reflect," said Ibrahim. "Verse twenty-one, chapter thirty."

It was Murray's favorite verse in the Qur'an. He'd had it embossed in raised burgundy lettering on the creamy background of their wedding invitations. To him, marriage was a spiritual partnership and to Jameela, anything spiritual was suspect, but she needed to soothe Ibrahim.

"And you're one of those who reflect, so what's the matter with you?" asked Jameela.

"It's just —" Ibrahim stared at a flashlight.

"You've never had anyone care for you."

"My mother —"

"Mothers don't count. It's our job to love our kids even if they hate us. Marriage, on the other hand, is about wanting a person to love you in the same crazy, uncontrollable way. And feeling like you'll die if they don't." Jameela thought about Murray and his utter devotion to her. Did he ever doubt her love for him? She needed to get out of this wedding to another man, which was a suspicious situation to be in when your husband already thought you'd abandoned him.

"Your dress is ready," said a voice behind her. Rashad was holding a large, bubble-gum-colored mass of fabric, which glinted with an iridescent sheen in the sunlight. Zayn came up to them and looked on with interest.

"The headpiece is sewn in for added convenience. You can lift the dress and put your head into it, and the whole thing falls into place. You will have to wear the pink veil to cover your face for the ceremony."

"So other men will not want to marry you as well," stated Zayn, as if it weren't obvious.

"We wouldn't want that," said Jameela, looking at the dress, which appeared so baggy almost two people could fit into it. Rashad had attached hoops under the skirt, *Gone with the Wind*–style, so she would have to be careful how she walked lest she knock over a table. "Where is my beloved?"

"He has gained weight recently because of his addiction to baklava, and now he cannot button his jacket. The tailor is making him a robe because it is . . . roomier."

Time is running out, thought Jameela. They were no closer to escaping, and the wedding was going to start in an hour. Zayn and Rashad left, leaving Ibrahim and Jameela staring at the pink behemoth.

"You are in trouble," said Ibrahim gravely. "You cannot marry this man. If you do, terrible things will happen to you."

"No kidding," said Jameela. She had almost forgotten about Ibrahim's lack of subtlety.

"I do not know what to do," he said sadly.

Until now, he had been the stalwart one, convincing her that faith alone would see them through their ordeal, but she could see he was wavering. Being in love and being in danger were proving too much for him.

"Don't be silly, prayers are always enough," she said, praying that they were. She hauled her wedding dress over her beige abaya. "Maybe this marriage is what God intended for my happiness," she said with the sincere hope that it was not.

"But Brother Murray is a very good husband. I am certain that marriage to him couldn't have been that unpleasant."

No, marriage to Murray was the best thing that ever happened to me, and I blew it.

Her nose started to tingle from the tears that were coming. She pushed back the stress and fear from the last few weeks that were threatening to erupt. Ibrahim needed her, and she couldn't let him down now. She took a few breaths like Murray had taught her, and she felt the despair melt away.

"I trust God completely, and we are going to get out of this unscathed. How do I look?" She tried to twirl the parachute dress out, but it was weighed down. There were old battery packs sewn into its hem. Rashad had mentioned a YouTube video that had gone viral in which Kate Middleton's dress had flown up in a gust of wind. Apparently, the queen had been displeased; there was a rumor that she had weights sewn into Kate's hems to prevent the travesty from happening again. He had taken this anecdote to heart, and Jameela found it hard to take even one step.

"You look beautiful. I remember once, as a child, seeing a hot air balloon floating in the sky above the minarets. You remind me of that."

"Thank you," said Jameela, genuinely touched.

Together, they turned and watched the men streaming into the tent and taking their positions at the tables. Someone started playing drums, and a wild ululating started. Abdullah, resplendent in a long white robe, was hoisted on the shoulders of his comrades. He looked like he could have been the wedding cake.

Talal was brought in, sheltered in a makeshift plastic bubble, Popemobile style, with the enclosure secured by duct tape to his wheelchair. He looked worse, his face even more gray and emaciated, although he'd had blood transfusions. Nusayba walked sternly beside him, wearing a lighter gray abaya as a nod to the occasion and perhaps her husband's pallor. She wore a matching gray fascinator that had ostrich feathers sticking out on top of her headscarf, complete with a black veil shielding her eyes. She was also wearing the most outlandish items from Courtney's pilfered suitcase: the shiny little green crocodile bag and a pair of towering platforms with a metal heel and studded leather straps that wouldn't be out of place in a sex dungeon. Her face was done in a foundation that was still too light, and she had on crimson lipstick. She looked like a cross between Camilla, Duchess of Cornwall, and Morticia Addams. Nusayba took out the diamond-encrusted cell phone and took several selfies.

Unbelievable, how vain was this woman? She was trying to upstage Jameela, but that was fine with her. It was probably Nusayba's idea that her face be covered with the pink veil. Jameela knew she looked like a giant piece of chewed bubble gum.

Talal and Nusayba took their positions at the head table, which was decorated with what looked like the antlers of an animal or a dried-up cactus — Jameela couldn't tell from behind the pink gauze. Amina had been banished to the barracks to think about her actions and wouldn't be joining them. Mercifully, Lee Lee was given a day of rest for all her hard work, and Jameela had told her to stay in the kitchens. She couldn't bear to watch Lee Lee suffer as she married for the second time.

Abdullah had now reached Ibrahim and Jameela, who were sitting at the front table. His comrades put him down gently, and he took his seat next to Jameela.

"It is time to begin," said Ibrahim solemnly.

Ibrahim, Silent Internal Prayer, 4:13 p.m., Oct. 20

My Lord, I have never doubted You before. But today, I feel despondent. I must marry Sister Jameela to this terrible man, and I do not know how to stop it.

What will happen to us? I know that the prophet and his companions were also tested by being banished by nonbelievers into the desert for two years because they believed in You. But I feel this is different. The prophet had his companions for support, but Sister Jameela and I are alone here, and the desert is full of dangerous men.

I am weak and feel that I cannot take any more tests. I see no way out for us. Sister Jameela and I are going to be defeated at the hands of these brutal people. And yet I believe in You. What does this mean? That prayer and patience are not enough? The one who is the cruelest will be victorious? The world does not belong to the weak and humble?

38

JAMEELA SAT IN A CHAIR DECORATED WITH STYROFOAM hearts. Someone had tried to paint them red, but the paint had flaked off. Her parachute dress seemed to be reverting to its original purpose. Every gust of air puffed it up, and if it weren't for those battery packs weighing her down, she would have been floating above her own wedding tent. Abdullah sat beside her in his freshly stitched white robe, paired with a gold-trimmed military vest. Someone had cut black plastic bags into strips and hung them around the tent. Giant fans were set up to make the strips flutter for a festive look.

Roasted lamb and steamed rice were placed on the main buffet table by burly men pressed into service as waiters. Platters of stuffed vine leaves and chicken skewers followed. But it wasn't the main course that held Jameela's attention. Zayn brought out the large assortment of desserts himself, carrying the trays with the concentration of a man holding live ammo. *You never know.* She stared at the red heart-shaped pieces of Jell-O. They were arranged in a heart-shaped circle like a moat with a pile of Oreo cookies in the center.

"There wasn't supposed to be any gluten at this wedding," said Zayn distastefully. "But Abdullah insisted, so Lee Lee made a Jell-O barrier to protect the other desserts from getting any crumbs."

"That's wonderful," said Jameela, wondering why she hadn't been consulted about her favorite desserts. But no, patriarchy extended into everything, including the pastries. A giant, towering croquembouche was brought out next. On closer inspection, there were no cream puffs; instead, Lee Lee had scooped out melon balls and drizzled them with butterscotch, a particular favorite of Zayn's.

The more delicate desserts, which needed extra care to survive the heat — chocolate pudding pops on Popsicle sticks, bowls of coconut rice pudding, maple-baked mangos, and bowls of pink sorbet — were stored in a portable walk-in freezer that had been brought to the tent for this purpose, along with a giant ice sculpture. Zayn emerged from the freezer with the pièce de résistance: the wedding cake in the shape of a giant teapot, with pink icing and sliced strawberries decorating the perimeter.

Abdullah and Zayn stared at the cake in awe. Jameela was certain they loved it for different reasons. Rashad broke everyone's reverie.

"Sister Jameela, as promised, we have choreographed a dance for you."

Jameela looked at him in astonishment. She had completely forgotten about her promise of a dance-off. For the first time, she noticed that all the guests were dressed in one of two different outfits. The Pakistani men wore white shirts with dhotis or sarongs at the bottom in various colors — lime green, red, orange, and yellow — with matching vests and turbans in deference to the Punjabi origins of their dance. The Arab men wore baggy Aladdin pants and vests with belts decorated with tiny coins that tinkled when they moved.

"Who would you like to go first?" asked Rashad.

"Would it be unfair to give the South Asians the first crack?" said Jameela.

A giant whoop went up, and music poured out of enormous speakers. The whole tent came alive with fast, furious drumbeats as men of South Asian descent lined up, and started kicking their legs and waving their arms. The joy and happiness radiating from them was infectious. Everyone clapped and tapped their feet to the beat; even Talal's lips looked like they were turned up slightly. Nusayba moved the feathers of her fascinator out of the way for a better view.

It was the most colorful and bizarrely heartwarming experience of Jameela's life.

When the bhangra number finished, the sweaty, exhausted Punjabi men took their places at the tables with looks of pleasure and exhilaration. Then the Arabs came forward, and the music changed to a slow, seductive tempo. Hips shook delicately as the coins jangled. Jameela couldn't believe she was watching men from DICK perform such a suggestive and sexy dance. But they did so with incredible precision and concentration. She couldn't figure out how they were able to isolate each muscle group to undulate in succession. But the best part was when they turned around and only the muscles in their buttocks vibrated as their arms swayed to the music. It was more sensuous than she'd expected. By the time the fiery music was finished, both groups of men were on their feet, congratulating their brethren.

"What did you think?" asked Ismail, dancing seductively toward Jameela with the tinkling of his coins, which, on closer inspection, turned out to be spent bullets.

"I've never seen anything so spectacular before. You guys are the most amazing dancers in the world. You should be on *Who's Got Talent* or something."

"Really, you mean that?" asked Ismail in astonishment. "She loved us!" he yelled to the other men, who whooped in response.

Jameela turned to Abdullah to see what he thought. His brow was knitted in consternation. He wasn't happy with the riotous and steamy dancing, or that her attention had been diverted toward sweaty men immodestly moving parts of their bodies; clearly, the wrong sex had been covered up. He grabbed an Oreo cookie from the heaping pile, shoved it into his mouth, and slammed the table, sending cookies and crumbs flying. This put Zayn into a panic.

"My cake!" Zayn screamed, running toward it.

"*My* cake," parroted Abdullah who was using the little English he knew for effect. He stepped in front of it while Zayn tried to push him away, but it was like a squirrel trying to push a woolly mammoth. "*My* wedding."

Abdullah crushed several cookies in his palms and poured them over the pink teapot cake, contaminating it.

Zayn took out his AK-47 and pointed it at Abdullah.

The wedding grew quiet.

39

ZAYN AND ABDULLAH CIRCLED EACH OTHER LIKE TWO lions in a cage. Jameela could see the anger on their faces through her pink face veil. Ibrahim gripped her arm.

"We must prepare ourselves to run," he said, looking at the open section of the tent. "If they start to shoot, we will be caught in the crossfire."

"You have never let me have anything that I want!" screamed Zayn.

"You always think of yourself, you son of a jackal," said Abdullah. Ibrahim quickly translated Abdullah's words for her.

"When I'm planning an attack," retorted Zayn, "you undermine me. You send out the men earlier than planned, so they think you are in charge."

"Because I am in charge! You are trying to become the next leader of DICK. But I see through you."

This statement apparently caught Zayn off guard. He looked uneasily at Talal, observing him through his plastic tent.

Talal was watching the exchange with great interest. Nusayba whispered something in his ear, and he nodded.

"You spoil the men by being so lenient," spat Zayn. "You are going to undermine this organization with your sloppy Western ways."

"What's more Western than your wimpy gluten allergy? You're jealous of me because I am more popular among the men," said Abdullah.

As Ibrahim translated, Jameela felt like she was in high school again, except the blond, big-haired girls had morphed into brown, hairy men.

Abdullah's eyes were red and defiant, his whole body tense. Jameela thought he was about to punch Zayn in the face, but he did something far worse. He smashed the teapot cake with his fist and threw a hunk at Zayn's head.

Zayn looked like he'd been shot. Pink icing hung in clumps from his beard. Halved strawberries stuck to his cheek and clothes like bright clots of blood. His cake, the one he had waited a lifetime for, was destroyed.

Flicking the icing from his eyes, Zayn raised his automatic weapon and unleashed a bloodcurdling war cry. The men, thinking this was their cue to attack, began throwing food: cupcakes, kebabs, stuffed grapevine leaves. Jameela ducked a volley of melon balls. Ibrahim tugged at her sleeve, and they ran, keeping low, moving around the outer perimeter of the tent. The guards were no longer in their places. They were simultaneously slurping crème brûlée from their beards while flinging Jell-O Pops.

"We can leave the tent and find our way back to the barracks, where it will be empty," said Ibrahim.

"But we still don't have a plan to get out of this place," said Jameela. "There's no way to escape on foot."

"You are correct, Sister Jameela. It is a hopeless endeavor. We are going to die here."

Jameela stopped and stared at Ibrahim. Not on her watch.

"Ibrahim, what's wrong with you? What happened to 'Pray and be patient, and God will take care of us'?"

He shrugged. "Does it look like God is taking care of us?"

Jameela was shocked. How was she supposed to respond? She had only known Ibrahim to be steadfast and faithful. Now he looked worn out and defeated. Had she done this to him? Destroyed the one part of Ibrahim that defined who he was? How was she supposed to respond to his lack of faith? She held his shoulders and looked at him as intently as possible.

"Have faith, for God is the true protector of every soul. You taught me that," said Jameela, holding Ibrahim by the shoulders. His eyes were glazed, and he looked pale. "It doesn't matter what the odds are, as long as God is on your side. It might look like it's hopeless, but it's just an illusion. Our faith in God is being tested, and we mustn't fail now." Jameela searched in Ibrahim's pockets and pulled out the piece of paper with Barkley's cell number, a miswak, and some lint until she found the blue prayer beads. She pressed them into his hands.

Ibrahim started to rub them, and after a moment, he relaxed and smiled. Some color came back to his face. *Thank God. I can't be the one who breaks him.* She racked her brains for stories of the Qur'an that would give him strength. "Remember when Moses was being pursued by the Pharaoh and his crew? He probably thought that it was hopeless, too, but he didn't give up."

Ibrahim perked up.

"Well, you're like Moses, all holy and God-conscious," said Jameela, on a roll. "God doesn't abandon people like you. Me, maybe. But you've done your time in the holy trenches, praying and believing. You're too good for God to abandon."

"Is he?" asked Talal, standing behind them with armed guards. He was wearing a face mask but had discarded his plastic wrap and wheelchair, and was leaning on Nusayba. Custard was dribbling down his neck, and there was a mini cupcake with tiny silver beads squashed on the side of Nusayba's head. He pulled a gun out.

Zayn came up to them, out of breath from his exertions. He pointed at Jameela. "She is the problem. Ever since she arrived with her friends, there's been no discipline in our ranks. Look at the chaos they've caused. And Abdullah is in cahoots with them."

Jameela felt like she was caught between a rock and a terrorist. Zayn was obviously trying to cover his ass because Abdullah had revealed to the whole camp that he wanted to be in charge. She was about to be shot. Ibrahim tried to shield her, but it was her time to protect him. Pushing him aside, she stood defiant in front of Talal.

"If you kill me, you'll have to answer to God."

"I don't believe in God, which is why it's easy to kill people." And then Talal fired his gun.

40

JAMEELA AND IBRAHIM STARED AT ZAYN, WHO LAY ON the ground with a bullet hole in his head. Talal put his gun back into its holster as the sound of the shot reverberated in the air. He turned to Ibrahim.

"Don't you have a wedding to perform?" asked Talal nonchalantly.

Ibrahim nodded. Like Jameela, he was dazed. Both had thought the bullet in Zayn's head was intended for them.

"I never liked him," said Talal, putting his gun away. "Too haughty."

Clearly, Talal felt that Zayn was more of a threat to his leadership than Abdullah, who appeared somber as he stood beside Ibrahim. An air of solemnity and terror descended, and everyone had become very quiet. The wedding tent had food splattered on its walls. The only thing that remained standing was the enormous ice sculpture of a mountain. The men still holding food discreetly threw it behind their backs. You could have heard a marshmallow puff drop. No one wanted to make a sound in case Talal was deciding who would still be alive by the end of the ceremony.

"Just do it," whispered Jameela to a shell-shocked Ibrahim. "We'll figure something out."

"Let's get on with it," said Talal, clapping his hands. "We have a city to sack, men to kill, and children to terrify, so chop-chop. Social media needs its villain, so let's not keep it waiting."

Jameela sat down at the head table, along with Abdullah and Ibrahim, who seemed comatose. Jameela couldn't get him to speak, but she remembered the ceremony from her marriage to Murray. The imam asks the bride if she accepts the marriage proposal.

"Yes, I accept his marriage proposal and the gift of an apartment complex in Dubai," said Jameela loudly. She grabbed the paperwork from Ibrahim's hands, signed her name, and gave the contract to Abdullah to sign. He did, and suddenly she was a married woman. Again. The men gave a sedated murmur. The joy and energy of the room had seeped away after Zayn's murder, and no one wanted to draw attention to themselves. All that was left was the consummation of her marriage. And Abdullah seemed to be in a rush. He grabbed her hand and started pulling her away from Ibrahim, who was frozen in place and didn't seem to notice. She was going to have to save herself.

"Wait a minute," yelled Jameela. "I want a piece of cake." She didn't know what else to say at a time like this. The cake was a soggy mess on the table. Abdullah scraped up a few pieces and presented it to her on a plate. She sat down and started to eat very slowly. Unfortunately, this just excited Abdullah. *What do I do?* thought Jameela.

The men began helping themselves to food that remained on the tables. They were eating, but being circumspect so as not to draw Talal's attention. Abdullah eyed Jameela hungrily while she looked around the tent. Talal's guards were stationed again at every exit. There was no way out, and Ibrahim looked like he could hardly move. She looked at Zayn's body, which had been covered by a white cloth. It was too bad he hadn't lived to taste his creations.

She felt a hand on her shoulder. It was Abdullah. Her cake was done, and she was out of excuses. He took her elbow and started leading her away from the table. The men parted for them. Jameela walked with a strange feeling of calm. He would still have to get this contraption off her, which could take a while. Maybe she could pretend that she was bashful. Did that even work anymore?

As they reached the tent opening, she saw lights resembling two fireflies, except they were moving rapidly toward her and getting larger. A rumbling filled the air. Everyone panicked, and Abdullah released his grip on Jameela. She ran back to Ibrahim and pulled him off his chair and down to the ground with her.

A giant fuel tanker crashed through the tent, running over the tables and chairs, the brakes desperately squealing, filling the air with a loud hissing noise as the tanker hit the buffet table, which went flying and finally slid to a halt. Most of the wedding guests were stunned at first, but then their reflexes took over, and they started firing at the truck. Fuel sprayed out of the tank from the bullet holes.

"What's happening?" asked Ibrahim. Jameela couldn't answer him; she was choking on the fumes that were overwhelming the tent.

Jameela could see a black figure barreling toward her. "It's about time," she thought, pulling out Courtney's iPhone from her utility pocket. Her last text read *Anytime Now!!* After stealing Courtney's iPhone out of Nusayba's purse during the dance-off, she had texted Barkley the coordinates of the wedding tent. Watching the ensuing chaos unfold, she wished God wouldn't make everything so hard.

Protected by the mayhem, Barkley managed to find Jameela and Ibrahim huddled at the periphery. He reached her and grabbed her arm. Thank God for the giant candy-colored contraption she was wearing. It doubled as a rescue flare.

"I came as soon as I heard from you," said Barkley, in a bulletproof vest and helmet, seeming very pleased with himself. "Feeling rescued yet?"

Jameela wanted to weep. Her plan had been to pack them all in the truck and leave, but Barkley had crashed it and now it was full of holes and leaking gas, making it unusable. Men were the biggest idiots that God ever created. How they had ruled the earth for so long, keeping women enslaved, boggled the mind.

A DICK operative's gaze zeroed in on Barkley, and he yelled to the other men to raise the alarm. Soon all the guns were trained on them.

"Nope. Not feeling rescued."

One hundred and fifty DICKs held their fire, waiting for a command from someone. Shooting Abdullah's bride could end badly for all of them, and no one wanted to take the chance.

She could feel a tickling sensation on her torso as tiny red tactical lights from many guns roamed her body. *Have faith, have faith, have faith.* She wasn't going to lose it now. Ibrahim and Barkley believed in her, and she wasn't going to let them down. Jameela raised her hands, and slowly stood up in her reflective pink dress. She moved herself in front of both Ibrahim and Barkley, becoming their bulwark against attack.

"You must kill her, Abdullah!" Talal, who was huddled with Nusayba in one corner of the tent, spoke up. "She's betrayed us too many times."

Abdullah looked furious at being thwarted yet again. He took his semiautomatic, aimed it at her, and then shot it in the air in frustration. The bullet ricocheted off a metal tentpole, and sparks flew to the ground, igniting the fuel that had pooled around the vehicle. Fire bloomed in blue and orange ripples around the tires, and in seconds, noxious black smoke engulfed them, blinding and choking everyone in the tent.

Jameela remembered her elementary school training: stop, drop, and roll. She flung herself to the ground and found Ibrahim unconscious nearby. Barkley was bent over him, calling his name. While the flames devoured the tent with alarming speed, Jameela and Barkley dragged Ibrahim behind the ice mountain sculpture. The melting water kept the flames at bay, but not for long; it would be only a matter of seconds before the fire reached them. So Jameela did the only thing she could think of and pulled her pink burqa over Barkley and Ibrahim. The flame-retardant material would save them, at least for the moment, but smoke inhalation was going to be a problem.

Ibrahim lifted his head. "We say a prayer when death is imminent."

"Say it," cried Jameela, overwhelmed with the heat and smoke. Her skin was burning, and she couldn't breathe. She had turned into the *Hindenburg* and could feel herself starting to lose consciousness as the fabric started to melt.

Liverspot Tribune, Obituary by Hank McMurty, Oct. 21

Jameela Green, 39, formerly beloved Liverspot local and the CIA's most dangerous Muslim terrorist, has been killed in a firefight between rebels in Raqqa, Syria.

Mr. Jed Smith, the manager of Act of God Insurance, where Ms. Green worked, said, "We'll have to hire counselors. We can't have our people running off to blow things up in the Middle East every time a farmer is unhappy with his soybean slug-damage payout."

The CIA, FBI, Homeland Security, and Pakistani officials are not giving any details as to the nature of their investigations into Ms. Green's case.

Ms. Green attended New York University, where she received her BA and met fellow student Murray Green. They married after graduation. Mr. Green converted to Islam, which caused his parents to question his allegiance to America. His mother, Trish Green, said, "We're the least racist people you'll ever meet, but we were not surprised to learn that Murray's Muslim wife became a radical Islamic terrorist and turned her back on America. Len and I pray every night that Murray will let Jesus Christ back into his heart."

Jameela's mother, Nusrat Butt, said she considers herself racist and didn't approve of Jameela marrying a white man. "Nothing good ever comes from these people."

After marrying, Murray and Jameela Green left New York for Liverspot, where Mr. Green opened his dental practice, All Smiles, All the Time.

Jameela Green is survived by her parents, husband, and daughter, Maleeha Green.

41

MURRAY SAT IN HIS MOTHER-IN-LAW'S KITCHEN, WHERE Nusrat served watery tea with store-bought soda crackers. Such substandard food would usually be a heresy in this house, but, given that their daughter was dead and granddaughter missing, it was a miracle Nusrat and Faisal were getting by at all. Nusrat's hair, normally styled in an immaculate, elegant bun, was uncombed and in disarray, and her eyes were red and swollen. Her hands shook as she poured Murray another cup. She was mispronouncing his name, but he didn't have the heart to tell her; at least she had stopped calling him You Idiot.

"Furry, I didn't have time to make samosas . . ." she choked, and her husband quickly removed the teapot, put it down, and held her. Faisal looked ill, and the buttons on his shirt were misaligned.

"I should have let her date," Nusrat wailed. "She would never have become a terrorist."

"You raised her well," said Faisal, in a voice cracking with emotion. "I shouldn't have lectured her so much about the American military. She was trying to get her revenge for us."

Murray stared at the green liquid in his teacup; it tasted like warm dishwater. He couldn't believe sadness could be so overwhelming. He was falling into a bottomless pit of loneliness, but he hung on to the only hope he had left. Lee Lee's calls had given them all hope that she, at least, was still alive.

The doorbell rang. Nusrat and Faisal were weeping and clinging together. "Please get that, Blurry," croaked Nusrat.

A short brown man stood at the door, wearing a dark-green double-breasted suit. His hair was cemented in place with gel.

"My name is Aziz."

"This is a bad time for us right now. Could you come back later?" said Murray as he started shutting the door.

"I work in Pakistan's intelligence force, the ISI, and I am the person who arranged for your wife to leave for the Middle East in order for her to rescue the imam."

Anger surged through Murray. It took everything he had to not punch the man. Violence wouldn't bring Jameela back, but it would help him feel better.

Aziz's arms rose in defense as he read Murray's mind. "Please do not strike me," he said. "Your wife made me promise to find you if something happened to her. I am here to fulfill her wish."

When Murray led Aziz into the kitchen, Faisal and Nusrat immediately stopped crying. Nusrat grabbed her frying pan from the stove and lunged at Aziz.

"You took my baby away from me," she screamed as Faisal and Murray grabbed her arms.

"Speak quickly, because I don't know how long we can keep her from hurting you," said Murray through gritted teeth.

"Your wife is not a terrorist. She met with me because she wanted my help to bring back her imam. The Americans had kidnapped him, and she was his only hope. Mr. Ibrahim would be dead by now if she hadn't intervened," said Aziz rapidly.

Murray felt Nusrat relax. She lowered the frying pan, and Faisal removed it from her hands.

"Does it have something to do with the homeless man Jameela and Ibrahim found?" asked Murray, remembering what seemed like a long-ago conversation.

"The homeless man, Barkley, was a recruit for the DICK," said Aziz, sitting down and acknowledging the sad crackers on the table. "Once your wife and Mr. Ibrahim visited the police to report his disappearance, the imam's name came up as a person of interest. No doubt he knew many men who joined the DICK, and one of them gave his name while under duress. The police had the imam deported under the guise of a trip to visit his sick mother, who had already passed away. Your wife was the only person who knew the truth. She said it was her responsibility to get him back. She was extremely motivated to do so, and I do not know why."

"I do," said Murray quietly, so no one could hear. "Jamal." He'd been trying to figure out how Jameela had been radicalized so quickly. It hadn't made any sense. Now things started to fall into place. She had felt guilty about ensnaring Ibrahim in her plan to succeed as a writer. She wasn't going to let him disappear if she was responsible.

"But none of this changes the fact that she's gone," howled Faisal, still holding his wife.

They all looked at Aziz, who had become as pale as a brown man could. Nusrat broke away from Faisal and grabbed Aziz's shoulders.

"You sent her to her death!" she screamed, shaking him furiously. Aziz let Nusrat expend all her anger on him, and when she was done, he spoke. "I have reason to believe Jameela is alive."

Murray wasn't sure his heart could take much more. "Please, don't give us hope unless you have real evidence. We can't take any more pain."

"There was only one female corpse found in the fire, and everyone assumed it was your wife. But our reports indicate that Talal's wife, Nusayba, was also present. American intelligence has little information about her, and in their arrogance, they believed the legend Nusayba created for herself, that she had died early in the war. The woman who was killed was burned beyond recognition, but we have obtained her dental records from the Syrian authorities, and they are a match. The Americans have misidentified her as Jameela."

Nusrat fainted. Faisal carried his unconscious wife to the living room.

"You seem to have a lot of knowledge about what's going on over there," said Murray.

"It is in our best interest to have knowledge about affairs that concern our country's well-being."

"And now you're going to do something for me to ensure your own well-being," said Murray.

"Yes," said Aziz, reaching for a dry cracker. "Anything you desire. But first, can we find a decent samosa? The freezer perhaps?"

42

INITIALLY THE CHILL HAD BEEN A RELIEF FROM THE UN-relenting heat, but now the cold was starting to penetrate their bodies. The portable walk-in freezer Zayn had used to protect his gluten-free desserts from the desert heat had been strategically placed behind the ice sculpture. Jameela gave a quick prayer of thanks and looked around at the piles of mini cheesecakes that had never been served.

"If we stay in here much longer, we'll freeze to death," said Barkley, his teeth chattering.

Jameela was also stiff from cold and turned to look at Ibrahim, whose lips were turning blue. The door was locked, and they were trapped inside. Zayn must have been paranoid that someone would steal his creations and made sure anyone sneaking into the freezer couldn't get out. Caught frozen-handed, as it were.

She heard a faint knocking.

"Is anyone in there?" asked a muffled voice.

"Yes!" squeaked Jameela. She could hardly move her mouth.

"Hang on, we have to shoot the lock, it's melted. Stand back."

Jameela and Barkley dragged Ibrahim away from the door. Bullets ricocheted off the metal handle. As the door opened, Jameela saw Lee Lee and Amina with their mouths covered by wet scarves, looking pale and frightened. Smoke and an acrid smell wafted into the freezer.

"You're alive!" yelled Lee Lee. She ran to Jameela and embraced her. "After the fire died out, we looked everywhere and couldn't find you—" Lee Lee sobbed into Jameela's shoulder and took a big shudder-ing breath. "Then, I saw a piece of pink fabric sticking out of the freezer door."

Jameela held Lee Lee as she cried. Giving her child comfort was a new feeling. She wanted to say something to help Lee Lee feel better, but she couldn't speak because her face was too cold. She rubbed Lee Lee's back with the little strength she still had. *I love you. And when my face thaws, I'll say it every day until you get sick of hearing it.*

"I love you, too, Mom." Somehow, Lee Lee had read her mind.

Lee Lee placed her hands on Jameela's face, trying to warm it. It felt good.

"Come on, we have to go now," said Amina, looking at Ibrahim, who appeared more and more like a corpse. Barkley helped Amina carry a catatonic Ibrahim out.

The tent was gone, burned up, leaving fragments of white plastic sticking to the poles that still marked the periphery. They stood outside with the stars above them. The tables, chairs, and catering equipment were blackened and strewn about. Black ash was still floating around. The giant fuel truck lay smoldering on its side, and the place reeked of diesel.

"Don't look," said Lee Lee to Jameela, when she saw her staring at a charred figure in a seated position in an overturned wheelchair. The metal skeleton of a pair of Louboutins stuck out from underneath, just like in *The Wizard of Oz*.

Fleeing the fire, the men must have abandoned Talal; only his wife had stayed with him. It gave her a sense of solace that the men hadn't been incinerated with their leader.

"Where are we going?" asked Jameela.

"The women have set up a triage station in the compound," said Lee Lee. "We'll go there and have someone look at Brother Ibrahim."

"I don't know what's wrong with him," said Jameela.

"He's in shock," said Amina, stroking Ibrahim's hair. "If we don't get him help, he may never recover."

43

JAMEELA APPLIED A COLD COMPRESS TO IBRAHIM'S head. Amina paced back and forth, while Lee Lee spread butter on bread. No one at the triage had any knowledge about how to treat Ibrahim, and it was too risky to stay after everything that had happened, so they had decided to leave DICK's compound. Barkley found a car and drove them to Sahar's apartment. She ushered them into the living room, where Ibrahim was put on the couch and covered with blankets.

"We don't have much time," said Amina. "There's a tiny window of opportunity where we can escape. This place is going to descend into chaos at any minute."

Jameela stopped short. "How are you doing with all this? I mean, your parents are dead. Are you okay?"

Amina stopped pacing and looked at Jameela. "Would you think I was a horrible person if I said all I feel is relief?"

"But she was still your mother," said Lee Lee quietly.

Jameela went over to the stove and touched Lee Lee's shoulder as she put a piece of cheese between the buttered bread and started heating it on the frying pan.

"Your mother loves you and risked her life to save you," said Amina. "My mom used to be good but left me when I needed her most, only to hurt people. So, no, I don't miss her or my father. Good people are hard to find in this world." She looked at Ibrahim. "But I'm glad I didn't kill them," she said, stroking his cheek. "He would never have forgiven me. In the end, they died in the world they created."

Jameela lingered on what Amina said first: *Your mother loves you.* After Jamal died, her relationship with Nusrat had deteriorated rapidly. Nusrat's grief had made her stricter and more protective. But her mother had always loved her, even if she didn't know how to tell Jameela, just as Jameela had never known how to tell Lee Lee. Loss and trauma could seep through generations. When Jameela thought of her mother now, she remembered the good times. All her favorite foods made with love. Her room, still full of her favorite things: awards, trophies, framed photos, and certificates. The FaceTime calls to make sure she was eating properly and not working too hard. These were the acts of a mother devoted to her only child.

"We need to get back home," said Jameela. *I want to see my mom.*

She walked to the bedroom to gather her things, and as she did so, the streetlights caught her attention. She looked through Sahar's window, across the street, and saw a little girl peeping through lace curtains, her big brown eyes radiating curiosity and wonder. A few hours ago, those eyes would have been full of fear and terror, Jameela thought. The girl waved her tiny hand, her mouth breaking into a big grin that exposed two missing front teeth. It was the smile of hope.

The apartment door opened, and Barkley strode in.

Jameela turned from the window. "What's happening out there?" she asked him.

"No one really knows. DICK's men had a contingency plan if things went south for Talal. They'll be meeting tonight at the barracks to decide on the next leader."

"Do you think we can get everyone out of here safely?"

"I've found another transport truck we can take to Turkey's border. The guards have given up their posts," said Barkley. "We could leave anytime."

The bread sizzled and then the kettle gave a shriek. Sahar poured the hot water into a large teapot, added teabags, and let it steep. Lee Lee brought her mother the grilled cheese sandwich. Jameela stared at it.

"What's wrong, Mom?" asked Lee Lee. "It's your favorite."

Amina, Lee Lee, and Barkley regarded Jameela as she continued star-ing at the sandwich. She finally took a bite. "Barkley, take everyone to-night."

"But you're coming too," said Lee Lee, clutching Jameela's arm.

"No, I'm going to the meeting."

44

EVERYONE REFUSED TO LEAVE RAQQA WITHOUT JA-
meela, so she was forced to let them come with her, on the condition
Lee Lee stay in Sahar's apartment and look after Ibrahim. Jameela, Barkley, and Amina found themselves in a large room in an abandoned building. Dusty black plastic foldout chairs had been arranged in neat lines.
Jameela poured herself a glass of water from a jug that had been left on
the table at the front. There was a tray of baklava and mini powdered
doughnuts beside a coffee carafe. White stickers with a wavy red border
were scattered on the table. Name tags? She instinctively took the black
Sharpie sitting nearby, scrawled her name, peeled off the adhesive, and
stuck it on. She felt as if she were at a twelve-step recovery program for
addicts, except instead of alcohol, drugs, or gambling, the men were trying to recover from thoughts of megalomania and world domination. At
least they all already had a hysterical belief in a higher power.

Slowly, the fighters started entering the room. Jameela recognized
some of them from her time in captivity. They seemed younger and
more frightened now.

"Are you leading the meeting?" asked one of the young men. His name
tag said ADEEL. Jameela almost choked on her doughnut. She had assumed that there would be some sort of an agenda prepared by an in-
terim leader. Other men also looked at her expectantly. She recognized
her bhangra belly-dancing performers, who, a day earlier, had been having the time of their lives.

"And you're Talal's daughter?" asked another man, named Musa, looking at Amina with intensity. "He said that you never really believed in his cause."

Amina and Jameela gave each other the side eye. They had assumed that the men would be angry and vengeful seeing them, but instead they seemed relieved. Jameela spotted the tailors Rashad and Ismail, their costumes blackened from the smoke. The men beamed and came over.

"You must have thought we were monsters, being in DICK," said Rashad. "But we're good people."

"I know." Jameela suspected the men needed to talk to someone who understood what they had endured.

"We were told that DICK was building a just society. And at first, they were," said Ismail. "They restored electricity, established regular garbage pickup, and gave us clean water. No one was allowed to take bribes, and the police had to investigate crimes properly."

Jameela had heard that the one thing that DICK got right was establishing an infrastructure that wasn't corrupt. At first.

"But gradually, they started to become more brutal and spread the caliphate through intimidation and cruelty. Talal indoctrinated people to carry out terror attacks throughout the world. In the end, we were used to build their empire." Rashad hung his head in shame.

"Once we figured it out, some of us tried to escape," said Ismail. "But if you were caught, you were killed."

"I'm sorry we had to hurt our own people," said Rashad, looking sadder by the minute.

"Should we be punished for what we did?" asked Ismail.

Jameela had no idea what to say. They seemed so innocent and young. Each one had a different history, a different motivation. Like Barkley and Reem or even Mr. Nehru, personal trauma had likely played a role in the decision to come here. They were either searching for a family that would love them or getting revenge for a family they had lost. Should they be punished? The question was too complicated and fraught, and another group of people would have to sift through the evidence and render judgment. All Jameela knew was that she wasn't that person.

"You need a good leader," said Jameela. "Elect someone you trust and follow them."

More men walked in. The room started to smell like a campfire.

"We trust you," said Musa. "Will you lead us?"

"But I'm a woman," said Jameela, steadying herself by holding on to the table. "Don't you guys want a man to be your next leader?"

"The Qur'an talks about the Queen of Sheba, who was a wise and just ruler," said Rashad, coming closer to her.

Jameela sucked air in as if the oxygen were being siphoned out of the room.

Ismail's eyes glistened with excitement. "And she wasn't arrogant because of her power. She listened to people and took advice and knew how terrible war was. Men destroy, women create."

"God sent you here to become the next calipha of the Muslim world," said Musa as the men became more animated.

The room started to spin. The anticipation around her was more than she could deal with. She missed her life of going to work, driving on a single-lane highway heading to a meeting with a farmer, alone on the road, with no one for miles, crops of bottle green and canary yellow swaying in the gentle breeze, the blue sky, an endless sea, giving her a sense of comfort. That was when she'd listen to one of Jamal's recitations of the Qur'an and cry, the colors of the landscape beginning to blur like a swiftly turning kaleidoscope. She'd arrive back home and be in her kitchen, reading the newspaper, her husband greeting her with a kiss, her face being tickled by his rough blond stubble while the smell of aftershave and Sensodyne enveloped her.

"Jameela, wake up! Jameela I'm here."

Jameela opened her eyes and saw Murray.

Jameela, Maghrib Prayer, 7:09 p.m., Oct. 22

You brought him to me! At first, I thought I was hallucinating and the whole thing had been a dream. But then I saw Ibrahim lying beside me on a cot. Aziz had arranged safe transport for Murray once news got out that DICK had been destroyed. He wanted to make up for perhaps 'not being forthright with regard to certain details' of the mission. Just when you think you know a guy.

I'm trending on Twitter. I'm the new calipha of DICK. That's totally insane. I can't be the new leader. I'm an insurance specialist for farmers. And I might find the best rates, but that doesn't qualify me to lead a caliphate. Please get me out of this.

One more thing, could You wake Ibrahim up? He's finally opened his eyes, but now we have to keep adding eyedrops and manually blinking him, which is a pain.

45

"THERE'S A GATHERING OUTSIDE IN FRONT OF THE apartment," said Lee Lee, peering through Sahar's curtains.

"It's probably just a farmer's market or something," said Jameela, joining her daughter at the window.

"They've got signs that say 'Jameela Is Our New Calipha,' so they're probably not selling couscous," said Amina.

Jameela felt riveted to the window. A new feeling came over her — could one be both happy and sad at the same time?

Murray was chewing the hard kernels of wheat in the tabbouleh salad Lee Lee had made for him. After assessing his waistline, she was trying to get him back on a healthy diet. Murray obliged but felt he deserved some slack. After losing your his wife and daughter to who knows what horrors, he'd been eating his feelings. And those feelings were easier to swallow when coated in batter and deep fried.

"We need to leave," he said. "Jameela, please, you can't be taking this calipha thing seriously. It can't possibly work. There's a complicated process to rebuilding a country. Plus, we don't belong here."

Jameela knew Murray was right but still felt conflicted. All her life she had felt unmoored, but here, in an unfamiliar country during a civil unrest, despite the terror, she had finally learned to bond with people — Rashad, Ismail, and Barkley, even Amina, not to mention Lee Lee and Murray. But that wasn't a reason to stay. She wasn't Syrian, she couldn't speak Arabic, and she was woefully unqualified. But then again, weren't politicians back home often the least qualified to lead? She peered through the curtains, and people cheered. The same feeling overcame her — she wanted to go home, but maybe this was home now?

Amina moistened a paper towel and wet Ibrahim's lips. "I hope Ibrahim can hear the noise and excitement outside." She moved his hair off his forehead.

Lee Lee added water to a bowl of whole wheat flour and started to knead the mixture into dough. She was going to bake high-fiber bread.

"I'm going for a walk," said Jameela, putting on her scarf. She couldn't explain how she felt; it was like someone had cast a spell on her and she felt a magnetic pull leading her outside.

Murray choked on his tabbouleh. Amina gave her a reassuring hand gesture.

"I'm coming with you," she said. "You don't speak Arabic."

As they entered the street, people started to gather around them. An old man touched her scarf, and Jameela could see the deep lines in his face. The crowd started to become thicker, which made it difficult for them to move. But Jameela didn't feel afraid; she felt loved and accepted.

"They're saying they prayed for a sign to deliver them from Talal, and all the signs came true."

"What signs?"

"That he would die a terrible death for all the crimes he committed. And that their stories and their truth would be heard." Amina turned to Jameela. "There are too many, I can't translate them all."

The mood of the crowd began to change as Amina spoke. People started to move closer, and she could feel her ribs being crushed as the crowd continued its inward momentum. It felt organic and frenzied. The spell had been broken. *This was a mistake,* thought Jameela. She'd deluded herself into thinking she was their savior. She wasn't a substitute for democracy and a coordinated rebuilding effort. Plus, she was from the West, which was problematic for many reasons.

"Leave my wife alone!"

Jameela saw Murray wading through the crowd, which parted as word of his status spread. Touching another man's wife was considered disrespectful.

"She didn't come here to lead you, she came to rescue a friend," said Murray. "You have to respect that."

Amina translated.

"Is that true?" asked the young girl with two missing front teeth. She held a small Syrian flag in her hand.

"Yes," said Jameela. "He lived in my city and was taken away because of me. I came to bring him back home."

"Who is this friend?" shouted a woman in the crowd.

"My name is Ibrahim." Jameela froze at the sound of a gentle voice behind her.

"My name is Ibrahim."

How did he recover so quickly? she wondered. For the second time, she hugged him.

This time, he hugged back.

Ibrahim, Isha Prayer, 10:32 p.m., Oct. 22

My Lord, I apologize for losing faith. I should have been like Prophet Yaqub who believed that his son Yusuf was still alive after he went missing for many years. I never believed that Sister Jameela would be the stronger one. This is a very good lesson for me. Never assume you are the spiritually superior person. You were protecting my brain because I was having a difficult time coping with the stress. Once I could hear the noises of happiness around me, I started to feel better and woke up.

I promise never to give up my trust and faith in You, but please never test me like that again. I am weak and would like to go home and not see the Middle East again for a long time.

Marriage counseling is a job the mosque board wanted me to take on, but I refused because I didn't believe I had the stamina. After defeating a terrorist leader, I'm ready.

I must learn the meaning of "microaggression," as I've only been exposed to the larger kind that involves much blood and holes in the body.

46

IT WAS THE FIRST DAY OF RAMADAN, AND JAMAL WAS tickling Jameela's feet.

"Jam Jam, wake up."

"But it's three a.m.," she protested.

"It's suhoor. I'm going to Denny's with my friends. You wanna come?"

Jameela's eyes snapped open and drowsiness disappeared in an instant as she dressed and got in the car with Jamal. Denny's was the only restaurant open at this hour, and it was packed with Muslim teenagers stuffing themselves with their favorite fast foods in order to survive eighteen hours of fasting.

Fluffy buttermilk waffles covered in whipped cream and strawberries, chocolate chip pancakes, and tubs of French fries surrounded Jameela as she sucked down her milkshake and watched Jamal laugh with his friends. He had grown his hair long that summer, and he kept brushing it out of his eyes. Finally, someone gave him a hair tie so he could make a man bun, which looked so ridiculous it made everyone laugh. The air was ripe with camaraderie as the young people talked about their college plans. Jameela felt the warm and safe in Jamal's company. She was so happy.

Afterward, they drove home listening to "Peace Train" by Cat Stevens.

"Physics sucks," said Jameela. "I failed the midterm."

"Really? My friend Breanne is a great tutor. I'll get her to help you."

"Why do I have to take it, anyway? It's totally useless."

"To be a great writer, you have to experience life, the fun parts and the hard parts. And don't run from the hard parts — remember what I told you?"

"But Ummi and Abbu don't want me to be a writer. They're obsessed with me being a doctor."

"Don't worry, I'll talk to them."

Jamal always made her feel better about her life, no matter how hard her problems were. They pulled up to the house.

"Aren't you coming in?" asked Jameela, yawning.

"I'm going to the mosque to pray Fajr. I'll see you in half an hour, inshallah. But listen."

"What?"

"Caltech starts soon."

"Yeah, so?" said Jameela, staring at her feet.

"I'll be gone for a long time, Jam Jam."

"I hate that nickname."

"Ummi and Abbu are gonna be really sad, so make sure you don't fight with them too much."

"But they never listen."

"You're whining again. Remember, wine is haram. I have to go now, Jam Jam."

"Goodbye," cried Jameela, giving her brother a tight hug before running into the house. She sobbed as she watched his car pull away through the window and disappear into the twilight.

Someone touched her face.

Jameela opened her eyes.

Murray was leaning over her, wiping away her tears as she lay in the bed in Sahar's bedroom.

"Are you okay, babe? You suddenly started crying."

"I had a dream about Jamal. I've never dreamed about him before."

"That's a good sign."

"Where's Lee Lee?" asked Jameela.

As she spoke, there was a soft knock on the door. Murray went to answer and came back with a peculiar look on his face.

"The president of the United States is talking about you on TV."

They raced out to the living room where everyone was crowded around Sahar's small TV set. "What's he saying?" asked Jameela.

Lee Lee jumped up. "The president just said you were a hero and that they want to send in a team to rebuild the country." Everyone's attention turned back to the TV, absorbed by the various politicians who were intoning their thoughts on what America should do to help Syria, but Jameela stood there, frozen. The Americans had bombed Iraq in 2003 looking for weapons of mass destruction that had never existed. As a result, one third of the country's population died, were injured, or exiled. The US never apologized for their mistake or offered citizens reparations for destroying their lives. And now she was bringing the Americans back.

She had to find a way to stop them. But she'd have to be furtive. Murray wouldn't be happy to see her go outside after what had happened a few hours ago. Jameela quickly put on her scarf, her hands shaking. When no one was watching, she slipped out of the apartment.

47

DOCUMENTARY TEAMS HAD SWARMED RAQQA TO FILM
the fall of the tyrannical regime. With so many men sporting big, bushy
beards, it was hard to tell the difference between a hipster and a re-
formed terrorist. The city was starting to return to normalcy. Young
couples held hands on the street, women dressed as they pleased, some
with niqabs, some with colorful hijabs, and some with bare heads. Children ran screaming down the street, playing tag with each other. The local cinema had managed to snag a copy of *The Battle of Algiers,* a 1966
film about Algerians fighting for independence from France. There was
a long line at the entrance.

Jameela made a silent prayer for guidance and clarity as she pushed
open the exit doors and she suddenly saw a brown-haired man with a
beard voluminous enough to house an entire family of quails and a T-
shirt emblazoned with an image of Malcolm X. He was talking to his
selfie stick. They made eye contact, and he started gesticulating wildly.
Jameela beckoned him inside the lobby before he attracted attention.

"You're Jameela Green!" said Bushy Beard. "I'm a member of the media and, OMG, totally fanboying out right now. You crushed a totalitar-
ian monster."

Could he be the answer to her prayers? Someone from the media could
get word out and shame the American government to keep them from
sending in troops and interfering with Syria's self-governance.

"Listen, I need your help."

"That is why I am here, my queen."

"Don't call me that. I need large-scale protests, the kind that happened during Vietnam."

"Vietnam, Vietnam, it sounds super familiar."

Irritation rose in Jameela. But today's news cycle turned so fast it was hard to keep track of what happened last week, let alone a war that happened over forty years ago. "Once upon a time, Vietnam used to be two countries. The north wanted to unite the two, but under Communism. And the US didn't want that to happen."

"Why?" asked Bushy Beard. "Did the Vietnamese threaten the US?"

"No, but the US had a serious hate on for Communism, so they sent in over five hundred thousand troops. Young people who looked a lot like you protested, but over a million people had already died by the time America withdrew."

His eyes bulged out. "Wow, it's not easy to get military to withdraw."

"No, so now I need you and your white, hairy-faced pals to make sure the American military don't come here. I need to harness your privilege."

"Every morning I flagellate myself for being born white."

"Good, but now do something more useful. Can you get someone prominent at the *New York Times* to write an article?"

"A hashtag would be more useful."

"You said you were a member of the media."

"Social media."

Jameela rolled her eyes. *What a waste of time.* She started scanning the crowd for a serious journalist.

Seeing his opportunity diminishing, Bushy Beard spoke up. "No offense, ma'am, but you don't understand the power of social media. You've probably never heard of me, because my demographic is . . . younger. My name is Aldrich Akenberg von Arx III, but on YouTube, I'm Mr. Aardvark and I have thirty-five million followers — that's half of the people who read the *New York Times*. And if you count my friends' followers, we have more influence in the US than any media source."

Jameela couldn't believe it. Gone were the days of Bernstein and Woodward. Now she had to depend on a man who named himself after a nocturnal rodent. But he seemed to have a point.

"Okay, but what have you done besides have a lot of friends?"

"Remember net neutrality?"

Now it was Jameela's turn to feel humbled. "John Oliver was doing a story on it, but I . . . fell asleep."

"No worries, my queen. In a nutshell, net neutrality forces internet service providers like Verizon or Comcast to allow everyone's websites to load and stream at the same speed. Like, what's your favorite website?"

Celebitchy, but she wasn't going to tell him that. "Save the Whales."

"See, nonprofits like that wouldn't be able to compete with streamers such as Netflix or Facebook or Amazon, which are super rich and would pay extra for faster access to their customers."

"Yeah, it would be terrible if I couldn't learn more about . . . sea turtles choking on plastic."

"Exactly. I belong to a nonprofit, Fight for the Future, and took our protest to the streets as well as government offices. And we won that fight, but it's an ongoing battle."

He was ingenious; Jameela was forced to give him that. And she was an ancient relic when it came to the world of social media. Lee Lee had to help her post on Facebook, and Instagram was just too scary.

"So what do you suggest?" asked Jameela.

"A hashtag."

"Can hashtags really be that powerful?"

"Remember the hashtag OscarsSoWhite? It was started by April Reign, who wasn't a journalist for the *New York Times* but an activist on Black twitter, and Me Too was started by Tarana Burke, also a Black woman who survived sexual assault. You don't have to be rich or powerful or white to mobilize people and create massive global awareness."

Jameela looked at him for a minute. She didn't doubt he could do it, but suspicion arose in her. "Why are you helping me? To get more followers?"

Aldrich looked aghast. "My queen! Never. You're the man . . . the woman, or whatever you choose to be."

Jameela glared at him.

"After the government declared you a terrorist, my people checked your Facebook posts, and we knew they had been faked. We checked DICK chatter to get more intel, and we pieced together what happened."

Jameela's mind went back to the room she'd seen where men from

DICK had been on computers constantly. It must have been there that the group's social media accounts were being managed.

"Do you really think you can help me?"

"We will marshal every resource we have, and you will get your protests. They will make Vietnam look like the Macy's Parade."

"For a bearded, nose-ringed, tattooed creature that resembles a goat, you're quite useful," said Jameela, relieved.

"Cool, the hashtag should be OurDemocracyOurWay."

Jameela grabbed a fistful of beard and brought Aldrich's astonished face to eye level. "And don't make this about yourself."

"I swear on Rumi's grave and Beyoncé's babies that I would never do such a thing. As Mao Zedong wrote in 1930, a single spark can start a prairie fire," said Aldrich, putting his tattooed arm over his heart, his eyes glittering.

"Yeah well, do everything you can, even if it means setting that beard on fire," said Jameela, releasing him.

"Your wish is my command, my queen."

"How fast can you do this? The American military is already strategizing."

Aldrich smoothed down his beard and then tapped on his phone. "It's done. You should hear something by the time you get back to your family."

Her family! Jameela realized she'd been gone too long; they would have noticed her absence by now. She turned and ran.

"Where were you?" asked Murray as Jameela opened the apartment door. "You can't just leave like that. I thought you got kidnapped. Or worse, you decided to run the country."

Jameela felt terrible after everything she had put him through. Before she could reassure him, though, there was a desperate pounding at the door. Murray jumped up. "I'll get that. Nobody move." He cautiously opened the door

Abdullah stood there in his burned wedding robe, his arm in a sling.

"Who's this?" asked Murray.

Jameela, Fajr Prayer, 4:30 a.m., Oct. 24

Well, that was awkward. Try telling your husband you have another husband. And I used to think women were jealous. Anyhow, once Murray realized that I didn't have much choice and that the wedding didn't progress beyond signing the contracts, he settled down.

Turns out Abdullah's life is in danger. He's running from people who want his head. He's basically Gaddafi and Saddam Hussein rolled into one. I can't throw him into the baying crowds. I don't want to make the same mistake the Americans made and punish all the men who were involved with DICK, because a lot of them didn't have a choice. DICK outlaws will just become bigger DICKs. So, we're setting up a Truth and Reconciliation Committee, like Desmond Tutu did after apartheid ended in South Africa. Abdullah's punishment will be to spend years listening to all the families he hurt.

But the bigger problem is that the Americans want to come, like a moth to a flame lit by a cheap oil field. You're going to stop them, right? Right?

48

SAHAR REFRESHED THE TEA AND PUT BESIDE IT A LARGE platter of cookies: anise tea crescents, deep-fried shabakiyah cookies, and a mini mountain of ma'amoul shortbread cookies. The aroma of orange blossom filled the room. Everyone gravitated toward the table like bees in a garden. Jameela could see Lee Lee stiffen as Murray stared intently at the cookies. He was knitting again, the lavender scarf almost done, but he paused mid-purl stitch. Sahar pulled Lee Lee aside.

"It is important to eat healthy," she said, smoothing Lee Lee's hair. "I admire you for working so hard and making good food for your father. But on occasion, it's important to give people what they desire so those things don't become like a mirage on the horizon, something a person longs for to save their life."

Lee Lee nodded. She turned to her father and raised two fingers. Murray replied with three. Lee Lee smiled. Jameela's vision blurred as she watched them. Jameela had spent more time with Lee Lee and Murray than she ever did back in Liverspot, where she had been so busy running from her past. Her self-absorption and lack of focus on her family had made Lee Lee become hypervigilant about Murray's health. But he indulged her so she'd have sense of control in her life. That was how Murray did things, sacrificed his own needs so he could give Jameela and Lee Lee what they needed most.

As Jameela bit into the rich, dark center of a ma'amoul, her favorite Arab dessert, she felt as if she were eating perfume. She dunked it into her tea and noticed Abdullah from the corner of her eye. He realized she'd seen him and immediately turned his chair to face the wall.

"What's wrong with him?" asked Murray, noting the odd behavior. She hadn't had an affair, and she didn't have any reason to feel guilty. But sometimes a husband doesn't need to know everything. "He's feeling bad for all the wrong he's done in the world and needs time to think."

Lee Lee was staring at her phone with a furrowed brow.

"What's wrong, sweetheart?" asked Murray.

"There's going to be a massive anti-war march in front of the United Nations on Tuesday. It's supposed to be the biggest protest since 2003 when the US was trying to get UN support to bomb Iraq. There are coordinated marches throughout the US and all over the world. And there's signs with hashtag OurDemocracyOurWay."

Jameela couldn't believe it. Aldrich had kept his promise.

"All the placards are gonna have a meme of a Syrian girl holding a flag," said Lee Lee, giving her phone to Jameela.

It was the same girl she had seen earlier, the one with the missing front teeth and infectious smile. She had become the poster child for noninterference in Syria's political process. Jameela tried to not be skeptical, but she remembered the record number of anti-war protestors who had tried to pressure President Bush to back down from his plans.

She turned to Murray. "The US invaded Iraq even after all the protests in 2003 and the UN saying it was illegal. Do you think this'll work?"

Murray held her hand. "Keep the faith, babe. It's what got you this far."

"Can we go and be part of the march?" asked Lee Lee. "Oh please, oh please!" She bounced over to her mother.

"Of course we can, it's time to go home," said Jameela.

Amina came into the kitchen with Ibrahim. "There's a hilarious TikTok of this famous YouTuber, Aardvark or something. He burned his beard in front of what used to be the American embassy screaming "For you, my queen," while holding up a placard with the slogan #OURDEMOCRACYOURWAY."

"Mr. Aardvark! He's my favorite YouTuber," squealed Lee Lee.

"That is a very painful way to send a message," said Ibrahim, rubbing his own beard in sympathy. "Did he get burned?"

"There were people close by with buckets ready to douse the flames so he didn't get hurt," said Amina.

"My God, who gives people these ideas?" exclaimed Murray.

Jameela avoided making eye contact with him.

"This is amazing," said Amina. "There are rallies all over the US. People are demanding that the US not interfere with the rebuilding process. The campaign forced the army chief of staff to deny all rumors that the Americans were going to send in their own team."

As Jameela swallowed her cookie, a glow thrummed through her. She looked at Abdullah, who was still facing the wall like a truant child, and walked over to him. He stared at her with sorrow. "Abdullah came with a message for Amina. That he wants to rally the hardcore DICKs and get them behind her to help create a temporary new government."

"They've done some pretty horrible things," said Murray.

"I know," said Jameela, "but we're going to take a page out of history. Ibrahim, when the Prophet Muhammad finally conquered Mecca, what did he do with people who had tried to kill him and had done terrible things to their own people?"

"He forgave them, and after his enemies pledged never to attack again, they lived peacefully in the city."

They turned to Amina. "I'll do it," she said. "But on one condition."

Everyone looked at her.

"I want Ibrahim at my side."

49

JAMEELA STOOD AT HER MOTHER'S FRONT DOOR AND rang the bell. She was glad to have a tall, blond FBI officer answer the door. He looked like he had just walked out of central casting, a perfect doppelgänger for Ryan Gosling.

Nusrat pushed past Gosling to greet her visitor. Jameela gasped. Nusrat's perfectly coiffed hair was disheveled, her face gaunt from weight loss, and there were deep circles under her eyes.

"Ummi," said Jameela, embracing her mother. They went inside, and Faisal emerged from the bedroom looking like he had just woken up. He had been put on tranquilizers to stay calm, but the fuss at the doorbell had woken him up. Jameela covered her mouth. Her father shuffled toward her with a bent back. His face had more lines than she remembered, and his pallor was gray.

Jameela hugged her father, and the three of them went to the kitchen and sat down. It took her parents almost half an hour before they could speak. Gosling's partner, a plumper version of Tom Cruise, was hovering around computer equipment near the main phone. It had been placed there to geolocate calls from Lee Lee, she had been informed on the way over by officials. Even the agents had a hard time gaining their composure. One of them made some tea, and the other went out to get a cheese platter.

"I'm so sorry," said Jameela, holding her mother's hand, marveling at its softness, a softness she hadn't felt in years. "I had no idea how much pain I'd cause by leaving . . ."

She wanted her mother to blame her, admonish her, anything to make her guilt to go away.

"You went to save the imam," said Nusrat. "You didn't know what would happen. I'm proud of you for doing the right thing."

This was unexpected. Her mother hadn't been proud of anything she'd done since she finished reading the entire Qur'an. Even then, her mother felt that taking five years was a bit excessive. Jameela realized she wasn't comfortable with maternal approval.

"I should have gone with Jamal that morning. I could have saved him." Jameela blurted out. It was the confession she'd been trying to make for years but hadn't had the courage for. Her hands were clammy, and she kept rubbing them on her pants while avoiding her mother's eyes.

Nusrat put her hands on Jameela's to quiet them. "It's our fault. If we had told you the truth —" Nusrat started to cry again. The FBI agents grabbed some tissues and snuck out into the living room.

Jameela hadn't heard her parents speak about her brother in years.

"What do you mean?" she asked. Her heart raced, and her head throbbed. On the way to the mosque, Jamal had stopped to pick up a hitchhiker. He drove Jameela nuts with his compassionate behavior. Anytime they planned to walk in the park, he'd fill his pockets with change to give to the homeless. It didn't surprise anyone that he would have wanted to help someone in need.

"We couldn't tell you the truth," Faisal murmured.

Nusrat continued. "Today, we would call it a hate crime, but in those days, police called it premeditated murder."

"I don't understand. It was random. How could it be a hate crime?"

"A young man was waiting by the side of the road, and Jamal stopped to see what was wrong," said Nusrat. "But he had been waiting for Jamal."

Jameela blinked. The room started to look hazy.

Faisal poured some water in a glass and held it gently up to Jameela's lips.

Jameela drank the cold liquid, which helped revive her, but she could hear an angry buzzing growing in her head. She didn't believe her parents. "No, he was killed by some delinquent who was angry that Jamal didn't have more money. He attacked Jamal because he was drunk, or high, or something that made him freak out. That's what happened."

"That's what we told you happened. We thought the truth would scare you, so we left out some details," said Faisal, rubbing her shoulders. Jameela felt like she would fall to the ground if it weren't for her parents steadying her.

"What details?" whispered Jameela.

"Jamal was stabbed and died from blood loss. This much you knew. But his death wasn't a random killing. The young man was part of an anti-Muslim group called the Cross Bearers. They were hunting young Muslims going to the mosque. Jamal was their first victim. If you had been with him, you would have died, too. The police caught the man, and he's serving a life sentence."

Jamal had been hunted like an animal? "Why didn't you tell me the truth?"

"You were only fifteen. Your therapist felt if you believed it was a random killing, you would heal faster. He said if you knew the truth, the anger would consume you," said Nusrat.

"We knew the world was going to get more dangerous for minorities. A few weeks later, a man in a synagogue was attacked. A year later, a Sikh temple was firebombed. The police acted as if these events were just incidental acts of violence, not part of a pattern, but we knew the truth. The FBI were so fixated on Muslims, they couldn't see the danger of white supremacy movements."

Jameela stared at the wrinkles in her father's face and blinked again. They had tried to protect her all these years. Her mother held her for a few moments, and the noise in her head began to fade away.

"Your mother became afraid of the world and what it could do to her children. She protected you the best way she knew how," said Faisal. He coughed. "We came to this country for a better life, but we didn't know that violence and hate would follow us here."

"It changed the way you raised me," she mumbled. The angst her parents felt when she got her driving license. The way they anxiously stayed up whenever she went out at night, just so they could greet her the moment she came home, even now.

She always believed her parents didn't want her to assimilate. And in a way, they hadn't.

Jameela looked at her frail, traumatized parents. "If I had known the truth..."

"Who knows," said Faisal. "Maybe we should have told you the truth. We didn't want you to become afraid of the world like we were."

After her brother's death, she'd refused to visit the mosque because of bitterness. She avoided places where the homeless congregated. Barkley was the first homeless person she'd met after Jamal died. Barkley had saved her life. Ibrahim reignited the faith that Jamal had nurtured in her growing up. They had made her whole again. Better than whole.

Nusrat got up and took out some garlic and a paring knife. She started to peel off the papery casings. Jameela did the one thing she had never done before: she started helping her mother.

"Finish peeling these, and then cut some onions and tomatoes," said Nusrat as she handed Jameela the paring knife. She left Jameela to her tasks and started sweeping the floor. Her cheeks began turning pink, and when she got to Faisal, he lifted his feet so she could reach underneath.

Jameela asked the question that she'd been dreading. "Did you think you'd never see me again?"

Nusrat abruptly stopped, put her broom down, and reached for a Kleenex. After dabbing her eyes, she turned to her daughter. "God doesn't test you beyond your limits. After Jamal, I knew he would never take the only one I had left. I prayed and waited, just like Yaqub. When Yaqub lost Yusuf, he cried till he almost lost his eyes, but he was rewarded for his patience."

"I thought you didn't like to compare us to prophets," said Jameela.

Nusrat took a large tuberous section of ginger out of her pantry and sat down. It looked like a giant three-fingered hand. She deftly peeled the dull gray papery skin to reveal the bright-yellow fibrous interior, and then grated it into fine shreds of blond hair. "If we can't read the stories of the prophets in the Qur'an to give us hope, what's the point?" Nusrat put the garlic, ginger, onions, and tomatoes into a waiting pot, covered it, and turned on the heat. A pleasant aroma spread through the house.

They were a family again. The house even looked brighter.

"Bread, come here," yelled Nusrat.

"I think his name is Brad," said Jameela, looking at the nameplate of the sheepish FBI agent walking into the kitchen with bits of cracker stuck to his upper lip.

"That's what I said. Bread, here's a hundred dollars," said Nusrat, pressing a green bill into his hand. "Go to the halal meat store and get me twenty-five chicken legs and twenty-five thighs. Tell the butcher I want them separated and skinned. We are having a party. My daughter has returned."

"Yes, ma'am."

Jameela could swear her mother was starting to inflate again.

"Can you make some pakoras, too?" asked Faisal.

"What was the other one's name again, something to do with a cracker?"

"My name's Graham, ma'am," said the red-haired FBI agent, jogging into the kitchen. "But you can call me Cracker. It works, too."

"Fine, Cracker, go with Bread and buy a big jug of canola oil, chickpea flour, and fresh coriander. If you hurry back, you can eat with us."

"Yes, ma'am!" said Graham Cracker. Both men practically ran out of the kitchen.

Okay, maybe some things hadn't changed that much.

"Mom! Cracker is offensive. You can't call him that."

"Why would calling someone a biscuit be offensive?"

"It was used to insult poor white farmers in the South back in the day."

"Well, he's not a poor white farmer, he's a rich FBI officer. Did you see his shoes? They're polished so well, I can see my face." She took the lid off the pot and stirred the contents with a big wooden spoon.

"Well, poor whites could reclaim it," said Faisal. "Like the gays have reclaimed the word *queer*. I was watching a homosexual Muslim man on a Netflix show that helps the crackers become more urbane. That's how I learned about the French tuck."

"May God forgive them for their trespasses," said Nusrat, adding two teaspoons of salt to the pot. "I should have gotten their phone numbers. I need cream. I want to make chicken korma."

Her parents were back. With each minute, they looked more and more like their old selves.

"It's almost Maghrib time," she said. "I'm going to the mosque before dinner. I haven't been to the Brooklyn Mosque since . . . a long time."

Nusrat and Faisal looked up for a moment.

"That's fine," said Nusrat. "Just make sure you're home by seven."

Jameela, Maghrib Prayer, 5:48 p.m., Oct. 26

I'm in the mosque in Brooklyn that Jamal and I used to go to when we lived here. It's smaller than I remember, but I guess that's a cliché. Imam Adam was very kind and understanding when I told him about Jamal and how I had been too angry to walk through the front door since he had died. I started crying, and he squeezed my arm until I calmed down. Then he gave me a Qur'an from a shelf. It had Jamal's name written in ink on the top left corner of the cover. He had been hired last year and hadn't put the owner of the Qur'an and our family together until now. The margins were full of Jamal's notes, done in his perfect cursive. The imam said he'd refer to the notes during sermons because they were thoughtful and obviously came from someone who was very close to God. I started bawling again. I told him to keep it. I wanted a piece of Jamal left in this mosque because it meant he still lived on in the place that he loved so much.

Lee Lee and Murray want to attend the biggest democracy rally in New York's history. I'm not going. I don't want to risk bringing any more attention on me.

But I'm working on being a better person. For real this time, no agenda. I signed up online to serve food at the Liverspot YMCA on Sundays, and on my way here I saw a person in need and I gave him money, just like Jamal and Ibrahim would have wanted. Speaking of which, I hope Ibrahim is happy with his new life. He didn't want to stay in Raqqa at first, but Amina needed the moral support. Plus, she's gaga over him.

It's gonna be weird going to the Liverspot mosque and not seeing Ibrahim. He left his favorite turban in his office, and I promised to mail it to him. I think he secretly believes it's his good luck charm, even though, as he says, Muslims don't believe in luck, just God's prayer. Luck is a Western invention.

I miss Ibrahim so much.

50

JAMEELA SAT IN HER PARKED CAR IN FRONT OF THE LIV-
erspot mosque. She had been sitting there for almost half an hour, staring at the cracked stucco. It seemed like years since she had been there
last. She willed herself to get out, to open the steel and glass doors, which
were heavier than she remembered. The shoe cubby had been changed.
It was a brown plastic structure with square holes for each pair of shoes.
No more rust. *Muslims can occasionally pull it together,* she admitted, but
that thought didn't cheer her up.

A trip to the mosque was supposed to help her feel better, but it was
only making her feel worse. As she bent to take off her shoes, she saw a
string of blue marble prayer beads lying on the ground. They looked like
the ones she gave Ibrahim when they were in Raqqa. She started shuddering as tears fell down her face. She had overcome unbelievable situations in her life — kidnapping, fire, potential beheadings — but staring
at those beads broke her, and she had to sit down and lean against the
shoe cubby for support.

"I think I'm having a nervous breakdown," she said to the beads,
which she picked up and looped around her wrist.

"Nerves do not break down, Sister Jameela. It is just a saying."

Jameela whipped her head up, and saw Ibrahim coming around the
corner, carrying the same miserable vacuum cleaner from a few weeks
ago. Was he a hallucination? All the crying she was doing was probably dehydrating her brain and causing it to malfunction. Just in case,

though, she put out her hand, and he took it and pulled her up. Ibrahim held her until she had calmed down enough to speak. He handed her a box of Kleenex, which was sitting on the shoe shelf, and led her to the stairs where they both sat down.

"I thought you weren't real," said Jameela, mopping up her face, which was swollen from all the tears.

"I didn't want to alarm you," said Ibrahim. "I saw you in the car and waited until you were ready to come in."

"I thought you were still in Raqqa. You came back so soon?"

"The two-for-one pizza deal was going to expire this week," said Ibrahim.

Jameela had forgotten how literal Ibrahim could be. If she hadn't been so overcome by joy, she would have hit him.

"But what about Amina?" said Jameela. "You were supposed to stay and help her."

"The UN has protocols in place to help a country restore its democratic institutions. I am an outsider. There were many Syrian and Iraqi Arabs with more knowledge and more experience in helping a country rebuild. I arrived last night but didn't have time to call you."

"So, what happened with the find-out-if-we're-compatible plan?'"

"We have decided to have what Westerners call 'a long-distance relationship,' during which I will watch Amina's hard work and honesty from afar. If she stays committed to doing good, listening to the people, and ensuring the peaceful transfer of power to a democratically elected government, she will come here, and we will be married in Liverspot."

"Okay, but no sexting. If that gets back to Al-Azhar, you'll never live it down," said Jameela laughing.

"She did ask me to take my shirt off once, but I thought it was to make sure my bruises were healing." Now it was Ibrahim's turn to look embarrassed. He changed the subject. "I have just read that your book is number one on the *New York Times* bestseller list. Congratulations."

"When it's reported that you've come back from the dead and become the next calipha of the Muslim world, people get curious about you."

"But this is what you wanted. And that man who created Bookface —"

"Facebook."

"Yes, that man has chosen you as his favorite author. God has answered your every prayer. People are saying your book will sell more copies than that of the woman you do not like. Courtney."

"Aw, Courtney's okay; we've become friends, actually. I always thought she hated me, but she was just lonely. We're going shopping next week. According to her, she's been wanting to give me a makeover for two decades."

"Will you write another book right away?"

"You know, I'm going to take a break for a while. With my luck, if I write another book, I'll wind up in North Korea strapped to a nuclear warhead. I'm thinking about trying something different for a while."

"You could help me with marriage counseling. It is a very intimidating process."

"More intimidating than dealing with terrorists?"

"At times, yes. Even terrorists don't get upset as much as people whose spouse picks their nose in front of them or leaves a sock lying around. They feel 'triggered.'"

They looked at each other for a long moment.

What Jameela wanted was for Ibrahim to always be Ibrahim.

He finally said what she had been waiting for. "I've always wanted a friend. I never thought it was possible to have a female friend. You are married to Murray, and I am, by the grace of God, soon to be married to Amina. But I missed you very much. You have taught me things that I could never have learned on my own. It is easy to believe in God and be grateful when you live in safety. But to have faith when there are bullets flying close to your head or when you are trapped in a fire and cannot breathe is much more difficult."

No kidding. "And God may not have made the fire cold like She did for your namesake, Prophet Ibrahim, but She put you in a portable freezer, which is the next best thing."

"I did not think of it like that," said a happy Ibrahim. "I came close to knowing what it is like to be a prophet. Thank you for supporting my faith when I needed it most, Sister Jameela."

"I missed you so much, Ibrahim."

"The youth did not miss me. They were not happy to learn that I had survived and would continue to teach them."

"Yeah, well, some things will never change in a house of God."

"And now I must prepare for this week's Friday sermon. Will you come this week?"

"Of course."

"I must vacuum the library stairs," said Ibrahim, running a critical finger over the wooden stair banister. "No one cleaned while I was away."

Ibrahim got up and plugged in the vacuum cleaner. As the loud grumbling sound began, accompanied by the smell of burned rubber, Jameela put on her shoes and walked back to her car.

She stood there and stared at the mosque for a few minutes, trying to figure out how she felt. It wasn't joy exactly; it was more like a sense of peace she had never experienced before.

Jamal was gone, but she had gained Ibrahim. She had learned to seek help in patience and prayer.

And, most importantly, she had learned to stop whining.

Wine is haram. Jamal was right.

Author's Note

To write a satire about Muslims, terrorism, and ISIS was not easy or necessarily advisable. When ISIS first appeared in the news in 1994, I wanted to understand the political context in which that group emerged. The big political movements that influenced this book were the Soviet invasion of Afghanistan in 1979 during the Cold War, and the two Gulf Wars that devastated Iraq.

During the Cold War, paranoia severely impacted American foreign policy. Americans were so worried about the Soviet Union spreading Communism, they either directly fought it (by supporting and funding South Vietnam's military in the Vietnam War) or supported proxy armies in various countries. A key moment that influenced American policy was the Soviet invasion of Afghanistan in 1979. Americans were petrified that Communism would spread to the Muslim world as it had in Southeast Asia. Mahmood Mamdani, author of *Good Muslim, Bad Muslim: America, the Cold War, and the Roots of Terror*, explains in his book how the CIA recruited, trained, and radicalized hundreds of Muslims from around the world, including Osama bin Laden, in order to defeat the Soviets; I owe a debt of thanks to him. He also mentions Arundhati Roy's famous quote, "bin Laden has the distinction of being created by the CIA and wanted by the FBI."

The CIA spent over fifty million dollars on a "jihad literacy" project to encourage young Afghan children to resist the occupation through violence. Malala Yousafzai discusses this project in her memoir, *My Name Is*

Malala. These books were filled with pictures of guns, bullets, and headless soldiers, and were published by the University of Nebraska Omaha and funded by the US Agency for International Development. Four million of them were shipped to madrassas in Afghanistan, where they became part of the Afghan school system's core curriculum and were used by the Taliban. They have been criticized for indoctrinating a generation of children in brutality.

But American involvement that resulted in increased regional violence wasn't just limited to Afghanistan. Saddam Hussein, like Osama bin Laden before him, was a CIA asset. However, he was transformed into America's foe when Iraqi forces invaded Kuwait in 1991. Iraq needed Kuwait's money; it had been an oil-rich country, but after a crippling eight-year war with Iran, was billions of dollars in debt to Kuwait, who had loaned them money for the war. Saddam wanted Kuwait to forgive the loan since the war had ultimately prevented Shia influence into other Arab states, but Kuwait refused. Edward Mortimer wrote in the *New York Review of Books* that Saddam's meeting with April Glaspie, the US Ambassador to Iraq, seemed to give Saddam the impression that the United States wouldn't react with anything more than a verbal condemnation. Nonetheless, President Bush Sr. launched the first Gulf War, known as Operation Desert Storm. This began a decade of crippling economic sanctions against Iraq, but they failed to remove Saddam.

Then, in 2003, President Bush Jr., under the pretense of destroying weapons of mass destruction, attacked Iraq again, removing Saddam and setting up a provisional government. In *The Extraordinary Journey of the Fakir Who Got Trapped in an IKEA Wardrobe* by Romain Puértolas, there is a reference to Paul Bremer, the chief administrator of the US Coalition Provisional Authority (CPA) in Iraq, and the disastrous decisions he made. Responsible for overseeing Iraq's transformation from an authoritarian state to a democracy, he decided that anyone associated with Saddam's Baath party would lose their pensions and couldn't help rebuild the country. But because belonging to the Baath party was one of the only ways to show loyalty to Saddam, and not joining was frowned upon, the ruling affected huge numbers of men. Some 250,000 of them joined the insurgency in the aftermath of Bremer's decisions, which ultimately destabilized, and, some say, created the conditions for the formation of ISIS.

The book *Guest House for Young Widows* by Azadeh Moaveni helped me understand how the world became transfixed by ISIS. Moaveni explains how "less attention was given to the group's origins in 'American policies and wars.'" Instead, "ISIS became, in the Western imagination, a satanic force unlike anything civilization had encountered since it began recording histories of combat with the Trojan Wars," requiring a new class of "demonologists" to study them.

It's been almost a decade since I began writing *Jameela Green Ruins Everything*. When I started, the news was filled with stories about ISIS, but when Donald Trump came into power in 2017, those articles disappeared and were replaced with headlines about the growing threat of white nationalist extremist groups. I never thought I'd live to see the day when headlines about Muslim terror would be replaced by white terror. The obsession over the surveillance of Muslims came at a cost as white nationalist groups went undeterred, and now we are in the age of Capitol riots and global far-right movements that threaten our democratic structures.

But I'm an optimistic person and believe in the goodness of humanity. And writing through the prism of faith helped a lot. It takes huge amounts to finish writing a novel. But not as much as to read one. Thank you.

Acknowledgments

I'm very grateful to finally be writing this. My first book, a memoir called *Laughing All the Way to the Mosque,* took two years to write. This book, embarrassingly longer.

It takes a village to write a novel. And I had a large and loving one. Many people read the manuscript over the years and gave me valuable feedback: My dear friend Claire Ross Dunn, who I met in *Little Mosque on the Prairie*'s writing room, was one of my first readers and believed it in instantly, as did my talented niece Raeesa Ashique, whose quiet and insistent urgings got me through the first draft. A big shout out to Adrienne Kerr, who gave me valuable feedback for deepening character; Emi Ikkanda, who taught me the value of shortening and "getting" to the story; and, of course, Sheila Athens, who is not only a fantastic editor but had to double as my therapist and listen to my constant bellyaching about never being published.

Thanks also to my sister-in-law Sabreena, who taught me to stop being so "heavy" with the teachable political moments. And to Uzma Jalalauddin, who never lost faith in me and invited me to her writing retreat with Sajidah Ali (S. K. Ali), who had to remind me that comedy is one of the most difficult genres to write.

To Laurie Grassi at Simon & Schuster Canada and Pilar Garcia-Brown at Mariner Books, who stewarded this project through to publication with their combined wisdom and guidance. And to Angela Lederwood from Sugar23, who showered me with kindness. To my agent, Samantha Haywood, who never gave up on me.

And to my family, particularly my husband, Sami, who was forced to listen to me sorting out the story as we walked around Wascana Lake in Regina, Saskatchewan, year after year. And, of course, my four children, who still mourn the loss of the original title, *The Rise and Fall of DICK,* and don't understand why the marketing departments would have had some "concerns" over wrong images popping up during a Google search.